"You look great, Suz. Beautiful."

Suz scanned him for obvious signs that pod people had taken over his body. *You look great, Suz? Beautiful?* These were not the words of the Max Trevetti she knew. He was more likely to tell her to tie her shoelaces so she wouldn't trip.

"Why're you looking at me that way, Suz?"

"Have you been drinking?"

"Sure I've been drinking. It's my little sister's wedding." He touched the tip of one finger to the spaghetti strap of her red dress.

She glanced at the spot he'd touched to see if it had caught fire. Nope. It just *felt* that way!

P9-CSF-024

Dear Reader,

Not only does Special Edition bring you the joys of life, love and family—but we also capitalize on our authors' many talents in storytelling. In our spotlight, Christine Rimmer's exciting new miniseries, VIKING BRIDES, is the epitome of innovative reading. The first book, *The Reluctant Princess,* details the transformation of an everyday woman to glorious royal—with a Viking lover to match! Christine tells us, "For several years, I've dreamed of creating a modern-day country where the ways of the legendary Norsemen would still hold sway. I imagined what fun it would be to match up the most macho of men, the Vikings, with contemporary American heroines. Oh, the culture clash—oh, the lovely potential for lots of romantic fireworks! This dream became VIKING BRIDES." Don't miss this fabulous series!

Our Readers' Ring selection is Judy Duarte's *Almost Perfect,* a darling tale of how good friends fall in love as they join forces to raise two orphaned kids. This one will get you talking! Next, Gina Wilkins delights us with *Faith, Hope and Family,* in which a tormented heroine returns to save her family and faces the man she's always loved. You'll love Elizabeth Harbison's *Midnight Cravings,* in which a sassy publicist and a small-town police chief fall hard for each other and give in to a sizzling attraction.

The Unexpected Wedding Guest, by Patricia McLinn, brings together an unlikely couple who share an unexpected kiss. Newcomer to Special Edition Kate Welsh is no stranger to fresh plot twists, in *Substitute Daddy,* in which a heroine carries her deceased twin's baby and has feelings for the last man on earth she should love—her snooty brother-in-law.

As you can see, we have a story for every reader's taste. Stay tuned next month for six more top picks from Special Edition!

Sincerely,

Karen Taylor Richman
Senior Editor

Please address questions and book requests to:
Silhouette Reader Service
U.S.: 3010 Walden Ave., P.O. Box 1325, Buffalo, NY 14269
Canadian: P.O. Box 609, Fort Erie, Ont. L2A 5X3

The Unexpected Wedding Guest

PATRICIA McLINN

SPECIAL EDITION™

Published by Silhouette Books

America's Publisher of Contemporary Romance

If you purchased this book without a cover you should be aware
that this book is stolen property. It was reported as "unsold and
destroyed" to the publisher, and neither the author nor the
publisher has received any payment for this "stripped book."

To Diane Chamberlain and Emilie Richards.

Friendship and fellowship beyond value…
oh, yes, and *great* chocolate!

 SILHOUETTE BOOKS

ISBN 0-373-24541-6

THE UNEXPECTED WEDDING GUEST

Copyright © 2003 by Patricia McLaughlin

All rights reserved. Except for use in any review, the reproduction
or utilization of this work in whole or in part in any form by any
electronic, mechanical or other means, now known or hereafter
invented, including xerography, photocopying and recording, or in
any information storage or retrieval system, is forbidden without
the written permission of the editorial office, Silhouette Books,
233 Broadway, New York, NY 10279 U.S.A.

All characters in this book have no existence outside the imagination of
the author and have no relation whatsoever to anyone bearing the same
name or names. They are not even distantly inspired by any individual
known or unknown to the author, and all incidents are pure invention.

This edition published by arrangement with Harlequin Books S.A.

® and TM are trademarks of Harlequin Books S.A., used under license.
Trademarks indicated with ® are registered in the United States Patent
and Trademark Office, the Canadian Trade Marks Office and in other
countries.

Visit Silhouette at www.eHarlequin.com

Printed in U.S.A.

Chapter One

"Hey, Suz."

The voice and the touch came from behind her. The voice was a rumble in her ear, the touch a warm hand on her shoulder. A hand not only warm, but large and strong. The kind of contact between a man and a woman that was a play all to itself, complete with three acts.

The opening was a faint caress, stroking across the skin left bare by the narrow straps of her dress, followed by the main act of its solid presence, telegraphing strength. Then, before the curtain came down, that little squeeze saying it sure would be nice to have an encore.

In the flash before she recognized the shoulder gripper, Suzanna Grant couldn't think of a single man who might greet her that way at her best friend's wedding reception here in Tobias, Wisconsin. Or anywhere else, for that matter. Not a one. And wasn't that a cheerful thought?

She turned at the same time the shoulder gripper dropped

into a seat beside her, and saw the familiar black hair, the dark eyes so thickly lashed they could look like smudges, the strong nose, the powerful shoulders. Max Trevetti, the bride's older brother. The best man. Oh, yes, and the man who at one time could have earned a standing ovation from her if that touch had truly carried all those hidden meanings.

But that time was years ago, before she'd figured out it wasn't going to happen. Before he'd established himself as a big brother in all but name.

"You look great, Suz. Beautiful."

She scanned him for obvious signs that pod people had taken over his body.

You look great, Suz? Beautiful? These were not the words of the Max Trevetti she knew. He was more likely to tell her to tie her shoelaces so she wouldn't trip, or to wear her gloves in the winter so she wouldn't catch a cold.

"Why're you looking at me that way, Suz?"

"Have you been drinking?"

"Sure I've been drinking. It's my little sister's wedding. And every time I finish my champagne, some waiter comes by with a new one." He touched the tip of one finger to the spaghetti strap of her red dress. Two touches in under a minute—that had to be a record.

She glanced at the spot he'd touched to see if it had caught fire. Nope. Must be the tactile version of an optical illusion.

"Looked like it was slipping," he said.

Of course, he had a practical reason for touching her.

That first time she'd turned from greeting the fellow transfer student who'd become her new roommate at Northwestern University and laid eyes on this roommate's older brother, she'd seen satin sheets and white picket fences.

He'd seen…well, she didn't know exactly what he'd

seen. His view of her seemed to alternate between honorary kid sister and androgynous robot. Neither did much to boost a girl's ego. But she'd recovered from that ages ago.

"You've been drinking, too," he said now. "When I gave the toast."

"That's what you do after a toast—and a beautiful toast it was. I was just surprised to see you so relaxed, and I was speculating on its cause."

"Isn't my little sister getting married enough? Isn't Annette's wedding cause?"

"Sure."

"Then why aren't you celebrating?"

"I am, in my own quiet way."

He laughed, full out, head thrown back. "Your own quiet way. That's rich. Your way's never been quiet. It's fireworks and confetti." He waved over a waiter. "So have more champagne."

He took another glass for himself and one for her. She didn't touch hers.

"Who's driving you home, Max?"

"I dunno. Somebody." He looked at her, and the flippancy vanished, his deep-brown eyes softening with familiar concern and sympathy. And with the memories. "Sorry, Suz. I wasn't thinking. Annette has seen to it that no one will drive out of here after drinking and meet some innocent... I wasn't thinking," he repeated. "I was just concentrating on gettin' through the wedding. And we did this time, even with..."

In a second display of unusual tact for Max, he took another sip of champagne rather than finishing.

Suz wasn't in the mood for tact. Besides, talking about today's wedding would keep him off the other topic.

"Even with my untimely arrival?" she asked.

She had certainly never meant to re-create the intrusion

that had stopped Annette's wedding to Steve Corbett nearly eight years ago. The first time, a pregnant woman had come in the side door while they were at the altar, declaring she had a reason the wedding shouldn't go on—the baby was Steve's. Annette had immediately left Tobias, she'd thought for good. But since Annette's return to town three months ago, Annette and Steve had gotten back together.

Gotten back together so well that they had arranged a new wedding, at a different church, heck, even in a different century.

Then Suz had inadvertently repeated the pattern—at least part of it—by arriving late and bursting in the side door at the moment the preacher asked if anyone had cause that these two people should not be joined in holy matrimony. At least she hadn't been pregnant. And she would never say there was reason Annette and Steve shouldn't be joined together.

The fact that they already *were* joined together in the ways that counted had been obvious in their reaction to Suz's arrival. Without hesitation they had looked at each other and laughed. After a moment everyone joined in.

Everyone except Max.

From his position next to the groom, he'd stood like a statue and stared at her as if he'd never seen her before—and never wanted to again.

"Your unexpected arrival," he corrected now.

"Unexpected? I was invited."

"Of course you were invited. If they'd had anyone more than Nell and me in the wedding, you'd've been in it—you know that." She did know that. And she thoroughly understood Annette and Steve's need to limit the wedding party to her brother and his daughter. "But you said you wouldn't be able to make it because of your family situation."

Ah, yes, her family situation.

"It turned out not to be as big an emergency as they thought. I left yesterday."

Actually, to her parents and four older brothers, getting her to stay safe at home permanently probably did constitute an emergency. And living back in Dayton, Ohio, would be easy in so many ways. But not when the timing of their "emergency" meant missing Annette's wedding.

"Yesterday? Then why were you late? Get lost?"

There *had* been that one wrong turn when she hit the edge of Tobias. But she'd already been late by then.

As she'd driven across Indiana yesterday evening, she'd received a call that there'd been a last-second snafu with a transfer of records to the corporation she and Annette had sold their business to. The administrator who'd slipped up said it could wait. But those records represented a score of small businesses that could miss a week's worth of potential work when jobs were assigned Monday. So instead of driving on to Wisconsin, she'd stayed in Chicago last night and insisted a VP meet her downtown this morning to finish the exchange, so those businesses would be eligible to work.

She'd changed clothes in the restroom of the office building and headed straight here.

But Max was right—she had a notoriously bad sense of direction.

"I could've been lying in a ditch somewhere and you wouldn't have cared," she said with mock tragedy.

"I'd've cared." It would have been a more touching declaration if it hadn't been so breezy. And it was followed by an abrupt "Let's dance."

Before she could answer, Max had her hand in his and was pulling her out of the chair with such ease that it jolted her. She'd seen him lifting a lot of heavy items, from suit-

cases to boxes of books to dressers in the moves he'd
helped her and Annette make over the years, so intellec-
tually she'd figured the guy had to be strong. It wasn't her
intellect responding now.

He took her left hand in his and slid his other hand
around to the middle of her back. Her left hand found a
natural home on his shoulder as they moved into the easy
rhythm of the dance.

Having the reception at Tobias Country Club was Annette and Steve's way of keeping his mother happy—as
happy as Lana Corbett got. They'd kept the ceremony as
they'd wanted it, simple and straightforward. The reception
was Lana's party. Afterward Lana was going to Europe for
the summer, which would surely be a relief for the newlyweds.

Suz had to give Lana Corbett credit—the food was delicious, the champagne plentiful and the service terrific. The
club's grounds, slipping down in a sweep of lawn to Lake
Tobias, were beautiful, especially lit with fairy lights and
a rising, nearly full moon. And the music was lovely.

Max's voice rumbled in her ear. "Can't believe these
idiots haven't asked you to dance."

"Some did."

"You said no? You're showing good sense now, Suz."

"You make it sound like I don't say no. I do."

"With all the dates you go on?"

"Your sister's always telling me I should go on more
dates."

Sort of. According to Annette, Suz was the queen of first
dates, having no trouble turning down a second invitation.
Annette kept urging her to give guys multiple dates before
she made up her mind.

It seemed to Suz that she was fated to have *possibles*

abound in her dating life that never advanced to *maybes,* much less *for sures.*

The situation had worsened when she and Annette formed Every Detail, which provided harried homeowners with all the legwork and résumé checking and estimate getting for any job they needed done. Under Annette's leadership they had worked so hard to get the business off the ground that there'd been little time for a social life. When it took off, there'd been even less time. Now they'd sold the business for enough money to keep each of them comfortable for a long, long time.

The good news was the money gave Suz the freedom to do whatever she wanted, starting Monday morning. That was also the bad news. And that was the reason her caring, protective family had manufactured an emergency.

Which was what she'd been thinking about when Max first touched her shoulder. She shivered. Couldn't be at the memory of that light touch. Must be getting chilly.

''You okay?'' His murmur in her ear was accompanied by a slow glide of his hand to the small of her back as he drew their clasped hands in closer to their bodies. ''Thought you might be getting chilly in that dress.''

That explained both her shiver and why he tucked her in closer to the warmth of his body. It was Big Brother Max taking care of all around him.

So, why were the tip ends of her nerves vibrating so hard that she was surprised the hum didn't drown out the band? Must be the surprise, that was all. He so rarely touched her—and when he did, it was always in that ''Hey, kid,'' manner—that her nerve endings were reacting now like a G-rated dance was something to write home about.

His breath stirred her hair. Or had his lips actually…? No, had to be him simply breathing.

The band abandoned a rendition of "Lady in Red" for a drum flourish.

"Attention everybody!" said the bandleader. "It's time for the throwing of the bouquet and the garter."

Suz backed a step away from Max. That was as far as she could go until he released her. He was looking toward the bandstand, apparently oblivious to the fact that he still held her.

"Members of the wedding party, c'mon up here. It seems the new couple's eager to get out of here. Go figure."

Over the laughter Suz said, "Max." She put her hands on his upper arms, the bulge of muscles solid through the material of his suit. It was like trying to shake Mount Rushmore. "Max! You have to go up there."

He faced her, at the same time dropping his hands. "Yeah. See you later."

He looked at her another moment, his face unreadable, then turned and headed through the guests on the dance floor.

She watched his progress, noting no impairment in his confident stride, not the least bit of clumsiness when he neatly sidestepped a woman who suddenly backed into his path. Still, judging by his behavior toward her, he must be feeling the effects of the champagne. He was as responsible as the day was long. Still, she was going to make sure he got a ride home.

She was dragged into the pool of single women for the bouquet-throwing. Annette gave her a sly smile, but if the bride had a specific target in mind, she was foiled by a pair of unlikely bouquet-nappers. Nell, who was Steve's daughter and Annette's seven-year-old maid of honor, teamed with Miss Trudi, an older woman dressed in flowing chiffon and sneakers, to capture the elegant collection of blush-and-cream roses.

Steve groaned as Nell immediately started describing a wedding extravaganza that would put a Super Bowl half-time show to shame. Miss Trudi, on the other hand, pro-claimed that she wanted only the flowers, because they smelled a lot sweeter than any man she knew, and when they died you threw them out and got new ones.

The garter landed in the startled grasp of Rob Dalton, a friend of Steve's who hadn't even been among the pro-spective catchers. He was a good sport about it, though Suz thought his smile covered unhappiness. She caught a com-ment about ''getting divorced'' from one guest to another and figured that explained it.

As Annette and Steve disappeared into the clubhouse, Max was caught in conversation with four prosperous-looking men. Somehow they didn't appear to be chatting about how lovely the wedding had been. Maybe it was the frowns, solemn nods and lowered voices. She was half tempted to march into the group and tell them this was no place to talk business.

Max said little. But when the one whose middle was broader than his shoulders addressed a question to him, he answered with a single word: yes.

She couldn't hear it from the far side of the dance floor, but saw it in his body language.

Just then, a stir presaged Annette and Steve returning in their regular clothes, ready to start their honeymoon trip to an undisclosed location. They wove through the gathered guests, shaking hands, receiving kisses on the cheek and sharing hugs. Max broke away from the group who'd been questioning him, and Suz lost track of him.

''Suz!'' Annette's eyes filled as they hugged. ''Thank you so much for coming. Thank you for dealing with the company these past months. And now I'm going to ask you another favor—tomorrow before you leave town, visit with Miss Trudi. It's been so hectic lately, and I worry—''

"Of course you do, it's one of your best skills," Suz said, hastily wiping moisture from under her own eyes. "Sure, I'll stop by and see her. We talked earlier and she invited me to come any time, so it's all set."

"Thank you."

"You go and have the best honeymoon to start the best marriage and that will be thanks enough," she ordered as she stepped back. Steve was grinning at both of them. "And you—you'd better be good to her or I'll…I'll…''

"Get in line with Max and Nell and Miss Trudi and Juney and a lot of others to—as Nell says—pulverize me." Steve gave her a quick hug.

"I'll call you as soon as we get back," Annette promised. Then her eyes widened. "Oh! I don't know where you'll be. The closing on the town house…''

"I don't know where I'll be, either." Suz laughed, despite the clutch at the pit of her stomach. "But I'll let you know when I do. I'll leave a message on your machine."

"But the number's changing and…I know, let Max know where you are. You can always reach Max."

Satisfied with her solution, Annette smiled and turned with Steve toward the exit. Guests trailed after them, forming an audience as Steve's car pulled up. The valet got out of the driver's seat, while Max and Rob Dalton piled out from the passenger side, both grinning like mischievous boys.

Steve escorted Annette to the passenger side, then went around the back, alternately examining the car and the trying-to-keep-a-straight-face expressions of the two men.

The car hid the usual Just Married sign on the trunk, innocuous shaving-cream decorations and a tail of tin cans and old shoes. One high-heeled red leather boot added a nice touch, but it didn't seem likely that would make Max and Steve's friend look this way.

Max held the car door for Steve. "Open the sunroof so I can say something to Annette."

Steve complied, and Max said another farewell to Annette. Then the car pulled away from the curb. It was halfway down the drive to the country club entrance when someone shouted, "Look! Bubbles!"

Bubbles were streaming from the open sunroof. Not a few, idly floating spheres, but bubbles like a washing machine gone berserk.

"We might have overdone it," Rob said.

Everyone burst out laughing as the car with its train of white froth disappeared from view.

Guests quickly returned to the reception's food, drink and music, but Max stayed where he was, staring after the car.

Everyone else had left before Suz saw him give his shoulders a slight shake, then turn. He stopped when he saw her standing at the arched entryway to the grounds. He manufactured a semblance of a grin.

"It's a good thing those bubbles are biodegradable, or the EPA would be hauling us off."

Suz ignored that. "Miss her already? I don't know Steve well, but…"

"He's a good guy. They'll be okay." For an instant she thought Max was going to say something more. Then she knew he wasn't. "Well, I've done my duty here. Think I'll head home."

"Who's driving you? You promised—"

"I'm fine. But I did promise, so I'll get one of the kids who works here to drive me. I'm not going to pull anybody from the party—folks from Annette's half of the guest list don't get to the Tobias Country Club often, and certainly not as Lana Corbett's guests.''

She believed him, but she wasn't taking any chances. ''I'll drive you.''

''You don't have to.''

''I'm going to. My car's right over there.''

She took the key from her tiny evening bag and opened the car door for him. The narrow skirt of her dress had to be pulled above her knees to allow her to get behind the wheel. And strappy high heels were not designed for a clutch. She unfastened them, slid them off and started the car. Max was looking out the side window, so at least she wouldn't get a lecture about driving barefoot.

She drove out of the country club and turned right toward Max's house on the opposite side of the oval lake.

Max remained silent as they passed the community swimming pool on the edge of town and slowed for the increased foot traffic around the Tastee-Treat Ice Cream Shoppe. She'd picked up speed—to all of thirty—and they'd passed Brecken's Boat Rental, which meant they were exactly one mile from the turnoff to his house, when he spoke again.

''Barefoot? That's how you drive?''

''Not always, but I can handle the pedals better this way than in these shoes.''

His grunt hovered between disbelief and resigned acceptance.

The headlights sliced against the shadows of both night and the overhanging trees, starkly lighting the path ahead. A driver had to be vigilant in case an animal strayed onto the road. So a vigilant driver couldn't afford to even glance toward a passenger whose thick hair was ruffled by the wind through the window, whose relaxed slump against the door somehow made him even more appealing.

''Annette'll have a good life now,'' he said as if to himself. ''Steve's a good guy. Steady. He'll always make a good living and make sure she has everything she needs, everything she wants. And being a Corbett still goes a long way around here.''

Was he blind? Steady and a good living were not what Annette saw when she looked at Steve. But that wasn't what Suzanne said to him. ''You better not talk that way around Annette.''

As she turned the car into the short road to his house, she was aware of him facing her, one brow raised in his I'm-prepared-to-be-amused expression.

She eased the car over a serious dip in the road. Her irritation was harder to smooth over. She was *not* amused.

''In case you didn't notice, Max, your little sister's been all grown up and able to take care of herself for a long time. It's great that she and Steve have fallen in love again—or still.'' She wouldn't be surprised if Annette could get drunk without a sip of champagne—just the way Steve looked at her could do the trick. Who needed alcohol with that kind of love shining from a man's eyes? ''But if she heard you saying that stuff about Steve being the one to make the good living and taking care of her, she'd hit the roof. She's perfectly capable of making a good living herself. And of taking care of herself.''

''I know, but—''

''We made a lot of money selling our company.'' She brought the car to a smooth stop and turned it off.

''Yeah, but she had to struggle to get there. Not just the company and the work you two put into it. I mean growing up. It was tough on her. Always having to stretch every dollar.''

''How about you? You had to bring in those dollars so they could be stretched.''

It was almost as if he didn't hear her. "I'm glad she won't have to do that now. She'll have a different kind of life with Steve."

Suz got out of the car, closing the door with more force than necessary.

"Suz..." He came around the car toward her.

She didn't know why, but she couldn't have him touch her right now. She backed away a step, then turned and started toward the closest destination that made sense—the house.

She'd been in this house dozens of times over the years. But she balked at the idea of going in now. She made an abrupt right turn onto the porch that stretched across the house and looked out toward the lake, as if the view had been her object all along.

"Suz, say whatever it is that's sticking in your craw." He'd stopped in the patch of porch floor between the stairs and door.

Max had built this porch, as he had built all of the additions and improvements to the house. When she'd first come here, it had been a small, sad structure, and Annette had told her that earlier it had been much worse. By applying his skills in patient steps, Max had turned it into a snug, comfortable home.

Now he was applying his skills and all the resources of his small construction company to the two-step community project Annette had come up with. The project would both provide Miss Trudi with a safe and comfortable place to live and give Tobias a year-round tourist attraction—a crafts center in the to-be-renovated nineteenth-century mansion Bliss House, built by Miss Trudi's family.

"I hope this is the champagne talking, because otherwise you're dumber than I ever thought, Max Trevetti."

"Those are my only choices? I'm drunk or stupid?" He

moved to the railing not far from her, seeming to look out toward the lake.

"Consider yourself lucky I gave you any choice, because this is the stupidest thing I've heard." She stepped forward to the rail, too, with a good yard between them. "Annette would tell you she's had a terrific life and it's all because of you. No, don't tell me about money or houses or clothes. I'm talking about feeling there was always somebody in her corner. Somebody who believed in her and loved her, even when he was driving her nuts."

Max's silence made her words echo starkly, as the darkness was more highlighted than lightened by the wash of moonlight on the rippled water down the length of the lake. The country club created a fistful of illumination, but elsewhere signs of humanity were solitary firefly pricks against the night.

The darkness here had texture and depth. And its smell had a moist richness to it, but also carried the sharp sweetness of new-cut grass. A spurt of wind rustled the treetops, broke apart the moon's reflection and scattered the scents.

"I'm glad she feels that way." His voice came slow, with a gruff edge. "I'm glad I was able to take care of her after Mom died and the county wanted..." He cleared his throat.

"Annette never doubted you could..."

He was shaking his head. "It could have gone wrong. Real easy. The county, yeah, but not just that. I've thought about it a lot since I broke my wrist. All the things I couldn't do." Helping him after his accident had pulled Annette back to Tobias three months ago. "What if that had happened when I was starting the company and we were hanging on by a shoestring—hell, a thread? What if it had happened before, when I was working every job I could get so we wouldn't lose the house, so we could eat? What if I hadn't been able to work anymore?''

Suz curved her hands around the porch rail, holding on to its solidity. She'd never heard Max Trevetti talk like this. Big brothers didn't talk this way to their kid sisters.

"You'd have found other work. And you'd have found a way to keep the business going if your injuries had been worse three months ago.''

A sharp expulsion of breath spoke his disbelief. "Construction's all I know.''

"You'd learn something else. You have so many abilities beyond your construction training. You can't limit what you can do to what you have done.''

They were talking like one adult to another—a definite first.

"I'm a little long in the tooth to try something else.''

"That's not true. If you want to, you could do anything.'' The breeze fluttered a strand of hair across her face and she tucked it behind her ear. "You know, I'm sort of wondering what to do from here on, too. Maybe I could form another company like Every Detail somewhere—but how could I pull it off without Annette? But what else can I do? So I do understand how you feel.''

She hadn't been aware of moving closer to him—or had he moved closer to her?—but the gap had narrowed to a sliver that barely kept their shoulders from brushing as he, too, rested his hands on the railing. She could feel the heat of his body, smell a woodsy soap on him.

"Breaking your wrist has shaken up the way you think about your life, Max. Selling the business has done the same for me. And maybe both of us are reacting to Annette's getting married. Let's face it, that's going to have an impact on both our lives.''

He was talking to her, revealing who he was, who he

might want to be. The dance hadn't been real—a figment of moonlight and wedding magic with a dash of champagne thrown in—but this was.

"You can be anything you want," he said. "But I don't have the same options. I'm just a guy who works with his hands." His left hand covered his right wrist—the one he'd broken. "I never got that college degree and—"

"That's exactly what I'm talking about." Impulsively she reached out and stroked her fingertips across the hard bones of his wrist, brushing the fingertips of his left hand still resting there. "If that's what you want, go back and finish your degree. But with it or without it, I know you can be anything you want. I believe that with all my heart."

"You think anyone can be anyth—"

"Not anyone, Max. But you can. I do believe that."

Their fingers tangled. Sliding across each other, curving to hold on, drawing them closer. Him to her, or her to him? Or both.

Her other hand went to his shoulder, as naturally as it had when they danced. Through the fabric, the bone and muscle felt as solid as the railing it had helped build, but warmer, so much warmer.

"Suz…"

It sounded bemused, totally unlike Max's usual certainty.

She felt the breeze across her sensitized lips first. Then a touch so light it might have been the breeze, except the tingling attention of her body knew otherwise. His lips brushed hers again, returning to press against her bottom lip, then retreated.

His arm came around her back, as it had when they danced. But now his hand spread wide in a declaration of heat and possession.

She didn't breathe, not wanting to break this particular bubble for anything in the world.

Then his mouth came down on hers, and she sighed her held breath into him, and it was like fanning a flicker into a flame.

That expressive, strong mouth brought sensations to her lips she was sure she'd never felt before. Sliding and tugging and pressing. So many times. Over and over. Then he opened his mouth over hers, his tongue lined the seam of her lips, and she parted them gladly. He stroked inside her mouth, the pleasure of it so strong that she moaned deep in her throat. The muscles holding her upright loosened, while other muscles, deep, deep inside, tightened around the promise of that caress.

The kiss ended on a gasp from two pairs of oxygen-starved lungs, but his hand splayed across her back still held her against him.

Shadows masked details of his expression, but she saw that his eyes seemed to follow the motion as his fingertips traced the line of her collarbone. He encountered the thin strap of her dress and hesitated.

Too short a hesitation for her even to draw a breath. And then his powerful fingers tweaked the strand, and it fell off her shoulder.

Ah, then she drew in a breath. A sharp, long breath, and felt the swell of her breasts rising against the layers of fabric that covered her.

He spread his fingers, a delicious friction across her skin. His thumb dipped to the top of her dress where her flesh swelled against the material. He shifted his hand to where the space between her breasts left a gap between skin and dress. If he slid his thumb under the fabric there, then stroked toward her shoulder again…would the bodice, no longer supported by its strap, stay up? Would she want it to stay up?

They were balanced. So finely balanced on the edge of

the unknown that the slightest breath of a breeze could drop them into the swirling, cloudy waters…or it could shift them enough to return to the firm ground of how it had always been between them.

The wind strengthened, bringing a burst of laughter from across the lake.

Max stilled. But that lasted only an instant, and then he stepped away. Bereft of his support, she sagged against the railing, trying to get her senses back in some kind of order.

"Sorry. Suz, I'm sorry."

That straightened her backbone. "It's okay."

"No, it's not. I shouldn't have…"

That got her moving. The taste of him was still on her lips and he already regretted it. She'd been wrong. It wasn't only the dance at the reception that had been a figment. This whole night had been a mirage.

"Suz—" He reached for her arm as she passed him. She eluded him and started down the stairs.

"Forget it. Forget the whole thing. I will."

He should have had a hangover.

Max sat on his front porch drinking coffee, watching the morning sun glint off the lake and considering the injustices of the universe.

A real doozy of a hangover. Worse than he'd had in his two and a half years of college. He *deserved* a hangover. It would have explained a lot.

Instead, his stomach had handled cornflakes, bananas and milk fine. His eyes didn't mind the sunlight. And his head wasn't pounding—except with one question: what on earth got into him last night?

No, not even a hangover would have explained that. The only excuse for his behavior would have been if he'd fractured his skull instead of his wrist three months ago. A good, solid blow to the head that could induce delayed lunacy. That might be an adequate answer.

Instead, he had no excuse. Absolutely none.

He wouldn't blame Suz if she used mace on him the next time she saw him. As for unloading his worries on her— she'd probably run the opposite direction.

His only redemption was that she'd left town by now and the next time they saw each other maybe she'd have forgotten. Just in case, he'd make sure Annette and Steve and other folks were around for that first meeting. That would help her feel more comfortable with him again. He couldn't expect her to forget his acting like a horny teenager right away, but she'd start to relax when she saw it wouldn't happen again. Eventually she would forget, as she'd said she would.

What about you? Will you forget?

He'd do whatever he had to. Always had. Put his head down and bull ahead. It worked when Robert Trevetti left the family for good and Max, at thirteen, had taken over the daily care of five-year-old Annette while their mother took on a second job. It had worked when Max took a part-time job, while looking out for Annette and keeping up with school. A second job during the summers had let him put away enough money to supplement scholarships and loans, and he'd made it through more than two years at the University of Wisconsin. Then Mom had died, her heart and will worn out.

That had been the hardest time.

But it had worked then, too. He didn't waste time about might-have-beens. Instead, he'd put his head down and charged ahead, quitting school and working construction because his kid sister had the right to expect his best from him.

Suz wasn't his blood, but she had that right, too.

She'd been a godsend as Annette's roommate right after the fiasco of the first wedding with Steve. Wry and upbeat, lots of energy, funny. But also warm and comforting. He'd still worried about leaving Annette when he'd returned home, but he'd felt better after meeting Suz. And the more he got to know her, the more he knew she was good for Annette.

Even though Annette was now married to Steve, she'd always need a friend like Suz. Suz had been a good friend to him, too.

A tightening in his groin provided a graphic reminder that *friend* was not what he'd been last night.

He didn't know what had gotten into him, but he knew when it started.

That moment she'd come into the church by the side door. He'd turned at the sound and there she'd stood with the breeze pushing the fabric of her dress against the back of her long legs. In that instant of surprise that she was there when he hadn't expected her, it was as if she wasn't Suz. She was simply a woman—no, not simply. Intricately, mysteriously a woman.

And that odd reaction had stuck with him all through the reception and the drive home—and the moments on the porch. A night of contemplating might-have-beens, of thinking the impossible.

Only this morning had the recognition fully hit of what his weird reaction might cost him.

He'd have to make damn sure his idiocy didn't push her away. Whatever weirdness he'd allowed yesterday, she was Suz, and he valued the trust she'd placed in him over the years. He wouldn't risk that.

A timer inside dinged. Time to head to town.

He took the boat across—his truck was still at the country club. It was a nice day and he enjoyed being on the water. That left him a walk from the town's waterfront, past the library, then up tree-lined streets to the blocks that held the old-line stores, the town hall, post office and bank.

A couple of more blocks and he paused to study the house and grounds designed and built by Miss Trudi's ancestor late in the nineteenth century. Not willing to wait, he'd plunged into converting a hodgepodge of outbuildings into livable quarters for Miss Trudi. When that was done, his company would take on renovating Bliss House into a crafts center for Tobias.

It was a great opportunity for Trevetti Building. If he could get the work done to specification and on time with the whole town looking over his shoulder every second.

He shook off that thought and pushed open the iron gate, bracing for the screech. He'd told Miss Trudi he could fix it, but she maintained that so much would be changing soon that she enjoyed holding on to that constant.

"Ah, my dear, we have another visitor!" Miss Trudi's voice floated to him from over a hedge that intruded on the walkway. "We're in the rose garden. Do come join us!"

Short of the house, he turned right, pushing through a gap insufficient for a man his size and busting into an area surrounded by leggy rosebushes.

Suz Grant was here, sitting on a folding chair.

That was the only fact that made the journey from his eyeballs to his brain.

Suz was here. Not gone. But here. The next meeting was right now.

"What was that, Max?" Miss Trudi asked.

He clamped his mouth shut before anything else came out. He hadn't been aware of saying anything, but he had a feeling it had been a curse.

"Do come join us, Max," Miss Trudi invited again. "We're having tea and these delicacies Suz brought."

He blinked and the rest came into focus. An old table and four folding chairs sat in the middle of an area made up of equal parts gravel and weeds. But the table was covered by a pristine white lace tablecloth and held a vase with roses in it, a crystal pitcher of what appeared to be iced tea, and a plate of pastries. Nell Corbett was wrestling with the pitcher and scowling at Miss Trudi, who'd made a move as if to help her.

And Suz…she sat there with her sun-streaked hair being feathered into lacy wisps by a breeze. Shorts revealed a length of tanned leg that ended in sandals, but a short-sleeved blouse covered her shoulders, as well as the delicate skin over her collarbone. The skin he'd touched not twelve hours ago.

She wore sunglasses, so he couldn't see her slate-blue eyes, but there was something about the position of her mouth—as if it had been sputtering futile *but*s—that made him think she was shell-shocked.

''Do sit down, Max,'' Miss Trudi ordered, ''and quit looming over us. You block the view of the roses.''

''Yes'm. Thanks,'' he said as Nell handed him a glass of amber liquid. He took a sip—too sweet—then as he prepared to sit, he said with forced cheer, ''So, Suz, when are you heading out?''

Her lips parted, then closed without saying anything. She turned slightly as if looking at Miss Trudi, faced him again, swallowed and said, ''I'm not. I'm staying in Tobias.''

Chapter Two

Max sat down. Hard. "Staying."

"Yes, isn't it wonderful?" Miss Trudi said. "I've persuaded her to stay while Annette's gone. Why, think of how much she can help."

Suz, still reeling from her encounter with Miss Trudi and Nell, watched Max get sucked into the Miss Trudi Word Machine.

Was this how a car felt going through a car wash? Steered onto a track that commandeered control, torrents of words rushing over, pelted with soap (of the soft variety), more torrents of words, a blast of hot air ("If the Bliss House project gets behind schedule while Annette's off honeymooning, whatever would we do?"), then a final jolt before rolling out into the wide world. With the sun drying up the words while their shine remained.

Having been there minutes ago herself, Suz could almost feel sorry for Max.

Almost.

Except that at the news she was staying, Max's tan regressed from June to February in the blink of an eye.

Okay, she had her doubts, too. Big doubts. But Max's reaction was more than doubt about her filling in for Annette. It was as though the man was afraid she'd jump him.

She would admit to having once dreamed of kissing him. She would also acknowledge that the dream wasn't half as good as the reality had been last night. On the other hand, she'd gotten over her yen for Max Trevetti years ago. *Years* ago.

At first she'd thought the best way to reassure him of that would be to leave town as planned. But this arrangement would give her and Max a chance to settle back into their familiar roles. His discomfort around her had made it clear he regretted what happened last night. And she...well, she and Max had been friends for a long time. She didn't want to risk that.

Besides, Annette had asked her to look after Miss Trudi, who had asked her—begged her—to step in for Annette during these weeks.

And, being honest here, she'd felt a level of relief. It would give her something to do without deciding if it was what she wanted to do long-term.

Come Monday, she had no business to run, no job to go to, no obligations. Next week, after closing on the town house, she wouldn't have a home, either. Not her own home, anyway. She could go home to Dayton.

She shifted on the folding chair. How could that thought make her long to sink into the warm embrace of her parents, brothers, sisters-in-law, nieces and nephews while it simultaneously made her want to run screaming in the opposite direction? Until she sorted out that contradictory reaction, not to mention what she wanted to do with the rest of her life, staying in Tobias seemed like a really good option.

As for the work, it would be following Annette's instructions. That arrangement had worked out well with Every Detail.

On top of that, dammit, *he* was the one who'd kissed *her.*

At least, to start.

Miss Trudi had been so busy extolling the benefits of having Suz pick up Annette's work that not even Nell had got in another word. But now the older woman left a gap, and Max repeated, "Staying?"

"Maybe I shouldn't—" Suz began.

"Yes, staying," Miss Trudi said firmly. She looked directly at Max. "Surely you're not saying you don't want her here."

From stunned, Max's expression quickly shifted to cornered. Then he brightened while still wary, like a man who'd spotted a door out of that corner yet worried what was beyond it.

"Suz knows she's welcome to visit anytime. But there's no reason for her to work."

"Of course there is. There's a great deal to do."

As an understatement, that ranked with saying Pavarotti could carry a tune.

Suz hadn't appreciated the depth of the challenge until Miss Trudi took her on a brief tour of Bliss House earlier, during which her hostess bypassed several doors with an airy, "Oh, we hardly ever use that room." If those were as bad as the rooms that were used, they were *bad*. She suspected they were worse.

Windows in some of the "good" rooms provided views of the carriage house and stables that Max had started renovating and connecting to create a new home for Miss

Trudi. That alone was a complicated project. Despite the work awaiting him, however, Max clearly didn't want Suz involved.

"Three weeks is a long time for someone who has a hard time staying in one spot," he said.

"Flit," Suz muttered.

"What was that, my dear?" Miss Trudi had better hearing than Suz had given her credit for.

"What Max is trying to say without coming out and saying it is that he thinks I flit from interest to interest. Have no stick-to-it-iveness. So he thinks I won't last here for three weeks. I'll flit away."

"One time I said—"

"One time was plenty—you used me as the definition when you used the word in Scrabble, Max."

"I like Scrabble," Nell said to the table at large.

Max faced Miss Trudi and repeated doggedly, "Suz doesn't have to work. Annette set it up so that—"

"So that when she returns from her honeymoon, she will require herself to work nonstop at a time she and Steve and Nell will want to spend time together."

"I'm not gonna call her Mom. I'm gonna call her Annette," Nell said. "She said I should only call her Mom if a spirit moves in."

A spirit moves in? Sidetracked, Suz glanced in puzzlement toward the girl, who had both hands on the pitcher's handle and was sliding it toward the table's edge in apparent preparation to refill her glass of iced tea.

"That's an excellent plan, Nell, to wait until the spirit moves you," said Miss Trudi. "It will be so much easier for Annette if Suz helps me work through the decisions remaining. That will expedite your construction schedule, as well, Max. You did say your schedule was 'twisted like a pretzel'—I believe that was your term—to deal with An-nette's absence.''

He opened his mouth, closed it, then muttered, ''We'd manage.''

Miss Trudi beamed. ''There's no need to merely manage now that Suz has graciously agreed to step in. I should like to start with my new kitchen. I confess I have not stayed abreast of developments in culinary appliances and…oh, my! Annette had my head positively whirling with the pos-sibilities. I shall need a great deal of help sorting out my priorities and desires. Why, the options in a microwave oven alone—tunning, positively stunning.''

With that, Miss Trudi produced another verbal funnel cloud, whirling around and around, uprooting any thoughts her listeners might try to hold on to. Nell's asides had the listener focusing on odd bits poking out here and there, and then—*wham!*—the funnel blindsided you.

For someone being whirled around in a funnel cloud, Max looked awfully good. His jaw was stubbled with the morning-after-wearing-a-suit-all-day-and-I'll-be-darned-if-I'm-going-to-shave reaction she recognized from her ''wild'' brother Tim. Combined with his fierce expression and his wind-tousled dark hair, Max looked like a pirate. Dark, a little dangerous—and in the middle of rough seas.

She gave herself a mental shake. She needed to tune back in to this conversation, to see in what part of Oz the funnel cloud had landed them.

''So, it's all settled, then,'' Miss Trudi was saying. *Uh-oh.* ''Suz shall have the room Annette was using. It will be marvelous to have her company. Now, what time should Suz come to your office in the morning?''

''Miss Trudi—''

''Give it up, Max,'' Suz muttered. ''You're not in Kan-sas anymore.''

"What was that, dear? Kansas? No, of course not, we're in Wisconsin." Miss Trudi patted her hand, as if Suz had lost her marbles.

However, Suz saw a glint of comprehension in Max's eyes, along with something that might almost be shared amusement.

But it couldn't have been, because he stood abruptly and backed up. There was no amusement in his eyes or voice when he said, "Be at the office at ten-thirty, Suz."

He strode off, pushing the overgrown bushes back with one arm hard enough that when he'd passed through, they made a *whap-whap-whap* sound as they settled into place.

Miss Trudi appeared totally unfazed. "More tea, Suz?"

"I'll pour!" Nell had a fascination with that pitcher.

"This isn't going to work, Miss Trudi. I'm sorry, but—"

"Not work? Nonsense. You haven't let Max scare you off, have you? Surely from years of friendship with Annette, you've come to know his ways."

"He's louder than a bark," contributed Nell, standing to drain the last dregs from the pitcher into Suz's glass.

Suz couldn't take her eyes off the operation, in morbid expectation that the pitcher could fall any second, and equally morbid expectation that she would be expected to drink the pale sludge sliding into her glass.

"His bark is worse than his bite." Miss Trudi nodded. "Max has a good heart that would never allow him to bite anyone—" Suz could swear the woman winked at her over Nell's head "—at least not in anger. But he does have a tendency to bark at times."

"Not when he taught me how to use a hammer," Nell said.

She demonstrated, only slightly hampered by having both hands wrapped around pitcher's handle. Suz barely flinched; somehow her imagination stuck on the idea of

Max Trevetti's big rough hands wrapped around the little girl's grip as he patiently demonstrated the use of a hammer.

"He said I was very good," Nell continued with pride, placing the pitcher on the table without mishap. "He said I could work for him anytime after I've graduated from school."

"He's not as eager to have me on his roster," Suz said to Miss Trudi.

"Whyever not? He knows you and Annette established a successful business—he must be aware of your abilities."

"Max knows Annette's the real whiz."

"Well, my dear, you must show him otherwise. A man can't know what a woman can do unless he's shown. Come to think of it, sometimes a man can't know what he can do unless he's shown—most often by a woman."

Suz knew there was an insurmountable flaw in Miss Trudi's reasoning in her case. Annette had been the driving force behind their business from the get-go. Oh, sure, Suz had worked hard, but Annette had run the show. God, she hoped Annette had left step-by-step instructions for this one.

Her stomach sank as a new thought hit her. Annette wouldn't have had any reason to leave instructions—she'd had no idea anyone might be filling in for her. Oh, God—

"You look a bit worn-out, Suz," Miss Trudi said. "I suppose it's all the excitement from last night."

Suz refused to let her mind dwell on the excitements of last night.

"Last night we caught the bouquet. Miss Trudi only wanted the flowers," Nell said, pointing to the wilting roses in the middle of the table. "But I might have a wedding— a *big* wedding. Maybe with a circus and elephants."

"A circus would be entertaining," Miss Trudi said, "although you must considered the drawbacks of including elephants. For now, let's show Suz where she'll be staying.'' She stood in a flutter of chiffon.

''I'll find Squid.'' Nell zoomed ahead.

''My cat,'' Miss Trudi explained. ''Come now, I'll show you the room Annette used, and we can freshen it up before you move your things in. Did I mention that it has its own exterior entrance?'' The woman's voice was as proper as a Victorian matriarch's, but laugh lines fanned from her eyes as she added, ''Leading up to the wedding, that was a feature Annette and Steve found to be of great convenience.''

He'd overreacted.

What had gotten into him? It wasn't a bad idea. It made sense to have someone fill in for Annette. Since Suz and Annette had worked together, she was the perfect choice to pick up where his sister had left off.

And while she was here, he would prove to Suz that he was still ''good ol' Max,'' that what happened Saturday night wouldn't ever happen again. He'd wipe out the memory of that kiss and the way she had felt against— No, better not to think of that.

Yeah, this was better. If she'd left, that would have been the memory Suz carried. But now she'd see that they were back to normal. They'd get past that strangeness…well, not strangeness. Nobody could call the way Suz had felt in his arms strange. Or the way she had parted her lips, and the taste of her. Her skin. God, the softness…

He'd forget all that. And when Suz left Tobias, they would be on an even keel once more.

But what had thrown them off that even keel in the first place?

An image popped into his head. As if it had been waiting for that question to cue it.

The side door of the Church of the Woods opening during yesterday's ceremony. The collective gasp of recognition of déjà vu from Annette and Steve's first wedding. Then turning and seeing that the latecomer was Suz.

She'd worn a red dress. A jacket covered the fact that all that appeared to hold the thing up were a pair of red strings that tended to slip off her shoulder and down the smooth curve of her upper arm—especially if a man's hands...

No, that had come later, after the keel was already uneven. He was trying to trace when it started. And that was when she'd walked into the church.

Laughter from the bride and groom had triggered a swell of amusement across the small church.

Except for him.

He hadn't laughed. He'd felt like he'd never seen Suz before. But why?

She'd said she couldn't come to the wedding because of that family emergency. He hadn't been prepared to see her. Not that he had to prepare himself to see Suz. It was simply the...unexpectedness.

Yes. Unexpected events could throw you off balance. Unexpected events could jostle your equilibrium, but only momentarily, then everything settled back in place. Like a faint tremor from the mildest of earthquakes. No structural damage, not even any cracks. A temporary shifting, then things returned to normal.

Max wasn't at the office when Suz got there at ten-thirty-one Monday. She would have been later if Miss Trudi hadn't pushed her out the door.

She'd awakened in plenty of time—who needed an alarm clock when nail guns started at seven-twenty-five—but she and Miss Trudi had matters to discuss.

She wouldn't hear of Suz paying rent or even contributing to utilities. After two meals at Bliss House, however, Suz knew they needed to work out something about food. Fried chicken with mashed potatoes for Sunday dinner could be seen as a rare treat. But this morning's breakfast had been fried eggs, bacon *and* sausages with crusty bread. She practically heard her arteries clogging as she ate every last sinfully delicious bite because she couldn't hurt Miss Trudi's feelings. Besides, she'd needed sustenance.

But if staying in Tobias meant packing away the calories the way she had the past two days, she'd be as big as Bliss House in no time. After she met with Max, she'd stop at the fruit stand by Brecken's boat landing.

Max's office was in the second bedroom in his house, the one he'd built for Annette when she was a teenager. After she'd left Tobias, he'd converted it to an office. From visiting with Annette, Suz knew it well.

Juney Lowe, his office manager, said Max would soon return from his early rounds of Bliss House and a worksite that Trevetti Building was wrapping up. He'd gotten a late start, Juney added with a piercing look, because he'd had to wait for Lenny to take him to get his car from the country club for some reason. He'd be back any minute, she said.

That was not all Juney said. Her commentary included the business, the wedding, the reception, her own wedding four months ago, her honeymoon in Hawaii, personalities of various guests at both weddings and their intertwined histories. All Suz had to do was sit back and listen.

She had started to relax when the back door slammed shut. Max's footsteps tracked through the kitchen, then across the living room.

"Don't worry, he's not his best in the morning, but he's not a total bear."

Juney's assurance made Suz aware of her hands tightly

clasped in her lap. She unknotted them, resting one on the couch's arm, and crossed one leg over the other beneath her cotton skirt.

She'd left Dayton in a hurry, packing her outfit for the wedding, then haphazardly adding mostly casual clothes. The one halfway businesslike outfit she'd brought she'd worn Saturday morning to meet that corporate VP in Chicago. After this skirt, she was down to jeans and shorts.

Max's gaze came to her, then skidded away. "Morning, Suz. I'll be with you in a minute. Any messages, Juney?"

"Nope. You're late. You made Suz wait ten minutes."

"That's okay," Suz said. "It doesn't—"

"Sorry. There was cleanup to do at the Dunwoody site."

"And I suppose you did it yourself," Juney said. "If Eric can't leave a clean site, you should remove him as a foreman."

"He'll be under my supervision at Bliss House. That should get him on the right track." Juney harrumphed, but Max paid no heed. "Will you call about getting the TravelinJohn removed?"

"I'll do better than that—I'll make Eric do it! Just because he got through college doesn't mean he's too good to do what he's supposed to."

Amusement glinted in Max's eyes. "Good idea." Then he turned to Suz, and a film of reserve covered the amusement.

Suz felt as if a weight dropped from her throat to the bottom of her stomach. Even in those first months, when she'd been attracted to her roommate's brother and he hadn't returned the interest, Max had never been reserved with her. He'd simply been unyieldingly big brotherish.

What if they could never get back to being comfortable? What if Saturday night had done permanent damage?

She blinked hard. She was here because Miss Trudi

thought she could help Max while Annette was gone. If it was awkward, tough.

"Juney, would you get a copy of the proposal and design plan for Suz?" He retreated three steps and propped his back against the filing cabinet, crossing his arms over his chest. "She's come by to see what we're putting together on the Bliss House project."

"Sheesh, Max, you make it sound like she's on a field trip or something. Miss Trudi said Suz is filling in for Annette. I hope she has better luck getting that woman to buckle down and make decisions."

The phone rang and Juney held up one exquisitely manicured nail to hold off Max's rejoinder.

"Trevetti Building, Ms. Lowe speaking." Her voice lost its starch. "Hi, Mom. What's up…? Yeah, he's here, why…? Oh? Uh-huh… Yeah… Yeah?" Juney's eyes went from him to Suz and back. "Is that a fact…? That, too, huh?" This time she stared at Suz for a long moment, before switching to him. "I can't wait. I'll be by tonight after work… No, that's not a good idea. They might, uh, disappear… Yes, I mean it. Make sure you keep the negatives in a safe place until we get plenty of copies."

She hung up. "Sorry. You were saying?"

"What was that about?" Max demanded. "You sounded like a gangster getting ready to blackmail somebody."

"Max! You know me better than that."

He snorted. "I know you all right. What were you and Gert cooking up?"

"I like that. Here Mom and I are just making sure Annette gets all the pictures from the disposable cameras that the wedding guests were given."

A trickle of uneasiness snaked down Suz's back. Though what on earth could photographs from the wedding show?

It wasn't until they were alone on the porch of his house that they…

Well, anyway, the pictures couldn't show anything to do with her and Max. It was much more likely that Juney and her mother, Gert, were interested in some local indiscretion caught on film.

Max pulled his gaze from Juney and said to Suz, "I can't work with you a lot to get you up to speed on this."

Apparently during the phone call Max had decided on a different approach. She recognized it as treating her as a kid sister he was letting tag along. Now this she knew how to handle.

Before Suz could respond, however, Juney spoke.

"Cut it out—you're breaking her heart." She looked at Suz. "Don't worry, Suz, I can fill you in on whatever you need to know. You'll be better off without Max hanging over your shoulder, anyhow. He's a real buttinski."

"Juney—"

"What stage is the work at?" Suz asked quickly.

"We've strengthened the walls and roof structures so the stables and carriage house meet code. Got foundation down for the new sections. We've started framing and— What are you frowning about?"

"I thought…wouldn't it help to have Miss Trudi's needs for the interior finalized? I was looking around the structures and—"

"Don't go near there without a hard hat. It's for your own good."

Oh, yes, Big Brother was back in full force. "Are you going to leave all those walls in the existing structure?"

"No. You'll see on the design. But we had to get started, because we've gotta get finished."

As matter-of-fact as his tone was, Suz thought she heard an undercurrent. She and Annette had talked about the project these past three months, but it had been a distant also-ran to Annette and Steve's relationship, their wedding and their future. She needed to find out more about the schedule and the financing to understand what Max faced.

"Then Miss Trudi can move into the new space," he continued, "and out of Bliss House so we can start that. We've gotta turn this around on a dime. We don't have time to—"

"Wait for Annette to come back. Told you so," said Juney, pulling a folder from the stacking baskets on her desk. She met Max's fierce look with no sign of wilting. "What? I did tell you so. Annette kept saying she needed to get more done with Miss Trudi and you kept telling her it could wait until after her honeymoon, and I said you were a great brother, but you were backing yourself into a mighty tight corner. And don't pretend you don't remember that conversation."

"I didn't say I didn't—"

"Good. So here you go, Suz." Juney extended the folder and Suz automatically took it. "Here are Annette's notes. That should get you started."

"Juney." It sounded like a voice from Mount Olympus. A decidedly cranky god about to hurl a thunderbolt or two at pesky humans.

"No need to thank me, Max. But you should be down on your knees groveling to Suz. She's going to save your butt."

He waited until the front door closed behind Suz.

"You were out of line, Juney."

"Baloney. You need help. She's willing to help. I closed the deal, like you're always talking about."

But he wasn't so sure Suz was willing to help.

Juney's line "She's going to save your butt" had produced a look in Suz's eyes that was almost panic-stricken. Clutching Annette's folder like a lifeline, she had not looked like someone eager to jump in.

He spotted Suz through the window by her car. She opened the driver's door and leaned over to place the folder in the passenger seat. Her light summer skirt rode up, the fabric skimming over her firm, round rear end and floating about halfway down her thighs.

"Annette says anyone who thinks Suz is just decorative is an idiot."

June's voice hit him like the flick of a whip. "I wasn't—"

"No, not an idiot. Something else, another word... I know, misguided. That's what she said—misguided."

He'd recovered enough to realize Juney had been too distracted by her pursuit of remembering the precise word to notice his disclaimer. That was a relief. Because a disclaimer made it sound as if he'd done something wrong. He'd twitched only because her comment was so unexpected.

Unexpected—there was that word again. "Nobody thinks Suz is just..."

From certainty, his voice faded into nothingness. Juney gave him one of those looks women give a guy they think is about a mile behind on some mental path and they're waiting to see if he'll pick up the next bread crumb she'd left to lead him along.

He glared at her. "Did you check on that framing lumber?"

"Lenny should be taking delivery at Bliss House right about now. The filled Dumpster's been removed, and an empty one's in place. He's finished fencing around the trees and bushes Rob's sister and Miss Trudi said to be especially careful about."

He should have known better than to test Juney's efficiency. He shook his head, trying to hold off a grin. "So what do you need me for, Juney?"

"To go meet with that group of vultures, because Steve's out of town, and above all else, to keep that Jason Remtree from the bank off my back so I can keep this company running."

He laughed. Everything else might change—his little sister could get married, his future could be sitting between the jaws of a vice, and he might act like such an idiot with Suz that he put their friendship in jeopardy—but Juney stayed the same.

"I'll say one thing for you, Ms. Lowe, you don't lack for confidence."

"Why should I?"

He was grinning as he headed out.

Max agreed with Annette's assessment that anybody who thought Suz was just decorative was misguided. On the other hand, decorativeness wasn't without its power.

For instance, he suspected his sister might underestimate the impact of Suz's decorativeness on a construction crew.

After grabbing a post-meeting fast-food lunch, he parked his truck and walked through a nearly deserted site, only to find his entire workforce clustered around the back corner of the carriage house. If this site had been a ship, it would have sunk from all the weight being in one spot.

It so happened that that spot was directly opposite the exterior double doors to the room Suz was staying in.

He was familiar with the room, because Annette had stayed there before her wedding. She wouldn't live with Steve before they were married because of Nell. She'd said Max's house was too small once Juney returned to work after her honeymoon. Max suspected this room's privacy contributed to Annette's decision, too. It was at the end of a one-story 1960s addition built for a live-in nurse when Miss Trudi's parents were failing. It boasted modern plumbing—modern compared to the rest of the house—but did not run to air-conditioning.

The workers didn't notice his approach. This was not because they were so busy with their air nailers that they covered other noise. It was because they were staring over their shoulders and were hardly working at all.

He reached a point where he could see what specifically held their attention. Suz had the double doors propped open to match the room's three windows, one of which had a box fan whirling away in it. He doubted it made much headway against the June sun beating down on the black roof.

Suz came into sight, moving around the foot of the bed. She had her shoulder-length light-brown hair pinned up and wore loose shorts and a sleeveless shirt tied at her waist. She plopped on the bed on her back, holding a sheaf of papers up to read and bending her knees so her feet were flat on the mattress. The fabric of her shorts dropped down, making her legs look—to a man with some imagination, and what man didn't have an imagination in this area—as they would if she had nothing on at all.

A sound like a sigh came from his crew.

A curse rose in Max's throat, along with a bloodthirst that was totally unlike him. He swallowed both, but they didn't go down easy. He coughed.

Every worker jumped as if that cough had been a rifle shot. They started scattering at a pace appropriate to responding to a rifle shot, too.

"Lenny!" he shouted to his long-time foreman, who happened to be among those making good time in the opposite direction. "Call a meeting."

He waved toward a spot under a huge old maple—and away from Suz's room. When the men had assembled, he let a silence broken only by foot shuffling stretch a full minute. Then he began in a low voice, "This is the biggest project Trevetti Building's ever taken on. The biggest project in Tobias in thirty years. The schedule is too tight for comfort, and the financing is going to leave us only about half the skin on our teeth.

"I'm not asking you to do work you won't get paid for—you've worked for me before and you know I don't operate that way. But we need every one of you to do all the work you are paid for.

"One more thing. The house is off-limits. No exceptions. Ms. Grant—" few of the men were looking at him to see him nod toward Suz's room, but he was certain they knew whom he was talking about "—is going to help Miss Trudi decide what she wants so we can keep to schedule. I expect everyone to treat her professionally. She's a friend of my sister's." In case that wasn't clear enough, he added, "I expect everyone to treat her with the same respect you give my sister."

"You got it," Lenny said, and others added murmurs of assent.

Max frowned. Eric hadn't been among the assenters.

The jury was out on Eric. Lenny admired his carpentry. Juney thought his ego interfered with his work ethic. Max could see both points. But what concerned him now was that Eric considered himself quite the ladies' man.

"Lenny, Eric, hold up a minute."

He asked for a status report and got a rundown of minimal progress.

"We need to do better. You both need to set the tone. Understood, Eric? Good. Everybody get to work."

They had barely turned away when he heard, "Max!"

Suz was coming across the open area toward them. This swallowing of curses was getting to be a habit.

Eric's pace slowed to a shuffle. "To work," Max said. "Now."

Eric sent another look in Suz's direction, then headed off at a speed that wouldn't have pressed a snail.

Suz, with Miss Trudi trailing her, zeroed in her target—Max.

"Do you have time to take us on a tour? It would be so helpful for Miss Trudi and me if we could walk through the area."

"Now?"

"Now works for us. If you can't, maybe one of the other men—"

"I can. But…is that what you're going to wear?"

Suz looked down in puzzlement. "Yeah."

"Don't you have anything longer?"

Puzzlement gave way to irritation. "It's not a Britney Spears belly-button-exposer, for heaven's sake."

"I meant the shorts."

"They're not that short."

"They're short. Where do you think they got the name? Don't you have anything longer?"

"Gee, I forgot to pack my tent. What is the problem, Max? It isn't like Tobias is a religious center. I've worn shorts around here before."

"Not around a construction site." *Not around a construction crew.* "There're a lot of dangers." *Some of them human.* "You could get hurt."

"I'll sign an insurance release if you want, but I'll be careful."

He'd opened his mouth for another comment when he caught sight of Miss Trudi's expression of rapt interest.

His mouth snapped shut, and he turned on his heel. They

followed him, with Suz satisfying herself with one comment about being glad he'd come to his senses, before segueing into what she and Miss Trudi wanted to see and why.

She was still going—how long did she think this tour would last?—when they reached the old gardener's shed they used for storage. He unlocked the door, eyed the options hung on nails, selected two, tucked one under his arm so he could relock the door, and she was still at it.

"…we also need to decide if there's room for a terrace that—"

He clamped a hard hat on her head.

"Hey, that hurts!"

"It's for your own good."

"Where have I heard that before?" she muttered, taking the hat off and rubbing her head.

Stifling an urge to do the same to Miss Trudi, who was grinning at him like a cat with cream, he handed her a hard hat.

"Put the hat on and keep it on, or we're not going anywhere. That goes for both of you."

Chapter Three

They had planned a wonderful space for Miss Trudi. A workable kitchen, a dining room that opened into a living room, an entrance hall lined with bookcases that she called "the library," a bedroom suite with vaulted-ceiling sitting area, bathroom and utility area all on the ground floor, plus a guest suite upstairs.

It would be so much more livable than the rambling, decrepit Bliss House. Yet Miss Trudi did not seem enthusiastic.

The older woman had come into Suz's room and said with such urgency that they should do a walk-through of the site with Max right away. So their work could proceed, she'd said. But if she didn't like the plan, why was she so eager for the work to proceed?

"The kitchen's too small," Miss Trudi said now.

From the expression on Max's face, Suz could tell this was an old discussion.

"Annette showed you how the windows can work as pass-throughs to the dining room, and—" His gesture to indicate the two rooms brushed Suz's shoulder. "Sorry."

"No problem."

Miss Trudi wasn't sidetracked. "I want visitors to be with me in the kitchen as at Bliss House. I don't want a wall there at all."

Max moved away, resting one shoulder against the weathered brick wall. "It's a load-bearing wall. Can't take it out."

"Can't another wall bear the load?" Miss Trudi asked. "Then the kitchen could be a more generous size."

"The working area's almost as big as you've got now. With the separate dining room—"

"A dining room is not conducive to casual interaction. I haven't served my friends in the dining room in decades."

"The Bliss House dining room hasn't been *safe* for decades."

Miss Trudi's face rearranged into the austere lines of a teacher who's a stickler for discipline. "Maximilian Augusto Trevetti—"

Suz would have to try that on him sometime to see if he looked as abashed when she said it as when Miss Trudi did. At the moment, though, she had another matter to pursue.

"What if you made that wall the divider between the library and the living room, instead of between the kitchen and dining room? As visitors came in and passed your collection of books, Miss Trudi, they would catch glimpses of the living room, and it would be like they were being invited in."

"An excellent suggestion, Suz! In speaking of the pass-through arrangement, Annette mentioned using shutters on the old windows to allow the option of leaving them open or closed between the two areas.''

''Shutters would work great. You could have them finished on the living-room side to match the walls so when they were closed, you would hardly notice them. That's—''

She bit her words off when she realized Max had pushed himself away from the wall about five sentences ago. He was looking straight ahead, but with the glazed expression of someone who's seeing something else entirely.

Like probably his entire construction project crumbling into dust. Taking with it the project's schedule and budget.

''It wouldn't work,'' she said quickly, trying to backtrack. ''I shouldn't have jumped in where I don't know—''

''Nonsense.'' Miss Trudi trained that stickler look on her now. ''Eliciting your ideas is precisely the reason we wanted you to stay.''

Suz gave a fleeting thought to how loosely Miss Trudi used ''we'' in that phrase.

Then Max was asking, ''Where would you move the other rooms?''

''Forget I said anyth—''

''Where,'' Max repeated, facing her, his full attention so concentrated it felt like a fifty-pound weight on her chest, ''would you move the other rooms?''

He wasn't going to let her bow out gracefully. He was going to make her expose how little she knew.

''Rotate,'' she said.

''Rotate? How?''

She gave her hand a halfhearted twist, like turning on a faucet. ''Leave the bedroom suite where it is and move everything else one room clockwise.''

''Show me.'' He took her copy of the plan and smoothed it out on top of a stack of lumber. When she hesitated, he handed her a pen from his pocket and insisted, ''Show me.''

She sketched a new wall for the other side of the library–entry hall and added shaky lines to indicate configurations for the rest of the downstairs.

''Sort of like that. But you don't have to tell me it's not practical, that it won't work, so—''

''Yeah, it will.'' He reached for the sheet. She reflexively held it down with her palm, but he slid the paper out. With his other hand he took back his pen and started tracing over her lines, making them stand out boldly, ''In fact, it puts the water and sewage lines for the bathrooms and kitchen in a better configuration.''

''How fortuitous,'' Miss Trudi said. ''Now aren't you glad Suz stayed in Tobias?''

''Yes'm,'' he said with mock meekness, a grin creeping up. But when he turned to Suz, his gaze was sincere. ''This is a great idea, Suz—a creative solution to several issues. You've more than earned your keep.''

Suz's stomach felt like a dish towel someone had twisted to wring dry.

''You have to check this out, Max. Make sure it will work. I'm not sure what I said about the shutters can be pulled off, much less moving the design. It was a…a whim, and you can't turn the project around on a whim.''

''Not a whim. A good idea. Can't you take a compliment?''

She waved that away. ''Off-the-cuff remarks aren't something you should rely on.''

Although focused on Max, Suz had been aware of Miss Trudi's gaze, going from her to him and back as she followed the exchange. Now Max looked toward the older woman, and Suz saw Miss Trudi, the brightness and sharpness in her eyes turned up an extra notch, give him a raised-eyebrow look with a little nod, as if encouraging a student on the verge of making some vital connection.

He frowned.

Suz matched that expression. What was going on?

"Why would you think it wouldn't?" he demanded abruptly.

"What?"

"Why were you so sure your idea wouldn't work?"

Trapped for a second, she quickly recovered. "I'm not an architect, am I. How could I possibly expect my idea to work?"

He studied her, the frown still tucked between his dark brows.

"Well, it's going to work. Yeah—don't bother to say it again—I'll check it out. But this is one off-the-cuff remark that I'm betting can be relied on."

Before Suz could do more than open her mouth to protest, Miss Trudi slipped her hand through Max's arm and started off with him.

"Once Max makes up his mind, there's no changing it, at least not without—" she gave Suz a look that Suz had no hope of interpreting "—a great deal of evidence to the contrary."

Their inspection wrapped up quickly, since Suz hardly said another word. He promised to let them know ASAP about the design change, so Suz and Miss Trudi could adjust their thinking about the interiors.

They started for the house, with Miss Trudi talking away. The material of Suz's shorts swayed and flirted with the back of her firm thighs.

A change in Miss Trudi's voice caught his attention. She was looking over her shoulder at him, talking still. She gave him that one-eyebrow-up expression and a sort of nod, as if acknowledging that he understood something just between the two of them.

He didn't understand at all.

Nobody thinks Suz is just decorative.

That was what he'd intended to say to Juney earlier today. But could Suz possibly think she was just decorative?

But that didn't fit with the Suz he knew. Sassy and bright and taking no guff from anyone.

A good offense made one helluva defense. The sports axiom wriggled into his head and wouldn't go away. Sassy and bright and taking no guff *could* be a way to keep people from seeing that you thought you were just decorative.

Was that the bread crumb Juney had hoped he'd pick up? But how could Suz think that after what she and Annette had done with their business? That took talent, dedication, creativity and hard work—a lot of hard work. Sure luck had a role, but without the others, luck wouldn't have mattered.

And look at the way Miss Trudi had perked right up at Suz's idea.

Boy, *she* hadn't thought it was a great idea. Not after he and Miss Trudi latched onto it. When he'd complimented her, she'd gotten worse, as if his saying he believed in her idea made her more skittish.

Just then Suz stepped back to let Miss Trudi enter the back door first. He thought she might turn and catch him watching her, so he looked away—and caught Eric watching her.

The younger man must have felt Max's stare, because he looked toward him, not taking the time to fully mask his pleasure at what he'd been ogling.

"Lenny!" Max called out, a decision suddenly made. "I'm leaving you to wrap up today. I've got things to buy."

* * *

The knock at her door Tuesday morning took a moment to register in Suz's consciousness.

Partly because she first took it to be an element of the syncopated hammering that had started at seven-thirty. And hammering was only one instrument in this building cacophony. Add in the thrum of the generator, the shrill two-toned pound of the hammer guns, the whine of a power saw, men's raised voices.

And partly because that seven-thirty start had come awfully early, because in a sudden craving for baked solace, she'd been up until three making chocolate-chip cookies in Miss Trudi's archaic kitchen—the stove had to be a throwback to Victorian times. The urge for cookies had followed several sleepless hours after a call to her family in Dayton with the news that she was staying in Tobias. There had been tears, flutterings about how the sale of Every Detail meant she could have a genteel life now if she would just put her mind to it and warnings about dangerous and dirty construction sites. Even the temporary nature of the situation hadn't reconciled her parents to this plan.

On the other hand, her parents hadn't been reconciled to her leaving Dayton for college, so that wasn't likely to change anytime soon.

The final part of the delay in that knock registering with Suz was that she wasn't expecting a knock, since the doors were wide open in a vain attempt to catch a breeze.

But sure enough, when she looked up from the stack of home-building and renovating magazines she'd purchased last night at the grocery store, Max stood beside the open doorway, knocking at the frame, a lineup of workers behind him.

"May we come in?" he asked when he saw he had her attention.

"Sure, that's why it's open."

For some reason that made him frown. An expression that deepened as she unfolded from sitting cross-legged in the center of bed.

She would almost think he was uncomfortable being in the same room with her with a bed in it—but that was crazy. Half the times she'd visited Tobias with Annette she'd slept on the couch in his living room. He never once showed the least discomfort about that. Heck, he'd push her feet aside so he could sit on the couch if she was too slow getting up for his taste.

Besides, for him to be uncomfortable because this was her bedroom, he'd have to be thinking of her as a woman. And he'd made quite clear that making that mistake Saturday night had been an aberration.

"Put that down over there," he told two workers carrying a large box, pointing to the floor beside the desk. To another pair of men carrying five boxes between them, he added, "Leave those by the door."

She retreated to the far side of the bed to avoid being trampled by the workers intent on following Max's instructions. One of them was his foreman, Lenny, whom she'd met at the wedding. He put two boxes, each about half the size of a shoe box, on her desk and set a toolbox at the foot of the bed. As he straightened, he met her eyes and winked.

"All set, boss," he said to Max. "If you need any more help…"

"I'll give a shout when I'm ready to put the unit in place."

It was a dismissal, and the workers filed out quickly. The only one who looked at her was Lenny. He tugged at his ball cap's brim and smiled. No wink this time. His eyes cut to Max and he seemed to work hard at suppressing the smile.

"Thanks, Lenny." Max pulled both doors three-quarters closed.

"It gets too hot in here with the doors closed," she protested.

"We're going to take care of that." He squatted down and started opening the big box. The position and movement drew the material of his white T-shirt tight. It conformed to the muscles of his broad shoulders and made his shoulder blades shift sharply under skin and fabric. Then it snuggled up to his backbone as the white cotton dropped into the gap left by the waistband of his jeans, sinking lower and lower, out of sight, until—

"Suz?"

She jumped—and was grateful the involuntary reaction took her backward, because if she'd jumped forward, she would have landed on him. She hadn't even been aware of moving closer, and here she was practically with her shins against his—admiring phrases from women friends spoken about some men's great butts floated through her head—his rear end. "What?"

"You're blocking the light."

"Sorry." She turned away at the same time she backed off. "Wanted to see what it is."

"Air conditioner. A stand-alone unit. It should keep this single room cool enough for you."

"But…why?"

"Because it gets hot. And fewer mosquitoes get in with the windows closed."

She stifled the urge to rap him on the head with a rolled-up magazine. Not because of any anti-violence concerns, but because that would have required looking at him while he remained in that position with his jeans pulled across his…rear end, and that darned T-shirt doing its hugging number.

What was wrong with her? She'd seen him in jeans and T-shirt hundreds of times. It was his uniform, his work outfit, his comfort outfit. No big deal.

"I mean," she said with forced calm, "why bother, since this addition's going to be torn down when you renovate the main house?"

"You could swelter to death by then and the mosquitoes would pick the bones clean."

Her heart did a jazzy little tap dance. Probably at the thought of sweltering to death and the lovely image of bone-cleaning mosquitoes. Certainly not because his comment implied she'd be here for some time. Before she could consider that, another angle hit her.

"Annette stayed in this room until last week."

"It wasn't as hot then."

She'd been in Dayton, so she didn't know, and it sounded reasonable. The kitchen had certainly gotten steamy during last night's baking.

"What about the budget? How can the project afford an air conditioner that will be used so short term? With Miss Trudi's house and Bliss House getting central AC, there won't be a use for it later."

"It's not coming out of the project budget. And before you say you can't accept it from me, you've got to. Annette would kill me if I let you suffer."

"Leaving the doors open has worked fine."

He pivoted on his toes, still couched down. "You left the doors open? At night?"

"Why not? This *is* Tobias."

"Tobias, not Utopia, for God's sake. From now on you close and lock the doors at night. Understood?"

She nodded. Only because she hadn't slept that well with them open. Something about the way the gauzy curtains billowed kept making her think someone—no one in particular—was walking into her bedroom.

"So what's in the other boxes?"

Apparently satisfied with his inspection of the AC unit, he stood—finally—and went to the toolbox. He started rooting around in it, then seemed to change his mind, put it on the desk before reopening it and rooting anew.

"Blinds," he said at last. Maybe "rooting" wasn't accurate. He seemed to know exactly where everything was. In quick succession he pulled out three tools and set them on the desk. She recognized the screwdriver and had a feeling one of the others was a wrench.

"Blinds? For where?" She looked around, as if she might somehow have missed a window without curtains on it.

"The doors and windows."

"There are already curtains on the doors and windows."

"You can't see through blinds."

How could she argue with that? "You didn't think this was necessary when Annette was here, but you do now?"

"Steve was looking out for Annette by then." He paused an instant, then started talking quickly—probably so she wouldn't think he'd meant to imply that their relationship bore any similarity to Annette and Steve's. He needn't have worried. "There weren't three-dozen men working outside the door then."

A lightbulb moment.

"Ah. So this is to make sure I don't mingle with the workers?"

"Something like that."

"I wouldn't take them away from their work."

"Right."

She propped her fists on her hips at that evidence of his disbelief. "I know how tight the schedule is, Max. I wouldn't— What's *that?*'' He'd opened one of the boxes Lenny had put on the desk and revealed a metallic gizmo.

''A dead-bolt lock.''

That was what she'd thought. ''You're planning on locking me in?''

Her amused challenge didn't rattle him a bit.

''Not a half-bad idea.'' He strode across the room and studied the doorway. ''Nah, I'll put the key on the inside.''

''Thank you so much.''

''You're welcome.''

''This is ridiculous.'' She scooped the magazines off the bed and propped the stack on one hip, feeling more off balance than truly angry. ''I'll be in the kitchen until you've finished this security frenzy.''

''Good. I could use some peace and quiet while I figure how the AC goes in.''

''Here.'' As he passed her on his return to the toolbox, she handed him the pamphlet that had fallen and was in danger of being kicked under the bed.

''What's that for?''

''The instruction booklet for the air conditioner.''

''Never touch the things. You need an advanced degree to figure 'em out and I never got the basic degree, much less advanced.''

The tone was meant to be joking. But after Saturday night she knew—he couldn't un-ring that bell—not finishing college bothered him.

''So go back and get the degree.''

''You'd have a hell of a long wait before I got this air conditioner in.'' His lips twisted into a half grin as he rubbed his right wrist before selecting a long, narrow, shiny tool. ''Nah, I think I'll muddle along on my own.''

And if that wasn't Max Trevetti's motto, she didn't know what was.

She teetered on the edge of pushing it. Of pointing out that after Saturday night it didn't make any sense for him to pretend he didn't care.

When she backed away and matched his joking tone, she wasn't sure if it was for his sake or her own. "Reading the instructions—what was I thinking? Actually reading instructions might dry up every bit of your testosterone."

"Not likely."

In the sudden silence, Suz heard a buzz in the room. It sounded vaguely electrical, but Max hadn't started fiddling with any cords or outlets. So what…?

Then their glances caught for an instant. That was all. An instant, before they bounced off like water on a hot plate.

On second thought, maybe the buzzing *was* something electrical.

She cleared her throat. "Max, I appreciate your concern. It's misguided, but I do appreciate it. But I can't take all this from you. There's no reason—"

"Annette never complained."

Ah, that put her in her place—right next to his little sister. She'd been wrong about that buzz. Must be an insect in the room—not that she'd tell him, or he'd have an exterminator on the doorstep in minutes.

"If you think you're the first interfering, overbearing, overprotective male I've had to deal with, you're wrong. I have four older brothers, remember? You'd have a long way to go to match them."

"Just trying to uphold the honor of big brothers everywhere."

"God forbid you let down your big-brother image." She didn't sound bitter, not enough that he'd take it seriously. But in case he misread her tone, she shifted quickly to business. "Miss Trudi and I are touring new houses and condos at Lake Geneva this afternoon to get ideas of her likes and dislikes. Would you be available to go over things tomorrow?''

"Eleven-thirty."

"Fine. Eleven-thirty here."

She'd taken one step into the hallway when his voice stopped her.

"Not here. At my house—office. Better to meet at the office."

"Good grief." Juney halted at the door to the office in exaggerated surprise. "Did you two beat me back or haven't you gone to lunch yet?"

As if on cue, Max's stomach grumbled.

"And the answer is, haven't gone yet," Juney said.

Suz chuckled, but continued making notes on her legal pad. She'd arrived with pages of questions about what could or couldn't be done in Miss Trudi's new space.

Juney had left after twelve-thirty to have lunch with her mother, Gert, who was taking care of Nell while Steve and Annette were on their honeymoon, with help from Miss Trudi and Fran Dalton, Steve's neighbor and his friend Rob's younger sister.

He and Suz had kept working.

They'd covered her original questions, then somehow started talking about plans for the main Bliss House renovation. Pretty soon she was making lists of things to check out for him—display cabinets, special lighting, wiring requirements for computerized cash registers and dozens of other details in his mental "deal with it later" file.

All the time they'd talked about the project, he'd second-guessed his insistence that they meet here. The round trip took a big chunk out of his day. But it got them away from that cramped little room that was three-quarters bed. And from glimpses of clothes hanging on the shower-curtain rod to dry. Some practical underwear, a blouse and a skirt. No big deal. He'd faced down women's underwear and paraphernalia in his bathroom before, so why had he worked at a snail's pace getting the AC unit hooked up until he'd closed the door to her bathroom?

Besides, meeting Suz at his office cut the time she was around the construction site for Eric and others who hadn't toed the line—yet—to stare at.

She was a beautiful woman, always had been, but she was *Suz,* for Pete's sake, someone he'd sworn to protect and look after—*not* lust after.

He stood abruptly. "I'm starving. C'mon, let's get something to eat."

"You go ahead. I'm going to finish these notes and then get the rundown on sources for material from Juney."

"Do that after lunch. You gotta eat, Suz. C'mon, we'll go to the Toby."

She looked up. "Is that the place whose menu consists of five dozen ways of serving fat?"

"That's the one," Juney said before he could answer. "The place where you can get more nutrition by drinking a beer than by eating some of their meals—and that's where Mr. Health Nut here eats most often."

"Uh, thanks but no thanks, Max," Suz said with a chuckle. "I'll get something later. And you should eat better than that, too. Why don't you try the vegetarian place down by the library?"

Juney coughed, which did little to hide her laughter.

He glared at her and said to Suz, "I'll go if you'll go."

"Call the funeral home!" Juney shouted. "The man who said he'd get dragged to the Better Veggie only over his own dead body is on his way."

Suz put down her pen and laughed. "Oh, no, I couldn't

make you suffer that way, Max. Besides, I don't want to go anywhere because I'd have to come back to get that information from Juney. How about a compromise—we get something here.''

''Here?''

''Yeah. I'll cook as a thank-you for the air conditioner. It made a difference last night. The blinds and the dead bolts are a little much—'' she shrugged ''—but thanks for them, too. So I'll cook lunch. You have a kitchen....''

''Barely,'' Juney said.

Chuckling again, Suz protested as she started for the door, determination in every step, ''Oh, come on, you always had plenty of food on hand when Annette and I visited.''

''Special circumstances,'' Juney said. ''You're about to glimpse the uncensored eating habits of Max Trevetti. You're a brave woman, Suz.''

Sure he stocked up for visitors, who didn't? Max thought as he followed Suz to the kitchen.

She swung the refrigerator door open with a flourish, then made a noise between a gasp and a laugh.

''Juney wasn't kidding. You really don't keep much food around here.'' She took out a container of yogurt. ''This expired two weeks ago.''

He shrugged as he took it from her and dropped it in the garbage. ''Must be Annette's. I don't buy that stuff.''

''Annette's? She moved out months ago!''

''She had lunch here sometimes,'' he said defensively.

''Not recently.'' She poked more deeply into the refrigerator, pulling out a bag of salad mix that had started to liquefy and celery that drooped over her hand. He held the garbage pail and she deposited them with a face of disgust.

''What do *you* buy?'' she asked as she washed her hands.

"Cereal, milk, bananas. Stuff for breakfast—most important meal of the day, you know."

"Breakfast?" She opened the fridge again, checking in the door, and found the eggs and butter he kept there. "An omelet okay?"

"Sure. But you know we could still make it to the Toby before they stop serving lunch."

"Forget it, Trevetti. You're going to have a lunch without brats and fries, *and* you're going to wash dishes. It's good for your soul."

With minimal fuss, she whipped the eggs with a fork, splashing in a little water, then trolling his cabinets and shaking in small amounts from spice containers Annette or Juney must have left. She muttered a couple of times about fresh not killing him. He leaned back against the counter as she started a pan heating, washed her hands again, then turned to him.

"So you have breakfast at home—one meal down, two to go."

"Lunch is whatever's near the site, and dinner's usually at the Toby."

Drying her hands, she prowled toward a basket in the corner. "Your bananas are all green."

"That's the way I like them."

"I've never had one that looked like a cucumber. May I try one?"

No. "Sure, go ahead."

He walked over to the table, spun a chair around and straddled it as she peeled back the first section of banana skin.

He did *not* want to watch her eat a banana, not because it meant anything. Just that…he'd have to go to the store a day early. He hated that.

"Tired?" she asked.

"I guess."

"You were working out at the site early this morning, weren't you?"

"We had a guy call in sick. I wanted to put in a few hours so we wouldn't get too far behind."

"You could have rescheduled our meeting. You know, if you need daylight hours to do other things, we can meet at night. That might work better for me, too. I can use business hours to see suppliers and meet with you when I couldn't see them."

She was leaning back against the counter. It was a small kitchen. There wasn't anywhere else to look. That was why his gaze locked on the sight of her mouth closing over the tip of rod-shaped fruit.

"Fine."

Her lips drew back as her teeth sank in, and his knees tried to clamp together in reflex. All that did was squeeze the back of the chair between his thighs. He slid back a couple of inches to ease his position.

"Good heavens." Her eyes had gone wide. "This banana is crisp. I've never had a crisp banana before."

"That's the way I like them."

He didn't mean anything other than what he'd said as it applied to bananas. Absolutely nothing.

He'd known she'd had a little interest in him when they'd met, and he'd been bowled over by her. But where would it have taken them? A fling? And when it was over, what would have happened to her friendship with Annette? Annette had needed her then. He never had gotten the hang of flings, anyway.

Getting serious wasn't an option—she was a college kid with a universe of possibilities. His possibilities had already narrowed to Tobias and Trevetti Building. What sort of slime would he be to have taken advantage of her?

Then, in Suz and Annette's senior year had come the accident....

He'd made it there in record time. After taking care of details, he'd brought the girls to Tobias for a few days. By the end of those days, it was settled without anyone saying a word—he'd be another big brother to Suz.

"Well, this one is making my teeth hurt. Sorry I wasted your banana." She started to pull the peel up. "I'll replace it."

"Give it here. I'll eat it."

After handing it over, she sat across from him.

He finished it in four quick bites. "Was this a sneaky way to get me to eat fruit in the middle of the day?"

"I hadn't thought of that, but it's not a bad idea." She stood, seeming to hear something. "Pan's ready." After she poured the eggs in with a smooth motion of her wrist, she turned toward him. He blinked away so she wouldn't think he was watching her. "I didn't see any, but in the hope that I simply overlooked it, since there's probably a law that as a native of Wisconsin you have to have some somewhere, do you have any cheese?"

"Do cheese curls count?"

Lunch was great. It was after lunch the trouble started.

It started with him saying lunch was great.

Suz had mumbled something about anybody could cook eggs and hurried off to the office.

As he'd loaded the few dishes and one pan into the dishwasher, he thought about her reaction. So it wasn't only in her work that she backed away from compliments as if they gave her a rash.

Suzanna Grant didn't think she deserved compliments.

Of all the cockeyed attitudes... The woman should have been taking bows on the hour and half hour all day long.

Instead, she shied away from being told she'd cooked a great omelet. Monday, when she'd come up with that solution for Miss Trudi's house and he'd said it was a great idea, she'd acted like she'd been tossed into a sizzling pan and cooked thoroughly herself.

He dried his hands.

The more he worked with her change in the floor plan, the more he appreciated it. She'd applied both practicality and creativity. He'd seen more of those skills in her questions today. She seemed always on the lookout to save money and time while producing a top-quality product.

Not that he'd tell her that after the way she reacted to "Great omelet."

He went to the office to get paperwork for tomorrow's deliveries. By ordering for both jobs at once, they got a volume discount, but more of a headache in storing and safeguarding.

Suz was stowing her papers in a leather case.

"You got everything you need for now, Suz?" he said.

"I think so. If not, I can always check with you when you're at Bliss House. Or I'm sure Lenny or Eric would—"

"Stay off the construction site unless I'm there."

"Or what?" Her eyes glinted with challenge. "I'm not your sister, so you can't disown me, and you aren't paying me anything, so you can't fire me."

"She's got—"

"Shut up, Juney." He didn't take his eyes off Suz. "It's for your own good."

"If I can't look out for my own good, don't you think I deserve whatever happens to me?"

Peripherally, he was aware Juney had started typing with great fervor.

"I mean it, Suz."

She stood, back straight, chin up. "So do I. Thanks,

Juney. Goodbye.'' She gave Max a cool nod as she walked out.

He stared at the floor a full minute after her car pulled away, leaving Juney's determined typing as the only sound.

''Sorry I told you to shut up.''

''Apology accepted.'' She kept typing, but at a natural pace. ''Especially since I've said the same thing to you. More than once.''

He looked up. ''You have?''

''You might not have heard me,'' she said with great dignity. ''I might have waited until you'd left the building.''

He laughed, and he realized that was what she'd been aiming for.

Juney had a good heart, in addition to a level head and a smart mouth. She was also a good judge of character.

''What do you think of Eric?'' he asked abruptly.

With her hands poised as if over the keyboard, she turned ninety degrees to face him. ''What brought that on?''

''Stuff at the site.''

''Stuff with Suz at the site?''

''Suz doesn't see…''

''Maybe she does see and knows she can handle it.''

He shook his head. ''She's used to a different kind of guy.''

''Well, I know Eric isn't exactly uptown, but he's not a sleazeball, either. He wouldn't hurt Suz or anybody else.''

Hurt Suz. His stomach muscles clenched at the phrase as if he'd taken a punch. And a memory clicked in. A long hospital corridor, with Suz at the end of it looking impossibly fragile. He'd pledged then that he would take care of her the way he took care of Annette.

''He's a bit of a hothead,'' Juney was saying, ''but his

biggest problem is he wants the perks without the responsibilities.''

Juney had hit it. The kid was good with the tools, good
with the other men on the job and customers. The trouble
was what he *didn't* do. He tried to slide by without attending to the grunt details, leaving them for someone else. As
owner and boss, Max had to do something about it.

''What are you going to do about the rest of it?''

Juney's question came as if she knew exactly when he'd
reached his conclusion. Now that was scary.

''Rest of what?''

''You putting your foot in it with Suz.''

''I didn't—''

''Oh, yeah, you did.''

He expelled an emphatic breath but didn't argue. ''Juney,
you said the other day about Suz thinking she's just decorative…''

''Did I say that? I don't think so.'' She shook her head.

''Well, something like it.''

''See, that's where guys get in trouble. Thinking that
saying something within the same galaxy is good enough.
Big difference, Max. Way big difference.''

''All right, what did you say?''

''What I said was that *Annette* said that anybody who
took Suz as being just decorative was misguided. I didn't
recall the word *misguided* right off, but that was the word
Annette used. And that's what I said.''

Misguided. Could that be what Suz was? He didn't think
she regarded herself as purely decorative, but she surely
didn't believe in her abilities the way they deserved. And
she didn't give herself credit for what she did.

He was more than willing to give her credit. Except he'd
seen that compliments did not convince her she'd done a

good job. If anything they seemed to make her feel less secure.

If I can't look out for my own good, don't you think I deserve whatever happens to me?

Max knew what Suz Grant deserved—the best and happiest of lives with someone to look out for her. For now that was him. So beyond making sure she wore a hard hat and stayed away from guys who wouldn't treat her the way she deserved, he'd have to convince her how good she was.

Chapter Four

White T-shirts should be outlawed.

At least as worn by Max Trevetti.

From the open Bliss House kitchen window, Suz had an unobstructed view of the so-good-it-had-to-be-illegal infraction as he worked harder than even the most hardworking of his hardworking crew.

In the bright midday sun, he would work beside one guy, make a comment or two, then move on to the next. Each one seemed to work with more gusto during and after his visit.

On his way to the next member of his crew, he spotted a short, dark-skinned man trying to balance on his shoulder a length of lumber so long that it teetered dangerously. Max caught hold of one end, the man moved toward the opposite end, and they easily moved it out of her range of vision.

She should get the material she'd gathered on kitchen cabinets and appliances prepared, anyway. Miss Trudi would be here any minute to go over them, then to take her on a top-to-bottom tour of the house to start deciding what furniture she wanted to take to her new home and—

Max strode back into view. He exchanged a couple words with the man using the saw, examined a piece of wood the man showed him, then clapped him on the back and moved to where Lenny and another worker were examining blueprints.

Max spread his arms in a gesture, and the shirt's short sleeves snugged along each swell and valley of his muscled shoulders and upper arms.

Sure, she'd seen it before. Just not in such repeated doses—*and not after being held in those arms, kissed by those lips and touched by those hands.*

She hadn't thought about daily exposure to this when she'd agreed to stay on in Tobias.

It wasn't right what he did to simple white cotton.

Heaven help her, *damp* white cotton.

She could start a petition. Surely women would sign it so they wouldn't be exposed to his broad shoulders and muscled back straining against oh-so-innocent-looking fabric. On second thought, most women wouldn't sign.

Maybe asking men to sign it would be the way to go. Most sure couldn't like having Max in a T-shirt to be compared to.

Unfortunately she didn't think she'd get many signatures from his crew. They all seemed to respect and like him. Even that kid with the cocky grin, the assistant foreman, Eric.

He'd come up to Max and was clearly explaining a problem. Max listened, head down, concentration complete. He said two quick words, then they walked away together.

Eric had the slim-hipped grace of youth. She preferred

Max's rear view. Solidified by years, firmed by wear. Oh, my, jeans needed to be outlawed, too.

Yeah, and a lot of good this did her. She needed a brain transplant if she thought Max would change how he viewed her because of that little episode Saturday. If she'd had any doubts, his message had come through loud and clear the past few days.

Just what every woman needed. A fifth big brother who made the four related to her by blood look like the kind of guys who'd throw her in front of a truck.

"What are you looking at, my dear?" Miss Trudi materialized beside her.

"Nothing." Well, that wasn't going to fly, since she'd been craning her neck to keep him in sight. "I was, uh, thinking about the design."

That response pleased her until Miss Trudi looked in the same vicinity Suz had been looking and asked, "The design of what, dear?"

She wasn't fooling her hostess one bit. But she didn't have to admit it.

"The overall design." She made a sweeping gesture that somehow caught her hand in the sapphire chiffon scarf trailing down Miss Trudi's back.

"Ah, yes. The overall design is pleasing." She stood patiently while Suz unwrapped her hand. "I beg your pardon for changing the subject, but catching sight of Max so hard at work reminds me of when he was a boy."

"Max was one of your students?"

"I never had him in a class, nor was he among the young people who regularly visited me here at Bliss House. Annette came for afternoon tea quite frequently, but never Max. Yet I felt I knew him. From observation," she added, the twinkle in her eyes becoming more pronounced. "So much can be learned from close observation, as you clearly recognize.''

Suz felt heat ooze across her cheeks.

''I observed that as a boy Max exhibited great determination,'' the older woman continued as she moved to the table. ''I saw a number of instances when his determination alone carried him past his family's difficult circumstances. But I won't bore you with those details.''

Bore her? The woman was a seventy-odd-year-old tease. She had Suz panting like a Saint Bernard in the desert.

''However, if those circumstances forced him to—I won't say give up, because that is contrary to what I observe in him—to *release* a goal, he accepted that with a finality that allowed no going back.''

All or nothing—that sounded like Max. Suz followed Miss Trudi to the table, taking the chair to her right. She clamped her teeth together to keep the million questions milling about in her brain from popping out.

Miss Trudi saved her from bursting by continuing, ''I have often wondered if it was the fact of his determination that prevented him from regrasping a dream or goal once he had been forced to release it. He gave his all, yet could not attain his dream for whatever reason, and thus classified it as unattainable. It would be a natural response,'' she added. ''Releasing a dream causes great pain, all the worse for having strained to the maximum to obtain it.''

You can be anything you want. But I don't have the same options. I'm just a guy who works with his hands. I never got that college degree.

From Annette she knew Max had worked hard for both the scholarships and money he'd needed to go to college. It had to have hurt to let that go when their mother died, though he never talked about either loss. No, not Max Trevetti. He'd pushed ahead to build a business and stable income—to give Annette a good life, including a college degree.

Could he be persuaded to wrap his hands around that dream again? What would it take?

"It was very difficult for Max when he broke his wrist early this spring."

Suz blinked. She had missed how Miss Trudi's talk had taken her to this point. "It seems to have healed well. And Annette helped a lot."

Yet she *had* noticed his habit of rubbing his right wrist, as if it hurt. Or perhaps a talisman of some thought plaguing him?

"Why do you think it was very difficult?" she asked the older woman.

"Crossroads are always difficult. Makes one question the path one has been following and wonder, not only about the outcome if one changes course at this moment, but what might have been if one had selected a different path in the past. Ah, yes—"

"Crossroads? But why would breaking his wrist…?"

"He has put a great deal of his own money into this project."

Miss Trudi had made a conversational right turn, which suited Suz—she was interested in the financial impact of the project on Trevetti Building. She doubted she could draw her hostess back to the original road, anyway.

"I thought it was financed with state and grant funds Steve and the others arranged, with matching dollars from local investors, like the bank."

Miss Trudi inclined her head in partial agreement. "I should have said that Max has advanced funds to cover the project materials and work hours. He started work well before all the paperwork required to release any money was completed. Also, it is my understanding that the manager at First Bank of Tobias has delayed payments for the most minute of details.''

''Why did he do that?''

''I fear that Jason Remtree did it because he could. He is simply not a gentleman.''

In other circumstances, Suz might have found amusement in Miss Trudi's scandalized pronouncement of that indictment. In these circumstances, she had other matters on her mind.

''Not Remtree. I mean, why did Max do that?''

''I believe he would tell you it was necessary in order to complete work to have the crafts center open for Christmas to begin attracting off-season visitors as it is designed to.''

''That's great—for Tobias. But how about for Trevetti Building? To put his company's balance sheet on the line…'' Even as she spoke, something nagged at Suz. She ran through Miss Trudi's words. ''Wait a minute. You said you believed he'd tell me that was why. What do *you* think?''

Miss Trudi's mouth remained solemn, but her eyes lit up. She'd clearly dangled that to see if Suz would bite and was pleased as punch that she had. And Suz felt an odd pleasure at pleasing her that way. Boy, the woman must have been one dynamite teacher.

''Because that is Max Trevetti. He is a man who sees the common good more clearly than his own benefit.''

Suz frowned. ''That works out great for the common getting the good, but how about Max? Unless he's running for sainthood, it seems to me that's not a great system for him.''

''Ah. Is this the material you promised to show me?''

Miss Trudi reached for the stack of glossy brochures and

printouts Suz had gathered. Suz crossed her forearms over the papers and leaned forward, blocking her access.

"That's it? *Ah?*"

"Well, I very much doubt he will change his inclination to look out for other people. He began performing that function at a young age and it is deeply ingrained in him. Annette did succeed in reversing the roles and caring for him after his injury, but that was only for a brief time."

And now Annette had a new family to look out for. While Max was still thinking of other people—his employees, the town—was that part of his thinking he couldn't go back to college?

"Even before his father left the family," Miss Trudi was saying, "Max carried more responsibility than many men three and four times his age. When Robert Trevetti left, some in Tobias felt the children should be taken away. That house was barely habitable then, especially in winter. Isabella Trevetti added a second job. But it was as much Max who was responsible for holding that little family together.

"At thirteen, he cared for Annette, still in kindergarten then. He persuaded a builder to hire him for the one day a week his mother was home to care for Annette. As he gained building skills, he improved the house. All the while he remained among the top students in his class."

Suz knew about the poverty the Trevettis had endured, but she had heard the stories only from Annette's viewpoint, with Max as her shelter from the harshest realities of their life. Max hadn't had that shelter.

Miss Trudi sighed, her eyes unfocused. "He was so thin. But he never stooped, the way some thin boys do. He always stood straight and tall and proud. So proud. Never had a warm enough coat, though he made sure Annette was bundled up against our Wisconsin winters. The principal of the high school told me how a teacher had put a new, warm jacket in Max's locker, hoping he could accept an anonymous gift. Max turned it in as lost property.''

Suz's eyes stung with threatening tears. But there was a deeper sting. Max's frame had filled out, hardened by labor, to a powerful force. Few would ever think he might require protection. But what of the thin, proud boy inside? He needed someone to look out for him. He needed someone to protect him.

Something fierce and warm flowed through her.

He had done a lot for her over the years. If she counted only the ordinary assistance with moves or broken-down cars, she owed him a debt. But he had done much more. At the worst time of her life he had buffered her from all the exterior consequences. For that she could never adequately repay him. But she could try.

The first step was to stop drooling over him. Poor man.

The second step was to relieve him of as much worry as possible about the Bliss House project.

She straightened in her chair and met Miss Trudi's assessing gaze.

"Shall we get started on this? We need to narrow down to a few so we can go look at them tomorrow. Max needs your final decision the day after."

"Yes, indeed." She emphasized her agreement with a nod.

Then Suz wondered, as she handed Miss Trudi the brochures grouped by price and features, if the nod was less about agreement than approval.

Guiding Miss Trudi through side-by-side versus top freezer, smooth cooktop or burners, preheating cycle versus crystal-gentle cleaning required constant vigilance. They had winnowed the possibilities to four in each category when Suz's cell phone rang.

She debated ignoring it and pressing Miss Trudi. But

she'd learned with Every Detail clients over the years that sometimes backing off for a bit accomplished more than pounding away. She could use a break, too.

Recognizing the voice clinched the matter. "Just a minute," she told the caller. "I have to take this call, Miss Trudi. When I come back, we'll pick the finalists."

Without waiting for an answer she scooted outside, but that was not an ideal solution. Not only was it noisy, but there was that white-T-shirt-and-faded-jeans problem in front of her.

"Annette? You're breaking up." She ducked down the path into her room—she hoped Max didn't notice that she hadn't needed to unlock it, since she hadn't locked it in the first place. "Okay. That's better. It's so great to hear your voice. But you're calling me from your honeymoon? What, are you nuts? You're not bored, are you?"

"Not nuts and not bored. Definitely not bored. But I wanted to talk to you. I hear you're staying in Tobias."

"How on earth did you hear that while you're on your honeymoon?"

"Oh, Suz, you have a lot to learn about Tobias. Steve's home answering machine had six messages by Sunday evening, and by Monday morning—"

"Wait a minute. Nobody knew about it until Monday except Max, Miss Trudi, me and Nell."

Annette laughed. "And your point is? Nell's a chatterbox. Miss Trudi can keep a secret when she wants to, but she often doesn't want to."

"Good heavens."

"Exactly. So watch your step—that is, if you're going to stay."

"Yup. For a while. And I have a hundred questions to ask you about this Bliss House project."

"Of course, but first…" A hum came through the telephone. It sounded faintly worried. But that was probably her imagination. "Suz, this wouldn't have anything to do with, uh…I mean what does it have to do with?"

"It has to do with building Miss Trudi's home in order to get started renovating Bliss House into the crafts center you, Steve and Max fought so hard for."

"It does?"

"What—you don't think I'll be a good temporary design assistant?" she asked with feigned indignation.

"I didn't know there *was* a design assistant for this project."

"I'm self-appointed."

Another worried little hum. She'd known Annette too long, worked with her too closely to even try to fool herself that this one came from the telephone connection.

"What's bothering you, Annette? I'm following your notes. I check everything with Juney even before I run it past Max. And Max said you weren't…but if I've horned in on your—"

"No, no. Absolutely not. I'm relieved about that. Max kept saying it wouldn't delay his work, but I worried… Even when I get back, I'm going to be busy with Steve and Nell—with my family." Suz had the feeling Annette turned and smiled at her new husband at those words. "And I can't think of anyone who'd do a better job. Only…are you sure this doesn't have to do with Max?"

Suz's heart gave a lurch. She hoped that reaction didn't creep into her voice. "How could it not have to do with Max? He's running the project."

"I meant something, uh, personal. You once had…well, I thought you felt, or could have felt if he—"

"Relax, Annette," Suz said with a casualness she didn't feel. Damn, had she been that transparent? "That was, what? Eight years ago? If I'd held a torch that long for your brother, I could have turned pro. Sure, I was interested in him when we met—I'm not blind, you know. But that's also the reason any natural interest never went any further. I saw he didn't return the interest. We became friends. End of story. So now can I ask you about this project? I'll limit myself to my top ten so you're not still answering when the honeymoon's over.''

''Sure. If I can help. I just…I don't want you to get hurt.''

''Are you kidding? With Big Brother Max around? I'm wearing a hard hat at all times, even in the shower.''

She knew and Annette knew—and Annette knew she knew—that wasn't the kind of hurt Annette meant. Annette chuckled, anyway. ''Okay, what are your questions—though you're much better with liaison work than I am.''

Right. Suz asked and Annette filled her in on local personalities she might encounter, gave her the names and numbers of additional contacts and promised to alert Fran Dalton that Suz would be coming by for the key to Steve's house to retrieve material Annette had. Annette also went over Suz's thoughts on what she'd done so far and what needed to be done next.

Suz felt like a fifty-pound weight had been lifted off her shoulders by the time they wrapped that up.

''Where are you guys, by the way?'' she asked with would-be casualness.

''Oh, no, I'm not telling you. As much as I love you, Suz. Somehow it would get out, and then the calls wouldn't be messages left on the machine, they'd be directly to us. No way.''

''All right, all right. It was worth a try.''

Suz heard a male voice rumbling in the background, ending with a chuckle.

''What's Steve saying?''

"Nothing."

"C'mon, Annette. Share the joke."

"Okay. But remember, this is Steve talking, I'm just repeating it. He said he hopes you're fibbing about there being nothing between you and Max. He thinks it would be great if you and Max got together, because he can't think of anyone more deserving than Max of getting involved with a woman with four protective older brothers."

Despite another heart-lurch, Suz chuckled. She made her voice as light as possible when she said, "You tell that husband of yours that he'll have to find his revenge another way because Max is like another one of my big brothers."

"Drive carefully!" Miss Trudi called from the back porch of Bliss House Friday morning.

Max swung around and saw Suz, wearing the same skirt she'd had on Monday, loading a duffel into the trunk of her small car.

They hadn't talked since she'd left his office Wednesday afternoon. He'd thought she was simply busy working. That had been the case with him. You'd think that with all his crews working in one spot and not needing to drive from site to site it would be easier, but keeping the work going as efficiently as possible took more coordination. That was why he hadn't checked in with Suz—more work to do than there were hours in the day.

He reached her car as she opened the driver's door. He pulled it wide, keeping a grip on the top of the door.

"Leaving?"

She flung her purse onto the passenger seat, then crossed her arms.

"You think I'm flitting away? Why don't you say it?"

"I didn't—"

"Don't bother to apologize. I don't have time. I have an appointment."

An appointment? With a duffel? A man? "I wasn't apologizing."

"That's your problem, Max." She sat and swung her legs into the car in a smooth motion that had his retort forming a lump in his suddenly dry throat. She heaved a dramatic sigh that raised her breasts so they pushed against her blouse, and that sent the lump plunging south. "I'm going to the closing on the town house, to pick up more clothes and clear out the things I left there when I hotfooted it to Dayton for my family's so-called emergency. I'll be back Sunday evening. Okay?"

When he didn't answer, she pulled the door from his now unresisting hold and closed it. He did produce a short, neutral wave as she backed out.

Friday morning to Sunday evening? It was only a couple of hours each way. How much did she have to clear out?

More likely she had dates for both nights. She usually did.

None of his business. None at all.

"Don't drive barefoot," he called after her.

The latch on Miss Trudi's back door stuck, so Max gave it a solid push with his shoulder Monday morning, propelling himself into the kitchen.

His abrupt entrance froze two of the kitchen's occupants in place. Suz was bent over the big table, with Eric on her right in a similar pose. He had one hand on her back and was leaning into her to point to something on her left. Practically wrapping her in his arms, he was hip to hip with her like—

"Eric, get out of here."

"Max, I asked Eric to show me something on the drawings," Suz said.

After the tension the last two times he'd seen her, he wished for a different mood this time, but no such luck. Not with Eric's hand on her back. Not with the guy's body crowding hers.

"The house is off-limits to the crew. You know that, Eric. Get out."

"Boss, I was—"

"Now." Max kept his stare pinned on Eric. He didn't need to look at Suz to know her reaction.

Sure enough, the second the door closed behind Eric, she was off. "Max, I won't countermand what you say in front of one of your employees—"

"Good."

"—but that was utterly unnecessary."

"I won't have him bothering you."

He moved to the opposite side of the table. A shadow slid from near the stove toward the hallway—Miss Trudi. She must have been there all along.

"Miss Trudi…" But she was gone. There would be no buffer.

"He wasn't bothering me," Suz said with something beyond irritation. "I told you, I asked him for information. But even if he had been bothering me, I know how to handle it."

"I've seen the line of guys around the block wanting to go out with you, so I know you're used to guys hoping to get in your, uh, life. But you've been dealing with an entirely different kind of guy. Eric is more than a little rough around the edges."

"You're saying he's not good enough for me?"

"Yeah, that's what I'm saying."

"Oh, for heaven's sake." She straightened and threw up

her hands, apparently not able to hold still with her disbelief. "I'm—"

"You don't have the best track record for good judgment when it comes to men."

The stricken look hit him full in the gut before it even finished blooming in her eyes.

Damn. He hadn't meant Tad and the accident. That hadn't been anywhere in his thinking. He'd seen Eric touching her, and he'd wanted to yank the guy away, push his face in and lock her in a tower for good measure. It was how big brothers felt.

But if he simply told her he hadn't meant the accident, she wouldn't believe it. Better to confess to the misdemeanor to avoid the felony.

"You're always falling in love," he said. "Then you fall out of love just as fast, because before I can turn around, you're in love with someone else."

"Me?" Surprise flooded out the stricken look, so that was a relief. Though why she'd be surprised... "What on earth gave you that idea?"

"You. You're always going out with somebody new." Like this weekend?

"Those are just dates. You know, having fun."

"Falling in love isn't about fun."

"*Dates,* not love. Did you ever think that's why you haven't fallen in love? If it's no fun for you, it's no fun for the other person, either." She picked up an empty glass from the table and carried it to the sink. "It'll take a real masochist to fall in love with you. Until you meet someone fond of pain, you won't be getting engaged or married."

He shifted his focus from her back to the plans spread on the table. The glass she'd taken had been holding one corner down. With the glass gone, it curled, covering part of the lettering, so it read Bliss Hou.

As close as his attention was to those printed letters, he knew when his silence became a kind of answer in her mind, because she went entirely still before turning slowly toward him. "You haven't, have you?"

"Haven't what?" *Deck chairs on the* Titanic, *Trevetti.*

"Max Trevetti, you're being..." She clamped her mouth shut and narrowed her eyes at him. "Have you been? Engaged or married?"

"Yeah."

Now her eyes were wide open. "You've been married?"

"No. Engaged."

She let out a huff of breath that could have knocked over a couple small buildings. "Engaged. You've never said...*Annette's* never said a solitary word about this in all these years."

"Annette doesn't know."

He braced for a sound-barrier-breaking screech, but her mouth simply opened and closed without producing a peep.

"I was at Madison, in school," he said.

"College," she got out on a second try. "What happened?"

"My circumstances changed."

"What do circumstances have to do with loving somebody?" The words were tart from a trace of accusation.

"A lot when you can't give your fiancée the life you'd planned together."

He saw her working that through. Saw the concern, confusion and doubt. If he stayed he would tell her. What he hadn't told anyone else. Ever.

He walked out before she could ask questions he just might answer.

Chapter Five

From the landing of the main staircase, Suz watched Max pace in the open center of the tangled rose garden.

She had watched from the kitchen window as he spoke with Lenny, including a curt nod toward Eric, working on the roof. Then he headed away.

As if keeping sight of him might provide answers to the newest riddle he'd made of himself, she had tracked him by moving from room to room. When he disappeared into the rose garden, she'd found this vantage point at the landing window.

"Max was engaged."

Perhaps hearing the words would make the fact more real. Max had loved someone. Had asked her to marry him. Had planned marriage, children, a life. And then…and then…

My circumstances changed.

He meant dropping out after his mother's death, didn't

he? It fit Max so well—he no longer could give the woman he loved the sort of future he wanted to, so he let his pride overrule his heart. Marriage became another of those goals, those dreams he'd let go of and hadn't tried to grasp again.

Max drew a deep breath and caught the scent of roses. Sweet and warm. Not at all like the clipped spicy scent Laurie had favored.

God, how had he remembered that? He hadn't thought of Laurie in years, not since somebody who'd known them both told him that she'd divorced the lawyer she'd married after graduation.

He'd been called back to Tobias when his mother was taken to the ER that Monday morning. She'd died just before two in the afternoon. He'd spent the rest of the day making arrangements and being with Annette. She'd finally fallen asleep, with one of his mother's co-workers staying with her. He'd driven to Madison to pack his things overnight and withdraw from school in the morning.

"You don't have to make a decision right away, Max," Laurie had said, standing against the wall beside the dresser. "Explore other choices…"

"You think I haven't? There's no choice."

"You could put her—your sister—in foster care. That's what it's for." At his look, she'd put her hands up as if to placate him. "For a few years. So you could finish your education and get the start we've talked about and—"

"I won't sacrifice my sister."

"No. You'll sacrifice your future and yourself and—"

"If I have to."

"—me! Everything we've talked about. Everything we've planned for."

"Annette comes first. After she's through college, I could finish and—"

"After she's through college! In ten years? *Then* you'll—"

"Eight years."

"Eight years. Fine. Oh, that's so much better." Her lush lips twisted with sarcasm. "And if I wait around for those eight years, what do I get? A maybe that you'd go back to school. Then how many years to finish? And how many more years to get established as an architect and start earning the reputation we've talked about?"

If I wait around... Now there was a phrase designed to cut into a man.

He wanted to reassure her. Wanted to guarantee that she'd have what she wanted sooner rather than later. But he didn't have those answers, and what answers he did have wouldn't have reassured her.

He gave her a level look, to let her know he was going to do what he said, no matter what. Anger flared in her blue eyes.

"You're a fool, Max. You're damning yourself to slipping right back to being the poor boy from Tobias. You'll never escape being blue collar. You'll never rise above what you were. *That's* the choice you're making."

He'd moved to the bookcase, loading the contents into a box to take to the bookstore to resell. They would need all the money he could get. From the desktop, he took his sociology textbook. Better put that in his suitcase, he had reading due— No. Not anymore. He dropped the book into the box.

"Like I said, it's no choice. I'm taking care of Annette. That's first priority. Whatever I have to do to see she gets what she needs, including somebody who loves her to raise her, that's what I'm going to do."

"Then you've made your choice. You can sacrifice yourself, Max—'' at the doorway, Laurie looked back ''—but I won't let you sacrifice me.''

Yeah, he'd made his choice. But it had come hours earlier when he held his dying mother's hand and made promises, knowing he couldn't keep them all.

He stared at a faded pink bloom right at eye level.

"Lenny said you wanted to talk to me?"

Eric's voice jolted him out of the past, but it took a good forty seconds to remember what he'd intended to say. "I've been letting you slide and—"

"Boss, I wasn't—"

"You can't talk your way out of this, Eric. Your only hope is to listen your way out. You broke a rule you're supposed to be enforcing."

"Suz asked me—"

"Listen. Not talk." Eric shut his mouth, and Max went on, "This has nothing to do with Suz—Ms. Grant."

Eric's expression said he didn't believe Max, but he didn't say it. There was hope for him yet.

"It has to do with you not following through on responsibilities. You're a good carpenter—if you want to be a craftsman, you'll make a good living. But you told me you wanted to work toward running or owning a company. You're not going to get there at this rate, Eric.

"You gotta be a good craftsman so that what you build lasts. But you gotta be a good businessman so you have a chance to build something that lasts. That means cleaning up a site every day. That means making sure the TravelinJohn is serviced right and off the premises on schedule. That means making sure materials are stored in a way that's safe and protected so the client doesn't have to pay extra."

Eric showed continued good sense by keeping his mouth shut.

''Here's what's going to happen. I'm not going to be dazzled by your crap anymore, and you're going to stop flinging it. You're on probation as assistant foreman on this job. When I give you a responsibility and you meet it, you stay assistant foreman. When I give you a responsibility and you don't meet it, you're not assistant foreman until I decide you've earned the right to be trusted with another responsibility and you meet it. Got it?''

He obviously wanted to argue, complain, do a little dazzling. He said, ''Yeah, I got it.''

''Good. Now go check the stacking job on that lumber that was delivered today. It looked closer to those flags marking the weak ground over the root cellar than it should be.''

It was probably too much to hope that Eric would respond with a crisp ''Yes, sir.'' He was satisfied the kid left without a protest or wisecrack.

Now all Max had to do was tell Lenny he had a now-you-see-him-now-you-don't assistant and tell Juney she might be changing Eric's base pay eight times a week.

It would be worth it if immediate, no-nonsense feedback straightened Eric out.

Max put his hand up to push back the overgrown roses, and stopped.

If this system worked on Eric, who thought so highly of his own abilities that he didn't think he would be held to account for his failures, would it also work on Suz, who needed to be held to account for her successes? He turned that over in his mind. How could he apply this to Suz's situation?

Did it have any hope if he didn't change how he'd left things with Suz a few minutes ago?

Pain penetrated his mind, because a rose thorn had penetrated his index finger.

"Damn!"

He had a feeling this was going to be a fun time, compared to making things right with Suz.

Suz didn't see Max for the next two and a half days.

A stomach bug was buzzing through Trevetti Building's construction crew, so he worked all day with the group that put vapor-barrier paper on and started the roofing.

She awoke the first day from a restless night and looked out at the early-morning light to see Max moving roofing materials into place so his crew could start right at seventhirty. He and Lenny and a few others stayed until dark.

So it wasn't accurate to say she hadn't seen him for two and a half days. More that they hadn't talked. Or made eye contact when she passed where he was working.

She had her own schedule to keep. She'd promised Max she'd have Miss Trudi's final decisions on appliances today, although a note from Max had rescheduled their planned meeting from two to eight-thirty. She was glad to have the extra time.

When she got to Max's house for their next meeting, she was surprised to find Juney there.

"I had appointments this afternoon, so I stayed late to catch up," she explained.

Juney had turned off her computer and pushed her desk chair into place when Max walked in. His hair was matted from sweat and the hard hat, his shirt was streaked with black goo, and even his tanned skin was tinged red from the day spent on a roof unsheltered from the sun.

"You look like—"

"Thank you, Juney." But one side of his mouth lifted. "I gotta get a shower before we talk, Suz. Sorry for the delay."

"No problem. Now, if you'd insisted we meet before you took a shower, *then* we might have a problem."

Juney laughed and the other side of Max's mouth joined the upward trend to create a real smile.

"Hey, you two, make sure you look at the photos from the disposable cameras." Juney gestured toward a stack of photographic folders on the corner of the desk. "Mom and I thought you both should get a preview before we give them to Annette and Steve when they come back."

She'd nearly reached the doorway when she looked from Max to Suz and back with a wicked grin. "But don't even consider trying to destroy the evidence. Not only do we have copies, we have the negatives."

Before she or Max could respond, Juney gave Max a push to clear the doorway. "Phew! Go take that shower!"

Max muttered something and headed toward his bedroom, while Juney left.

Suz stared at the folders, started to get up, then sank back to the couch. Instead, she pulled out Miss Trudi's appliance-choice list and went to the copier.

When Max returned, in a fresh white T-shirt and jeans aged to a grayed blue, with his hair just dry enough not to drip, she had his copies spread on the coffee table in front of the sofa and she'd taken the side chair.

"Look these over and tell me what information you need that I've missed, and I'll—"

"Can this wait? I've got a frozen pizza in the oven, and this'll make more sense if I've had food."

She drew a breath to say he needed something more nutritious than pizza, then used it to say, "Of course."

"I, uh, also wanted… Look, I'm sorry if I overreacted the other day with Eric."

"Shouldn't he be the one you apologize to?"

"No. He knew the rules and he broke them."

She almost smiled. No chance he'd ever be Max the Wishy-Washy.

"I know you don't want the crew tromping through the house, Max, but I did ask him to come in to show us the location of the pantry closet on the plans because it affected which way the refrigerator would open."

Something in the way his gaze slid away from her combined with his earlier reference to rules—plural—jangled in her head. What other of Max's rules could Eric have broken?

"You told him to stay away from me," she said with sudden certainty.

"Not just him," Max said, as if that were an improvement.

"What? You think I'm some siren trying to lure your crew onto the rocks?"

"You don't have to try. With all the dates you have, you know that."

He held up a hand as if to stop her response. But she wasn't giving in to that temptation this time. She'd almost slipped the other day—she'd almost told him that far from falling in love with her various dates, she seldom saw any of them a second time.

"Before you get really angry at me for my first apology," he said, "could you let me finish the second one?"

She advised, "Better make it snappy."

One corner of his mouth lifted again. The left side. The same side he'd lifted at her earlier comment. She was starting to feel as if she had a claim on that side of his grin.

"Okay, I'll spit it out. Sorry I walked out that way. It was rude."

"You had every right to feel I was being intrusive about your personal life and to get away."

"I...I don't talk about that," he said, not denying she'd been prying.

"Apparently not, since Annette doesn't know."

"I hadn't thought about it in a long time. It caught me...by surprise."

"Okay. Now about these appliances...how soon should I order—"

"Apology accepted?" He stepped forward, hand extended.

There wasn't anything to do but to put her hand out, too, and let it be swallowed in his work-hardened grip. "Sure."

For an instant they connected. Her hand in his. His eyes on hers. For an instant she thought she saw confusion and heat and hunger in his eyes. Thought she felt warmth and desire and possession in his hand.

The trouble with instants is they're gone as fast as they come. And the next instant he had released her hand.

Swallowing, she got out, "The appliance colors—"

He cut her off. "You don't have to keep asking me about every detail."

"I'm sorry I've been bothering you."

"Did I say that? I said you don't have to ask me about every detail. You've got a grasp on this project. You know what's within the scope and what's not. If it affects construction, I sure as hell want to know about it. If it moves electrical outlets a few inches, run it by me in a batch of stuff. But if it's stuff like colors, don't bother."

Why did she feel as if she'd been attacked when his words and tone were matter-of-fact?

"Fine. How about another kind of question, then? Why haven't you gone back to school and finished your degree? You could have after Annette left home."

His left hand massaged his right wrist as he backed up,

leaning against the filing cabinets the way he had at that first business meeting here.

"Told you, that fork in the road is way behind me."

It clicked then how often he took that position—resting against something and rubbing his wrist.

"You're not getting enough rest," she blurted out.

His eyebrows shot up. "You want me to go back to college to get more rest?"

"Max, I'm not blind, I see the signs that you're working too hard. Your wrist aches, doesn't it." He released his wrist and dropped both hands to his sides. "You rub your wrist a lot."

"It's a habit. From when the cast was on and it itched. I'm making up for then."

He was actually proud of that excuse. Pathetic. "Retroactive scratching? Right, Max. In addition to your wrist bothering you—"

"It's not bothering me."

"—you're tired all the time. So tired you can hardly stand up."

"What in hell gives you that idea?" More than his words, his expression of utter astonishment dented her certainty. But she had the evidence of her own eyes.

"You keep leaning against things."

He gave her that are-you-nuts look.

"Whenever we're talking, like just now, you backed up so you could lean against the filing cabinet."

His mouth opened and she fully expected another emphatic denial with a side order of Suz-is-nuts. Before the words came, however, his expression changed. He knew what she was talking about.

He clamped his mouth shut and looked away from her. "Maybe you're right. Maybe I haven't been getting enough sleep."

What the heck just happened? She had no explanation—not for his reaction, his about-face or her sense of deflation.

That did not mean she would pass up an opportunity.

"Max, you can't fill in every time someone's sick and then do your own work, too."

He gave a small shrug. "If I don't do my work, no one will."

"I will."

Oh, God, what was she thinking, making a promise like that? What if she failed? Another time when it had mattered desperately, she had failed. Then, the cost had been horrible, unforgivable. If she failed Max... No, she couldn't risk it. She'd have to tell him, have to take it back.

"You're going to work construction?"

"What? No. I meant your other duties, some of your other duties, but—"

"Okay."

That stopped her for a full three seconds. "Max, I don't—"

"First thing you can do is order these appliances. Then take over the ordering for the flooring and carpet. That would help."

"But—"

A timer went off in the distance. "That's the oven," Max said, not looking at her. "I'll get the pizza, then we can get to this work and make it an early night."

How could she argue with that?

Leaning on things because he was tired. If that had been true, he might have admitted it. No way was he telling her that her comment had made him realize he'd been backing away from her—in the office, at the site, in the kitchen. Just to gain space. And equilibrium.

Maybe he was more tired than he'd realized.

Although the reason he'd taken her up on the offer to help wasn't so he could get more rest. It was because she'd wanted to retract and it gave him a chance to try out his Eric method on her.

The pizza revived him a little, but after a couple of hours, that lift was long forgotten.

She went over every expenditure, explaining why each dollar was needed. He'd said that as long as Miss Trudi came in within the budget allowed for appliances and it fit in the kitchen, he didn't much care if she got a purple stove shaped like a toadstool. Suz didn't listen. In all the permutations, she added the figures in her head, then checked them on the calculator. She wasn't wrong once.

They still came in under budget. That seemed to make her nervous.

"I'll check these numbers one more time."

He took the calculator from her hand and put it out of her reach.

"Ten times is enough." Maybe he'd been careful not to touch her. So what? He rubbed the back of his neck. "Anything else?"

"There might be an eight-inch gap between the end cabinet and the wall."

He stopped in midrub and stared at her. "Might be?"

"That's how my figures added up, but...you need to check my math."

He swore under his breath. What was going on in that head of hers?

"Check your math? You've been outcalculating the calculator, Suz. I trust your figures. So—" he pushed out the rest of the sentence over the first syllables of her protest "—what are we going to do about it?"

It was a risk. Tossing in that compliment, then trying to redirect her thoughts. But if he could slide it in and not give her a chance to bat it away, maybe it would sink in. The *we* ought to help, too.

"If the counter can be ordered longer..." At his nod, she went on, "Then what do you think of adding a space for trays and cookie sheets and such?"

"Sounds useful." This noncompliment giving was tough work. He couldn't just say "good" or "great." He had to think of something that she'd accept but that would also let her see it was good or great.

She got up, as if even "useful" made her edgy. She picked up the top folder of photos Juney had left. He suspected it was simply for something to do with her hands.

"There's nothing available in that line of cabinets that would work, but I can get the hardware to match, and you've said Lenny's a good carpenter..."

"I'll ask him tomorrow, but I can't imagine it'll be a problem. It's a good solution and—"

She slapped the unopened photo folders down on Juney's desk.

"You have a hell of a nerve giving me grief about my love life."

He felt as if he were in one of those dreams where you're lazily walking down a deserted path and the next step puts you in the middle of a highway with eighteen-wheelers whizzing past.

"Where did that come from?"

"You said you were sorry for jumping all over Eric..."

"That's not what I said."

Had she been stewing about this since the beginning? Or could this be another case of her using a good offense as her defense? But why in the heck did she think she needed a defense against compliments?

She gave no sign of hearing his objection. "And for

walking out. But you didn't apologize for your cracks about my dating. Especially—''

''They weren't cracks. More like—''

''—when you called it off with your fiancée because of your pride.''

''Huh? Where'd you get that?''

''I know you, Max. When you didn't get your degree on schedule, when your circumstances changed, your pride—''

''You've got it all wrong. I asked Laurie to wait until I could support us and Annette, then we'd get married. She said no.''

Suz's eyes widened. At what he was saying or that he was saying anything at all?

It was over a long time ago, and it had been his pain. His alone. Who could he have told, anyway? Annette? It was his job to protect her, not go moaning to her. He'd cut ties with his friends from college; they were part of what he'd left behind. The adults around Tobias were mostly adversaries to be shown that he could take care of Annette and himself.

Besides, he'd never been much for confiding. Telling Suz in the first place had been an accident.

''She said no?'' Suz demanded. ''Why wouldn't she wait for you? What did she expect you to do?''

''She wanted to put Annette— She wasn't willing to wait. Not any longer than we'd planned. She broke the engagement and walked out—no, ran out.''

''Put Annette where?'' She spun away from him, paced two steps, then spun back and retraced her steps. ''No, don't tell me. I might have to hunt her down and hurt her.'' Suz was back to pacing. ''The witch. The unmitigated, selfish witch. Maybe I'll hunt her down, anyhow. How anyone could— What are you laughing at?''

''You, Suz. You.''

He hugged her.

For a handful of seconds it was the way it used to be. A warm, affectionate embrace between pals.

Then his hand covered the point of her shoulder, migrating from the softness of fabric to the smoothness of the skin beyond the sleeveless blouse. He remembered this sensation from the night of the wedding.

He remembered not only the sensation being absorbed by his fingers and palm, but the sensation rioting in his gut. Rioting almost uncontrollably.

From that fleeting instant when he'd replaced the narrow strap of her dress higher on her shoulder at the reception. And from the infinite moments when he had drawn it down her arm, giving him more to touch, leaving him wanting it all.

He dropped his arms and backed off half a step.

"Tha—that's me," she said, not looking at him as she gathered up her purse. "Laughable Suz. I say I want to hunt somebody down and everybody laughs."

"That wasn't how I meant it, not at all. I was laughing because you're such a good…friend. Loyal."

"Great, now I sound like a dog. No—" her traffic cop's hand stopped him "—it's okay. There are worse things. Besides, it's time for me to go. And you probably have a baseball game to watch."

"Yeah. Brewers are on the West Coast."

"See? I knew it. I might not fetch your slippers or newspaper, but after a lifetime with older brothers I do know sports schedules."

He escorted her to the front door, watched her get safely into her car and back out before he went to the living-room couch.

She'd left with a smile. Everything was fine. She didn't know how he'd reacted.

That was good. Essential.

He picked up the remote and clicked on the game. Lit only by the glow of the television, his hand looked pale in contrast to the black plastic.

Suz's skin was pale next to his. The fairness and delicacy of her shoulder, such a contrast to his big, tanned hand gliding across…

Big deal. A lot of people's skin was pale compared to his. His Italian heritage contributed to that, so did working outdoors. He took precautions, but he was still out in the sun a lot more than Suz. She wasn't one to put on a bikini and fry herself.

Suz in a bikini. The curve of her belly, so milky white that his hand there would be a stark contrast. As soft and pale as the line he'd traced, the night of the wedding, from her throat, across her collarbone and down. The creamy smoothness of her thighs clear up to…

Cursing, he shifted on the couch, accidentally hitting the button on the remote and momentarily losing the game.

In the time it took to locate the remote and click back to the game, he caught a few frames of some long-haired blonde jogging through surf wearing an economy-size swimsuit.

He'd seen Suz in a swimsuit—not a bikini, but still showing a fair amount of skin. And a fine sight it had been. But he hadn't gone nuts. He hadn't forgotten that she was Suz, for Pete's sake. And that had been a lot more than some wild thoughts from putting by his hand on her upper arm. That had been seeing her in the flesh, smooth, soft—

No. What the hell was the matter with him?

He'd get past this. He'd get back to being able to look at her and smell her scent and hear her voice without thinking anything other than that was Suz, his sister's best friend, and someone he cared about and wanted to watch over.

He had to put his mind back to how he'd dealt with her all the years before he'd tasted her and touched her and held her the way a man holds a woman.

Taking a break from checking online sources for display racks, Suz wandered into the kitchen Friday in search of something to drink.

Fran Dalton and Miss Trudi were sitting at the table chatting, with a five-gallon thermos and what looked to be glasses filled with lemonade between them.

"Oh, Suz, dear, come and have lemonade," Miss Trudi invited. "Fran makes excellent lemonade, and she brought some for us."

Suz liked Fran, who visited Miss Trudi regularly, and she loved lemonade.

Before she reached the thermos, the back door gave its grumbling rattle before abruptly swinging wide open. Max marched in with Nell slung over his shoulder in a fireman's carry. Giggles echoed from the vicinity of Max's back. His face was stern except for his eyes.

"Max, Nell, do come and join us for lemonade," Miss Trudi invited as serenely as the hostess of a party who could see more of one of her guests than her shorts-clad rear end. She handed Suz a glass.

"If you'll take delivery of this errant package, I'd be happy to have some lemonade," Max said.

He swung Nell down in an arc that increased the giggles. Max would make a great father.

The thought hit Suz like a blow to the stomach, expelling air from her in a spurt. Since she had the lemonade at her lips, it sounded as if she was blowing bubbles.

Max and Fran looked at her in surprise. Miss Trudi smiled benignly. Nell tipped her head as if judging her technique.

"Are you okay?" Max asked, stepping closer and raising his hand as if anticipating he might need to thump her on the back. Or maybe perform the Heimlich maneuver, wrapping his arms around her ribs, her back pulled snug against his broad, hard chest. Her rear end cradled against— She yanked the glass away as she gave another sputter.

Max took another step toward her, and she held up a hand.

"Fine. I'm fine. Just a little, uh, cough. Sorry."

Dismissing a cough as mundane, Nell turned to the lemonade and asked, "Why would you rent air, Mr. Max?"

"Huh?"

"Errant," Fran said. "He said he had an errant package—you. Errant means gone astray, or someplace it wasn't supposed to be, which you were. You were told not to be in the construction area, Nell. You promised."

"I didn't bother anyone. They didn't even see me."

"Max must have seen you," Miss Trudi said.

"But—"

"No buts." To be eye level with the girl, Max bent and propped his hands on his thighs, their power clearly defined by the stretch of the material. "You are not to come into the construction area, not unless I'm with you and have said it's okay. Remember how important it is to be safe with tools, like when you use a hammer?" He waited for her nod. "This is even more important. The men are using tools that could injure them if they're distracted by you or, uh, anything."

Had Suz imagined it or had his gaze flicked toward her? She propped her free hand on her hip, but he went on, "There are dangers to you, too. Things can fall or boards you step on might look solid, but aren't. Even the ground. You know there's an old root cellar out near where we're working?"

"What's a root cellar?"

"It's a big hole in the ground where people used to store food before they had refrigerators."

"Like in *The Wizard of Oz,* where Aunty Em got in, but Dorothy didn't because she chased Toto? Is that why they had one here? Did they have tornadoes?"

"Tobias has never had a tornado. One theory is that Lake Tobias, as well as all the trees, protect us. Indeed, Wisconsin does not get a great many tornadoes. Certainly not as many Kansas," Miss Trudi said. "Although I remember stories about a deadly tornado that struck New Richmond in the western part of the state. People were attending a circus and more than one hundred died. That was in 1899. Perhaps that did influence my grandfather to build a root cellar. I must check his journals and—"

"Whatever reason they had for building it," Max interrupted, dragging the conversation back to his lecture, "the ground's not as strong over it as it is other places. If that caved in while you were standing on it, Nell, you could be hurt badly. Nobody wants that. So I want you to promise me that you won't go inside the yellow tape ever again without me saying it's okay. Promise?"

Nell gave one decisive nod. "Promise."

Miss Trudi handed Nell and Max glasses of lemonade. The little girl and the big man smiled over the rims.

"Oh, whose UW course schedule?" Smiling, Fran reached out to the stack of mail Suz had forgotten to take to her room after opening it over breakfast. "Mind if I look?"

Suz's pause was so short she didn't think anyone noticed. "Go right ahead. I didn't know you were interested in courses at the University of Wisconsin, Fran."

Max had noticed. He shifted position to get a look at the materials that had come in today's mail, then swung his gaze toward her. She looked away before those dark eyes met hers, feigning great interest in Fran's answer. At least she'd left the application forms inside the envelope.

"Probably a pipe dream. I audited a few as a guest student while I was living in Madison after graduation, but I didn't even make a dent in my wish list before I moved back here. I loved having a university so handy."

"It doesn't need to be a pipe dream." Suz carefully did not look at Max, but she was aware of Miss Trudi's gaze shifting in that direction. "You could always go back to Madison. Pick up where you left off. There's no time limit."

"I know," Fran said. "I suppose the limitation is in me."

Not looking at Max was a physical strain on Suz's muscles. Not shouting "See! See!" required clamping teeth onto her bottom lip.

Fran gave a surprisingly wistful sigh for the pragmatic woman Suz had come to know. "Maybe I should be thinking about that more seriously."

"What a splendid idea," Miss Trudi said. "I have always held that ending one's education at any arbitrary point is unwise."

Fran chuckled. "What we should do is persuade Steve to get a college to come here—a UW-Tobias Lake campus."

"Wouldn't that be marvelous," Miss Trudi said. "With a strong botanical department. Oh! Fran, I would so much like your opinion on my rosebushes. I'm afraid the aphids are feasting. Do you have time to come look at them?"

"Absolutely."

The two women headed out with Nell zooming ahead.

Silence settled around Suz and Max, left alone in the big kitchen. The kind of silence as thick as Jell-O. So the least motion caused viscous ripples and waves that sloshed against any inanimate object—like Max—and echoed back to her. She would drown in Jell-O. What a fate.

"Are they for you?"

"No."

He lightly slapped both palms on the table, sending the Jell-O rocking and rolling. "Suz—"

"Why not?" she demanded, cutting to the chase. "What does it hurt to look?"

"It's a waste of time." The Jell-O was sloshing over the edges now.

"Not if you'd open your mind to—"

"I'm not going back to college."

A rhythmic motion caught her attention. Max's left hand wrapped around his right wrist and moved forward and back, forward and back. Yet he showed no sign of pain. She thought back, trying to remember when he did it.

Not a lot. Just…just… Good grief, how had she missed that?

"Why do you do that?" She kept all accusation out of the question.

"Do what?"

"Rub your wrist whenever the subject of returning to school comes up?"

He looked at the hand covering his wrist with apparent surprise, then dropped it to his side. "One time, I rub—"

"You do it every time, Max."

"That's not pos—"

"Every time."

He looked a question at her and read the answer in her nod.

"I didn't know I was doing it, so I don't have any idea why."

"Does your wrist hurt?" That might make sense, equating a physical pain with the emotional pain wrapped up with events surrounding his withdrawal from school—his mother's death, his fiancée's desertion, his taking on responsibility for raising Annette and his giving up his dreams.

"No."

She interpreted that bald statement to mean it didn't hurt so much he couldn't stand it. She didn't take the time to argue, since it wouldn't change his mind. Plus, she had other things on her mind—including what he'd said the night of the wedding, standing on his porch:

I've thought about it a lot since I broke my wrist. What if that had happened when I was starting the company and we were hanging on by a shoestring—hell, a thread? What if it had happened before—when I was working every job I could get so we wouldn't lose the house? What if I hadn't been able to work anymore?

Were those questions tied in with why his never finishing college seemed to bother him now when it hadn't any other time she'd known him?

All I know is construction...long in the tooth to try something else.

That was bunk.

But it went back to what Miss Trudi had talked about—dreams he had been forced to release and didn't know how to grab on to again.

She grimaced. It had to be even harder to grab hold of something with a broken wrist. Well, he'd just have to borrow one of hers.

"Since your wrist doesn't hurt, you shouldn't have any trouble holding on to this course schedule."

"No thanks. And I don't have time to talk about it. I've got work to do." His long strides slowed as he neared the door, as if he awaited her reply.

"No problem."

"Glad you got it now." He gave a decisive nod, but she saw by his eyes that he wasn't as certain as he tried to sound.

She gave him a sweet smile and had the satisfaction of seeing uneasiness edge into his expression before he pulled the door closed.

"You won't take it?" She addressed the closed door. "Then I'll deliver."

Chapter Six

"**I**'m starving. Let's go."

Max said the words without advancing past the office threshold. It didn't matter. A breeze brought her the scent of soap and clean clothes from his post-work shower and change.

Suz didn't look up from Juney's desk. Because she was busy. Not because of what she'd been thinking while she'd listened to the water running.

When he'd hugged her the other night, she'd thought for one wild second that he was going to kiss her again. He'd put his arms around her, sure. But the flourishes were all in her head. It had been a hug between friends. Nothing more.

"This needs more work."

It was Sunday evening and she'd been using design software on Juney's computer to calm Miss Trudi's latest worry, which was that the furniture she wanted from Bliss

House wouldn't fit in her new space. No matter how many times Suz had explained, Miss Trudi had fluttered her hands and said she simply couldn't visualize it. Not even drawings worked.

Then Miss Trudi had mentioned this afternoon that she'd heard about the software on Juney's computer, and she was sure that if Suz used that, she would feel reassured. Bubbling over with her idea, she'd rushed out to ask Max if Suz could use the computer. Max, of course, was at the site working. The man never heard of a day of rest, though his crew was off.

Accompanying Suz to her car later, Miss Trudi had said she was concerned about Max not eating, so she thought it would be a good idea if Suz stayed at his house until he came home and suggested they get a bite to eat.

Suz had given the older woman a sharp look, but saw no guile—that didn't mean it didn't exist, just that Miss Trudi was good at hiding it. Still, she was concerned about Max's eating habits, too.

Besides, Suz hadn't minded the opportunity to be in his house alone.

Max hadn't said anything about finding the course schedule she'd tucked into the guide to television listings that sat between his remote and the battered video of his favorite movie, *Casablanca*. It wasn't there now. What were the chances the course schedule was still in his possession and not in the garbage? Not likely.

That was okay, since she'd requested four more copies. She'd put another one there.

Max had come in twenty minutes ago, announced he was taking a shower and afterward they were going to dinner at the Toby. Because *she* wasn't eating right. She'd called out a pithy comment about black pots and kettles, but he'd already headed for his bedroom—and the shower.

"You've been working on this all day," he said now.

"A job takes as long as it takes."

He grunted and picked up a handful of pages she'd printed out at various stages. He shuffled through them, then plunked two on the desk.

"This one's got the earliest time stamp and this is the latest one. There's a hair's difference. It was good to start with, and by now it's got to be as good as it's going to get."

God, she hoped not. This version had to be better than what she'd had before. Maybe she should start over, take another run at it from a different direction.

"A little longer. I bought fruit on the way over here. It's in the fridge. Have that as an appetizer. I'll be ready soon."

Because the more she thought about it, the more she thought starting all over made sense. She'd start fresh after dinner. No, not after dinner, she wasn't coming back here, not at night with only Max, because—

"Is that an order?"

"Yes. Your arteries have got to look like the Dan Ryan Expressway at rush hour if you've been eating regularly at the Toby."

She'd save all the material on the computer now, and tomorrow, during Juney's lunch break, with Max at the site, she'd try for something truly good.

When she walked into the kitchen, Max was partially turned toward the sink, halfway through eating one of the overripe bananas she'd bought to make banana bread, and he looked as if each bite made him want to gag.

"Max? What are you doing?"

He swallowed hard and gave her a forced smile. "Eating the fruit you bought."

She took the banana from his unresisting hand and threw

it out. "I said in the fridge—grapes, peaches, nectarines. The old bananas are for baking."

"Sorry." He filled a glass with water and gulped. She had a feeling he would have spit it out to rid his mouth of the ripe-banana taste if she hadn't been there.

The man definitely didn't like mushy bananas. So why on earth had he forced himself to eat it? He couldn't have been that hungry for dinner.

"Don't apologize. It's a ten-cent banana. Just tell me why you would eat it when you prefer bananas with their own snap, crackle and pop?"

"Didn't want them to go to waste. You ready? Let's go."

End of discussion.

She could try to pry it out of him and get hungrier while making no progress. Or she could go eat dinner and at least be satisfied in one sense.

"I think Miss Trudi must have a mysterious past. She's traveled to exotic countries, probably tamed a maharajah or two. Wrote dispatches from the Congo, learned the tango in São Paulo, that sort of thing." Suz bit into another French fry.

Max put his napkin on the table, his burger and fries long gone. Suz wasn't one of those women who picked at food, but she didn't keep up with him. For one thing she talked a heck of a lot more than he did.

"She's lived most her life in Bliss House."

"Oh. Well, then, she probably had a tragic love affair. Her young lover was torn away from her by a disapproving despot of a father. He went off to war and never returned. Or returned a shell of a man who withered away before her eyes." She pointed the decapitated French fry at him. "What about that?"

"I've got my doubts."

"Hah! You see her as the role you've got her pegged in now. You don't see her as a woman. You never think that she was once a girl or cherished memories of her girlhood."

Suz was in one of her fanciful moods. Usually he let them fly over his head, like jets bound for destinations unknown. For some reason tonight he felt obligated to defend himself.

"I don't know anything about her girlhood. She had to be near forty when I was born."

"You're so literal, Max."

Max rubbed the back of his neck. Why the heck was he having such a hard time dealing with Suz? He never had before. Somehow things had changed. Like one of those weird movies where somebody making a train changes lives. Or someone arriving unexpectedly at a wedding…

Maybe that was the key. If he could understand that, everything would return to normal.

"What was the emergency your family wanted you to come home for?"

Her eyes widened. "What does that have to do with Miss Trudi's past?"

"Nothing. Just something I've wondered. You said you weren't coming to the wedding because of a family emergency, then you show up saying there was no emergency, after all. It's natural to wonder about the emergency."

"Nothing much."

"Then why did they call you to come home?"

"You've met them, Max. You know how they are—their darling little Suz can do no wrong. Except they're not entirely sure I'm capable of feeding myself, much less being out in the world. And…"

The word trailed away to nothing as she stared over his shoulder.

He twisted in his chair to follow the direction of her look. Rob Dalton and his sister, Fran, were drinking coffee two tables away. Fran came by Bliss House a couple times a week to see Miss Trudi, and he knew Suz had gotten to know her some, but as far as he knew she hadn't seen Rob since Annette and Steve's wedding.

Max, being older and from a different part of town, hadn't known Rob for more than a hello until recently. But Annette had known Rob since college; Rob and Steve were close friends, and Annette had been engaged to Steve. After that blew up, Rob remained friendly with Annette and consulted on Annette and Suz's business, Every Detail, before they sold it.

Rob's treatment of Annette had predisposed Max to the younger man. Working with him on the Bliss House financing had confirmed that impression. He was a nice guy.

Looking at him now, Max recognized he was also a good-looking guy, who wore clothes with ease. He worked for a financial firm in Chicago and made big money. And the last Max had heard from Annette, Rob's marriage was over.

"Want dessert?" he asked Suz.

"What? No dessert, thanks." She put down the French fry.

"How about some coffee?"

"No thanks. Let's get the check and…" She looked at him. "Mind if we stop and talk to Fran and Rob?"

He had a sudden urge for dessert and coffee, but said, "No problem."

He put his hand on her back, only to guide her through the chairs left all over the place. She could have tripped over one on the way, her focus was so tight on Rob's table.

Rob's frown dissolved into a smile aimed at Suz.

Max stepped in. "Fran, Rob, good to see you. You both know Suz Grant?"

Fran smiled in welcome. Rob stood and held out a chair. "Suz and I go way back—to when she and Annette started Every Detail."

So, the same time Rob had earned Annette's gratitude, he must also have been winning Suz's. Max took the remaining chair, opposite Suz.

"How are you, Rob? I was surprised to see you. Pleased to see you both—" Suz smiled at Fran "—but surprised."

"I'm spending the summer in Tobias on a leave of absence from the firm." Rob's voice was entirely neutral.

"That's great. You could use a break. You work too hard."

Rob exchanged a look with his sister.

"Yeah, well, it's not exactly a vacation. You've probably heard rumors… If not…my marriage is over."

Accompanied by words of solace, Suz put her hand over Rob's. Max couldn't take his eyes off the slim, smoothness of her hand curling around the other man's, still wearing a wedding ring.

"Sorry it didn't work out, Rob," Max said gruffly.

"So am I. I thought… Anyway, it seemed like this summer was a good point to take some time, assess where I am, where I want to be." His mouth twisted in a self-aimed grimace. "All that mumbo jumbo. So, Max, if I can help any keeping the funding straight on Bliss House, let me know. Hell, if you need unskilled manual labor, I could do that. I don't want to get in Fran's way around the house."

"You won't be in the way." Fran's usual calm held both an undercurrent of concern and a glimmer of amusement. "I'll put you to work."

Rob grinned. "Please, Max—I'll do anything."

They all laughed. That started the conversation shifting directions and darting around like a bird. They walked out together, calling good-night as Fran and Rob got in Rob's car, while Max watched to make sure Suz got in hers safely. He could swear she was humming under her breath.

As for him, he needed serious attitude adjustment. It was plain wrong to be so damned pleased that she'd talked more to Fran than Rob.

"Anything else?"

Suz scanned the papers spread around where she sat cross-legged on the bed. "I think that covers it."

Annette had called shortly after Suz returned from the Toby to confirm that she and Steve would be back in a week. Suz jumped on the chance to go over details with her. But her head must not have been in it, because she had hardly anything to ask Annette.

Holding the phone with one hand, she used the other to flip through the pages again.

"So, I hear you were part of an interesting quartet."

"Huh?" With her focus on the Bliss House project, Suz didn't follow Annette's conversational drift.

"The Toby. Tonight. You were there, right?"

"Good grief. The grapevine must have been burning up."

"You better believe it. I never thought I'd find any speck of redeeming value in Tobias gossip. But I've gotta say it's been fun to keep track of the important stuff going on."

"I don't see dinner at the Toby qualifying as important."

"Oh, I don't know. When you and Rob Dalton, and Max and Fran are there, it can be downright fascinating. I've always liked Fran."

If Suz had harbored any thought that Annette's pairings of the names had been accidental, that comment ended it.

Her friend was pairing her brother off with Fran Dalton. Why did that feel like a betrayal?

"She's great," Suz agreed, although she couldn't muster much enthusiasm at the moment.

"And I bet it was great to see Rob."

"Yeah, he's a good guy," Suz said absently. She could go over the lighting considerations with Annette a second time. Well, third, actually.

"He sure is. And with his divorce from that robotic wife, he's available again. I always thought you two would make a great couple."

The sheet with her notes on lighting fell from Suz's hand. "What? Tell me you didn't say that. Tell me you're not becoming one of those married-lady matchmakers after a grand total of two weeks of wedded bliss."

"I thought—"

"No, no and *no!* Am I getting through? Rob Dalton is a great guy who's had a tough time, and I hope I can be his friend. I don't want anything messing that up."

"You mean because you shut out guys after the first or second date, so you'd never see him again and that would mess up the friendship."

"I mean," Suz said with deadly calm, "your matchmaking would mess it up."

Annette ignored that accusation with the blitheness of old friendship.

"You know, Suz, you divide guys into two camps— friends and potential dates. With friends, guys you're confident won't ask you out, you're your charming and open self. With potential dates, you get all stiff and closed off. And the few who make it past those obstacles, you discard after a date or two."

"I've heard this first-date lecture before, Annette. I don't—"

"It's true! You were at ease the minute you met Steve back in March. It was because you thought he wouldn't respond. Because you thought he was taken. So he was safe."

"I don't know what you're—"

"That's what you've been doing all along! Keeping every man at a distance unless he was already taken—at least in your mind—so there was no chance you could get involved. But...but Max isn't taken, and you still flirt—"

Heat surged up Suz's throat. "I do *not* flirt with Max."

"I didn't mean flirt in a bad way. I meant you're open, comfortable with him, you let him see who you really are. Like you did with Steve. Like you did with Rob because he was married. And like you don't do with available guys."

"Sure I'm comfortable with Max." Having told that lie, she might as well pile on the rest. "He's like another big brother. Treats me exactly like they do."

"But do you want him to treat you that way?"

"Of course. That's how things always have been between me and Max."

"I knew at the start you had feelings for him, but...oh, Suz—"

"Don't 'oh, Suz' me. There's no need. Absolutely no need. I had a little thing for Max when I met him. He made it clear he didn't see me that way, and I moved on. End of story."

"Moved on to a never-ending stream of first dates."

Suz uncrossed her legs and slid them over the edge of the bed, needing to move. "Right. Meet 'em and leave 'em, that's my motto."

"But that didn't start until later." Annette's voice had the dreamy quality of someone mentally leafing through the past. "You weren't doing it that much right after you met Max. It wasn't until… Oh, Suz…"

"Don't." It was sharper than she'd intended. But at least it stopped Annette from following that track. Suz pulled in a quick breath and forced lightness into her voice. "Listen, girl, if you don't get off this phone, I'm going to think you're badly neglecting your groom. You are having a good time, aren't you?"

There was a pause, then the silence changed even before Annette spoke. Suz could imagine her smile and the love in her eyes as she said, "Oh, yes, I'm having a good time."

"Great. You keep on having a good time and we'll see you in a week."

And then it would be time for Suz to move on.

Suz watched the figure approaching the back door and swore under her breath.

Max was not supposed to be here, even if it was his house. Miss Trudi and Juney had both said no chance, no chance at all that he'd arrive before she finished. He would be at the Toby until at least ten, since Monday night was a special darts night. But here he was, at not quite eight-thirty.

She might have given them the impression her project was a surprise for Max. In reality she hadn't intended to share one bit with him. He was the cause of her urgent need for baked goods, and she saw no reason he should benefit from driving her nuts.

He stepped in and stopped, sniffing deeply. "Hey, what's that? Smells great."

"It's banana bread. Should be out of the oven in a few minutes." Which would have left plenty of time to clear out if he hadn't come back so early.

"Oh."

"Juney said I could use the oven. Miss Trudi swears the oven at Bliss House is fine, but I used it once and she had so many warnings about be careful of this and don't do that, I kept expecting it to explode. Plus, without air-conditioning, it makes that kitchen so hot, so…" She was overexplaining. She gulped in a breath and finished, "I hope you don't mind."

"No problem."

"You like bananas, so I'll leave you a loaf for…" She risked a look at his face. "You don't like banana bread?"

"I, uh, haven't had it in a long time."

"Since your mom made it?"

"How'd you know that?"

"Annette's talked about lying in bed and remembering the smell. It's a good memory for her." But clearly not for him.

"Yeah. Mom used to make it when Annette was little."

"But you didn't like it."

He glanced toward her, then away.

"Because of the bananas?" Yet it couldn't be the banana taste he disliked, since he ate those unripe ones on his cereal. "The old, soft bananas?"

"Old bananas." He spoke so softly it was as if he was talking to himself—or a memory. "My father came home with bags of them. When they were too rotten to sell, the store gave them to Robert Trevetti. Mom used them every way there was—bread was the best, but you needed flour and sugar and butter for that, and a lot of times we didn't have that. One time…four days. That was all we had. Old bananas."

Suz could see him then, a thin boy in a one-room shack, forcing down yet another banana. Needing the food. Hating the taste and the poverty it represented. She'd seen the echo of that boy when she'd walked into this kitchen and seen him nearly gagging on an overripe banana. She'd bought it and he'd felt obligated to eat it—the old necessity of gaining sustenance from where he could hadn't released him.

He was so thin. But he never stooped, the way some thin boys do. He always stood straight and tall and proud. So proud.

"I would never have made banana bread if... As soon as it's done, I'll get it out of here. I'll air it out so you won't smell—"

"It smells great."

She released the dial for the stove's fan. "Uh, okay. But I'll get it out of here so it's not around to—"

"Maybe I'll give it a try."

Slowly she smiled at him, which was quite an accomplishment, since she wanted to fold the little boy he'd been in her arms and make sure nothing ever hurt him again. "Sure, add flour and sugar and butter to almost anything and it's pretty good. You know my theory about baked goods."

"That they can cure anything?"

"Exactly." Even pain dug in thirty years deep.

The oven timer dinged, and she had an excuse to turn away, an excuse to blink her eyes hard and fast. It could have been from the heat as she opened the oven door. Could have been.

With the two loaf pans cooling on a rack, she rinsed out the mixing bowl, squirted dishwashing liquid into it and filled it with hot water, using it as a mini-sink for washing the utensils.

"Want a beer? Or something else?" Max asked, trying to sound casual.

"No thanks. I have to let the bread cool, but I'll clean up in the meantime and be out of your hair as soon as possible."

"No hurry." Max opened the refrigerator and pulled out a beer.

Moving behind her as she washed a knife, he reached next to her left leg for the cabinet door that hid the garbage pail. She edged to the right, but the turn of the counter didn't allow much room.

"You could put those in the dishwasher." His words stirred the hairs along the back of her neck.

"Doesn't take but a minute."

He leaned against the counter to her left and took a pull from the beer bottle, watching her. She dropped the spatula twice. When she finally succeeded in holding on to it long enough to rinse it, he wordlessly took it out of her hand and dried it. All the dishes except the pans were done in no time.

She tested the bread, but it was still too warm to take out of the pans. What was she going to do with herself now?

"Want to watch TV?" Max asked as if reading her thoughts.

"Don't worry about me. But isn't there a ball game to watch?"

"Monday night. Travel day. I could put a movie in." Max headed into the living room and she trailed after him because she didn't know what else to do.

"Casablanca?" she asked.

"You don't like *Casablanca*?"

"I'm not saying that. It's a good movie. But I can't watch it over and over the way you do. I want to shake them and tell them not to be martyrs."

"Martyrs? They're sacrificing what they want for the greater good."

"Hogwash." She welcomed the dispute and the change of atmosphere it brought. "They could have figured out a way to save the world without giving each other up if they'd worked at it. Okay, Rick was selfish at the start, so he *needed* some self-sacrifice.'' Unlike Max, who would have high honors wrapped up if they gave degrees in that. ''But…''

Wait a minute. Was this one of the reasons he wouldn't go back to school? Not going after his dream again because of all the people who relied on Trevetti Building? That meant that if she wanted to give him a hand in grabbing hold of that goal again, she'd have to figure how he could take the courses he needed without hurting his employees. Or she had to find a way for Mr. Responsibility to transform into Mr. Me-First. Fat chance.

''But what?''

''What good is the greater good if everybody's sacrificed their love?''

''Not everybody. That's the whole idea.'' His focus shifted toward the bookcase holding a recent snapshot of Annette and Steve with Nell cuddled between them. ''Like the first unit over the barricades in a war. There are a lot of casualties, but the guys that follow get through, and that's the greater good.''

''Like you quitting college—you were first over the barricades so Annette could follow.''

''That's a stretch.'' He dropped to the couch, started to reach for the TV listings, seemed to think better of it and drew his hand back.

Stretch, my eye.

''Why haven't you gone back, Max?''

''Annette's the smart one in the family. I trudged along.''

''You're kidding. I've seen you with building plans, the budget for this project and the proposal you and Annette put together. Nobody who can build a house, not to mention what you do with numbers, can be anything but smart.''

"I'd just squeaked by an English course when Ma died. Withdrawing probably kept me from flunking out."

"One course—"

"Let's face it. I wasn't cut out for that kind of life. I'm a blue-collar sort of guy. That's okay. I do good work. I earn an honest living. It's not so bad."

Not so bad. If Max really felt that way about his life…

"What would you have done if you hadn't had to quit college?"

"Build."

His answer, immediate and certain, surprised her for only a moment. His integrity would prompt him to do a good job even if he hated it, but reviewing these past weeks, she recognized a love for his work standing shoulder to shoulder with that integrity.

"So you are doing what you wanted to do."

"I would have been designing what I built."

"Big projects? Office buildings, shopping centers? Things like that?"

"No. I like building things for people, not corporations."

That didn't surprise her. "But you would have liked wealthy clients so you could do avant garde designs?"

"Not especially. Too much avant garde architecture is about the architect, not about people kicking off their shoes and living in their houses. I like helping people make their homes work better for their lives."

"So, you would have liked to have your own business— which you do. Building for ordinary people—which you do. Designing the projects—which you mostly do."

His brows dropped. "I suppose so. But if something happened to me and I couldn't do the physical work, it would all disappear."

Something physical like a broken wrist if it hadn't healed right?

''Then go back to school so you can design, even if you couldn't do half the manual labor anymore.''

''I don't do half the—''

''I've seen you out on the site, Max. You're into everything.'' And he was avoiding the other part of what she'd said—going back to school.

He'd started into an explanation of how vital it was for a builder to know what his workers were doing. She cut across his words ruthlessly.

''It must have been hard when your mother died.''

''—because redoing work is… What?'' He stiffened, suddenly wary.

''When your mom died and you were in college. I always thought about that from Annette's viewpoint—losing her mother, but having her older brother step in and take care of everything. But from your standpoint… You were, what? Twenty?'' She waited, but he shifted his gaze away, apparently developing an intense interest in the top of the television, or perhaps in the uneven stack atop it. She didn't bother to check out what it was precisely. She had more important things to do. ''To give up what you'd dreamed of, what you loved, *who* you loved…''

''It wasn't love. If it had been, she would have understood about taking care of Annette.'' Before he'd finished the sentence, his brows slammed lower and his gaze snapped back to her. ''Annette doesn't know about that.''

She heard the request he couldn't bring himself to make—that she keep this secret from Annette. What he didn't know was how many secrets she already kept from her friend.

''I wouldn't tell her or anyone.'' That Max had been engaged to a woman so dense that she hadn't seen the greater value of the man for the sacrifice he was willing to make for his little sister. That Max had been engaged to a woman who could have had Humphrey Bogart *and* won the war and she'd walked away from both. Idiot. "But Annette already knows you put her first. She knows how lucky she is to have you as her brother."

His shoulders twitched. In another two seconds he was going to make an excuse and end this conversation. Part of her wanted to let him. There were already so many new insights to consider. Not to mention the chance he might get the idea to turn the tables and quiz her.

And that could get into dangerous territory in no time. But she couldn't let this go. Not quite yet.

He took a step toward the TV.

"Your mom," she said abruptly.

That stopped him. "What about her?"

"Annette doesn't talk much about when your mother died. I know she wasn't sick long. Was it her heart?"

His mouth twisted as he picked up the stack from atop the TV—the folders of wedding photos, she saw now. They never did get around to looking at them. "I guess you could say that. She got the flu, but kept working—two jobs. It became pneumonia. She still worked. Annette tried to stop her. I came home that weekend and tried to stop her. But Monday morning she went to work. I got a call from the emergency room. She'd collapsed and been taken to the hospital.

"When I walked in, I knew...she'd given up the will to live."

He put the photo folders down without looking inside.

"I've never been sure if it was because she was so worn down or because the doctors said she needed to be hospitalized. I said we'd manage, told her for once not to worry about anything but getting better. It was no use. She didn't have medical insurance, and she was worried about the money."

He rubbed the back of his neck.

"She had me bring Annette in. She kissed us. Said to take care of each other..." He seemed to gather himself before continuing, "She said she loved us. She died an hour later in the ER before they could admit her."

Tears burned Suz's eyes. That burn would go away, but the searing in her heart would remain.

"No medical insurance, but she'd taken out a small policy on her life—enough to get us by until I got work, until I proved I could take care of Annette."

She rested her hand on his arm, absorbing the warmth of his skin through her palm, feeling the dark hairs tickle her fingers. She needed to touch him, to take in that heat and return it to him, to make him see that he was not alone. No longer the twenty-year-old taking on the rearing and care of his young sister, no longer fighting the world to keep her.

He looked at Suz's hand, then raised his head. If their eyes met, would her touch become something far beyond solace?

She looked away and removed her hand from his arm. She reached for the photo folders to occupy her hands.

"Your mother would have been so proud of you—both of you. And so happy at Annette's wedding."

Max watched as Suz put space between them.

She didn't meet his gaze, yet her fingers had trailed off his arm. Had she been reluctant to let go?

Maybe he shouldn't trust his impressions. He wasn't operating at full capacity, that was for damned sure.

"Look how beautiful Annette is and how happy—Steve, too." Suz laughed, a little forced, flipping through photos. "Not the beautiful part—the happy part."

He could have driven away when he saw her car parked by his kitchen door, gone back to the Toby for one last round. He could have gotten out of the kitchen pronto. He could have turned on any channel. He could have done a lot of things other than spilling his guts. Suz didn't need him unloading ancient history on her. What she needed was—

"Suz?"

She'd been viewing the photos, turning them one by one from a faceup pile into a pile of facedown photos, when she went as stiff as a garden hose in February.

"What is it?" He moved to her side.

"Nothing. Nothing." Her lips had frozen, along with the rest of her, because the repeated word came out garbled.

He reached for the photos, specifically the last one she'd looked at. She tried to slap the ones she'd already seen on top of the unviewed stack. Their competing actions collided, and photos went up, down and sideways. Not only her two stacks, but also photos from other folders landslided to the floor.

In a dozen poses from the reception, Annette's beautiful smile and Steve's beaming face looked up at them from photos scattered on the floor. A few caught Nell, Miss Trudi, even Steve's mother, as well as other guests, talking, laughing—well, not Mrs. Corbett—and dancing.

But all those seemed to recede into so much wallpaper as his eyes picked out photographs of Suz. Smiling with Annette, listening to Miss Trudi and Nell, looking pensive by herself. And then he saw what she must have seen. A picture snapped as he'd approached her from behind while she'd sat alone.

He'd told himself he'd responded to her that night because her arrival had taken him by surprise. But it wasn't surprise on his face. And it wasn't a man contemplating the unexpected.

God, he hadn't known, he swore he hadn't known, he'd

ever looked at her that way. It was as much of a shock to him as it must be to her.

As much of a shock, maybe, but not—obviously—as disturbing.

Clearly it bothered her that he'd looked at her that way. Bothered her? Hell, she was probably wondering if he was about to jump her right this minute. He had to reassure her.

"Suz, cameras can lie."

"Can they?" She didn't sound like Suz. She sounded vague and disoriented.

"Yes. At least they don't always tell the truth. You know me better than that. You know me better than the story one picture tells."

Her head snapped around and she stared at him.

"Yeah, I know. I know what it looks like." He pushed at the photograph with the side of his shoe, sliding it under one of Nell with Steve and Annette. But the photo revealed under it was identical. Damn. Juney and Gert had multiple copies of each shot. With his luck, they'd spotted this one and had a dozen copies made. So that was what Juney had been gloating about and why she'd been so insistent he and Suz look at the wedding photos.

"What *you* look like," Suz said, as if to verify something that didn't make sense.

She was right. It *didn't* make sense. He was supposed to look out for Suz. If he'd caught any of his crew looking at her like that, they'd be gone.

"Pictures can catch a moment out of context. That moment can look like it contradicts everything that came before and after—but they're the real truth, and that one moment's the lie."

She was still watching him. "Is that what happened when you kissed me later that night on the porch? Was that one of those moments that lied? One of those moments taken out of context?'' She paused. ''What about that, Max? That wasn't about a camera lying.''

''It didn't mean anything. It won't happen again.''

That was wrong, he knew even as the words came out, but he didn't know how to make it right—not what he'd said, not what had happened.

''Well, thanks a lot. You sure know how to flatter a girl.''

Her attempt to sound flip didn't quite come off. For some reason that made him angry.

''Don't fish for compliments, Suz. You don't believe them, anyhow.''

''I am *not* fishing! And that's—''

''You know damn well you're a beautiful woman,'' he growled. ''You've got three-quarters of my crew panting at the thought of you in those short shorts of yours.''

''They're not short sho—''

''Oh, hell, it doesn't matter. They could be down around your ankles and it wouldn't matter.''

Her eyes popped open wide. That made him think back over what he'd just said. He swore under his breath.

''I didn't mean it that way—not dropping them. I meant shorts that long. To your ankles.'' Words were tangling and choking him. He had to get free of them. ''I…men would still look at you and see you're beautiful. And—''

''That's—''

''Don't tell me they wouldn't be shorts then, because… Oh, hell.''

He spread one hand across her shoulder blades, the other around the back of her neck, cupping the base of her skull, and brought his mouth down on hers. Her lips were parted—still arguing—and he took immediate advantage.

His tongue plunged into her mouth, finding her tongue, sliding along it.

And she kissed him back. Not merely pliant or accepting, no, not Suz, but exploring and enticing and exultant.

Each touch, each shift of her tongue against his, left him hot and starved for more.

He hadn't forgotten the taste of her—a concoction of vintage champagne, sun-warm grass cooling in the night breeze and moonlight, all sparked by the catalyst that was Suz.

Hadn't forgotten the curve of her back flowing under his palm from her shoulders to her waist to below.

Hadn't forgotten the smooth, warm flesh of her shoulder. Not like silk, no—softer, warmer, much more alive.

Hadn't forgotten an atom.

So how come he wasn't prepared? How come it hit him with the same fireball as the first time?

It couldn't be like this every time, could it?

Sin and salvation together.

He was crowding her, he knew it. The press of his body against hers was tight and hot. She wasn't backing away from the contact. He could feel that in the way she softened against him. But his weight, his power moving against her tilted the balance, even with the desk behind her.

He felt her shifting, adjusting—not against him, *for* him—and the need surged through him so powerfully he couldn't hold it back. She moved again…and everything changed.

He felt her slip, felt her foot shooting out from under her. She must have stepped on the slippery pile of photographs scattered on the floor around them. If he hadn't been holding her, she would have gone down. Just that quickly, his hold on her changed.

He released her mouth, squeezing his eyes shut so he wouldn't see the temptation of her mouth so close. He still had his arms around her, but it was different. Now he was supporting her, protecting her. Holding her the way he always had before.

The only way he ever should hold her.

He heard a gasp from her, but kept his eyes closed.

She pushed hard against his chest, yanking herself free.

"Don't do that again, Max. Not unless you... Just don't do it again."

He opened his eyes and she was gone.

Photos spread across the floor like the remnants of a rock slide. Without looking at them, he left the damned things where they were.

Let Juney think whatever the hell she wanted. She would, anyway. And right now he didn't care.

Chapter Seven

Suz braked to a stop near the back door of Bliss House and let out a jerky breath.

She'd held it at bay—thinking, feeling, *being*—as she drove around the lake. She'd barely breathed, keeping every sense, every conscious thought on her driving and pushing back the unconscious with every bit of her will.

Now it all came in, intoxicating her.... This couldn't be right, could it? This sense that her body had found a new pulse, a new rhythm? As if it had become a series of clocks and they were all set to Max Time. *Tick-tick-tick.* Breath, heartbeat, the heat at her core—oh, most definitely there— all wound up and keeping time to something Max had set in motion.

She wasn't naive, wasn't inexperienced, but the way she felt with Max... And that was from kissing. If he really touched her, if they ever...

The clocks ticked faster.

He felt it, too. She didn't doubt that. But he didn't want to feel it, so he fought it.

If they could just go to bed… Men were notorious for no-strings sex. If she could have that with Max, she'd take it and be more than satisfied. Just until the end of this project. And then they could go back…

It wasn't the idea of returning to being treated like Max's kid sister that stopped the fantasy. It was trying to imagine Max playing his role in this scenario. Men might be notorious for no-strings sex, but Max? No way. Max who'd had his heart broken by that idiot girl in college. Max who kept *honorable* polished bright and visible on the mantel.

It would have to be a relationship for Max. A real relationship. On a level where he would see her with absolute clarity. Even if she could batter down Max's reluctance, she couldn't let that happen.

Max had a problem.

Actually he had several. But the big one was himself.

He wished he could say it was Suz, but it wasn't. She was still Suz. Still funny and bright, and so damned much better at everything she did than she had the slightest idea she was.

No, the problem was him.

He wished to hell he were better at lying to himself. That might solve the whole thing. But after kissing Suz a second time, and the kind of kiss it had been and what it had done to him—was still doing to him—his damned inconvenient honesty told him that pretending the kiss on the night of the wedding had been a fluke wasn't going to fly.

He'd meant that kiss. He'd meant this one. And his reaction to both kisses was as wild and rock-him-back-on-his-heels powerful as he'd been telling himself that it wasn't.

And it was just as impossible.

Suz, for God's sake.

He'd been ready to hog-tie Eric for thinking of Suz, and at least Eric had a college degree and all the potential in the world.

What did he have? The thin edge his small company resided on was getting shaved away day by day. If it went under, he'd be back to trying to catch jobs—a beat-up, aging, uneducated general worker.

The part of him that had been looking out for Suz for eight years knew the score on this one. It didn't make him a bad guy. Like Eric wasn't a bad guy. But they weren't enough, either one of them. Not for Suz.

She deserved a great guy and security and the luxuries.

All he could give her was the comfort of knowing he wouldn't try to pursue whatever the hell it was that had sent him reeling whenever he kissed her.

So the next day he made sure to see her first thing, going into the Bliss House kitchen for the tea Miss Trudi was forever offering. Suz had been uneasy at first. But he'd treated her as he always had, and when Miss Trudi left the room, he'd looked straight at Suz and said he was sorry. He had no excuse, unless it was possible to get intoxicated on the aroma of banana bread.

He'd put the two loaves, wrapped as best he could, on the table in front of her. She pushed one back toward him, telling him to keep it if he wanted it.

"Better not. Next thing you know, that aroma will have me pulling a Rudolph Valentino routine with Juney when she does the payroll."

Suz's eyes flashed to his, then back to her cup.

"I sincerely hope you don't make that mistake," she said in a voice close enough to the usual Suz to fool most folks, ''because I would hate to pick up the pieces after Juney ran you through the shredder.''

They both chuckled. A little rusty, a little awkward, but still laughter. That was how they'd been handling it. Light and easy. Nothing to get worked up about. Nothing to make anyone think something had changed. Changed along the lines of the earth beneath his feet heaving and buckling. Nope. Just a couple of pals, that's what he and Suz were.

And that was his problem.

It was killing him.

Racing from her car through pounding rain Thursday afternoon, Suz reached Bliss House's kitchen door at the same time as Max.

''You shouldn't be out in this. There's lightning,'' he said as he made room for her on the step.

Part of Max's unrelenting campaign to prove that nothing had changed between them with that second kiss had been to be even more big brotherish than usual. It was getting annoying. Especially since nothing had changed between them.

He didn't want to be anything but buddies, even if his hormones voted otherwise. She wanted him the way she had the first time she'd seen him. Again.

She searched her heart and her memory, and she was sure that she had not spent these years pining for Max. But apparently that feeling for him had been lying in wait like a bear in hibernation. The first warm breeze from his direction and out it came. The photo of her face as they danced at the wedding proved that. He'd called that picture a lie, contradicted by the truth on either side of it. But she couldn't kid herself—the picture she'd carried in her head of them as buddies all these years was the truth, but so was that photo from the wedding.

"You've obviously been out a lot longer than I have." Oh, now why did she have to go and say that? It made her more aware of the rain-plastered state of his T-shirt, which made her even more aware of the body it showcased. "Can't the state safety people get you for exposing your workers to danger?"

"Sent them home when it started thundering."

She rolled her eyes.

"But you stayed." As she'd driven in, she'd seen him attaching blue plastic covering more securely to a pile of lumber. She realized now that she hadn't noticed if anyone else was around because she hadn't looked beyond Max. "You'll protect them, but not yourself? That makes sense."

"This rain is costing us time and that costs us money. I've gotta use every minute I can."

"And if you get hurt or worse, then what happens to the project? Seems to me you're the most important asset and you should protect it. Not take stupid chances."

"Right now we're both being stupid, standing out here in the wet when we could be inside."

He had a point.

They reached for the door handle simultaneously. They both jumped back as if the handle was electrified. Suz felt a drizzle from the edge of the porch's overhang slide down her back. Good. Maybe it would cool her off.

"After you," Max said.

"Thank you," she said with equal formality.

But each step became an effort—lifting the foot, moving it forward, placing it firmly on the floor. He was too close behind. She was too conscious of him. The porch was too small. The air was too heavy.

"What's wrong?" he asked from over her shoulder.

She said a quick prayer of thanks to whatever god arranged it so there was an answer to give—a legitimate answer that still wasn't the true one.

"The door's stuck." She rattled the handle for good measure.

She had a sudden urge to kick the door. Could that be what psychologists called displacement? Could she actually want to kick something else? Something big and solid and as bulky as the door?

Muttering something about it always being stuck, he moved to her far side and turned his shoulder to the door's surface. "On the count of three, press the lever and push. One. Two. Three—"

She pushed with relish—it wasn't a kick, but it was letting the door know who was boss.

Perhaps Max experienced similar feelings, because he gave a good, strong push, too.

Or maybe the door had a lousy sense of humor.

Whatever, it unstuck so suddenly she didn't have time to let go of the handle. The door yanked her inside at the same time Max's momentum carried him in on a collision course with her. He grabbed her shoulders, no doubt in some protective instinct, which turned her just enough to face him, probably not at all what he'd had in mind. But even Big Brother Max couldn't undo the laws of momentum. The door crashed against the wall, followed in quick order by her crashing against the door and him crashing into her.

Her head went back with the force of the double whammy, which also sent the air out of her lungs in a whoosh, leaving her lips parted and inches below his. He exhaled sharply, whether or not from the impact she didn't know.

She did know the brush of his breath across her moist lips sent a streak of heat through her.

His hold on her shoulders pressed them back against the wood.

She was pinned between the door's unyielding surface and Max's equally unyielding presence. No, that wasn't quite right. Because the door just stood there, unchanging. Max breathed. The motion of that basic physiological fact pushed and pulsed against her in ways that triggered an answering pulse deep inside her and—oh, lordy—a desire to push against him. To rock her hips, to press her breasts into him. To feel what that contact did to her and to hope it did the same to him.

He sucked in a big breath, pushing his abdomen harder against her, and heaven help her, there was no stopping her response this time. Every action has an equal and opposite reaction. She remembered that from science class, too. She couldn't help it, her hips tilted against him.

And she felt the proof that Max was unlike the door in another important way.

It stood, he moved.

It remained unchanged, he grew.

A growl of what sounded like pain came from deep in his throat.

He pressed harder into her and lowered his head.

"Ah, there you are children. I thought I heard someone come in."

Miss Trudi's fluting tones from across the large room could have been a foghorn and delivered less of a shock.

Suz jumped, which increased the friction and contact between them for one stroke longer. Then Max stepped back, dropping his hands from her shoulders.

"I, uh…" Max, his color heightened on his tanned cheeks, looked toward the open doorway. "I was just leaving."

His gaze swept across her face like a searchlight. The seconds it met her eyes were almost blinding.

But not quite. Because she saw clearly enough that whatever their bodies craved, Max Trevetti was not one to give in to a matter as trivial as desire.

Suz also saw that he was cravenly walking out and leaving her to face Miss Trudi.

"You only just arrived, Max," Miss Trudi said. "Why, how strange he's already gone. Suz, do you have any notion what could have induced him to leave so precipitously?"

"Not a clue."

"Good morning."

Max jumped, the screwdriver skipping off the worn head of the screw and gouging the door.

He wished he could swear. But with Miss Trudi standing beside him smiling benignly, it didn't seem the proper kind of greeting.

"I didn't hear you, Miss Trudi. What are you doing up so early?"

She shifted her weight, her slippers peeking out from under her long blue-print housecoat. He should have heard those slippers scuffing along the floor a mile off.

"It is I who should ask that question, Max. You certainly arose early to be working at this hour. May I make you tea?"

"No, thank you." He'd already dosed himself with coffee, using caffeine to offset a restless night. "I need to finish here before the crew arrives."

"My dear Max, truly there was no need for you to add to what is already a long day solely to adjust that door."

Hell, yes, there was need. So no more accidents like yesterday happened. No more opportunities to feel Suz's body, warm and lush—

"No problem, Miss Trudi."

The screw was so beat-up it was hard to find the groove to fit the screwdriver in. Each turn was a delicate matter of finding the right balance and pressure. It required patience and calm, neither of which he felt at the moment. Must've had too much coffee.

"As I told you when you first offered, there is no necessity to fix a door that will be replaced in a short amount of time."

"I'm doing it so it doesn't kill somebody or drive me crazy, both of which could happen before we get this damned door out of here."

"Ah." She scuffed off toward the stove.

He didn't look up in the hope that would discourage her from continuing the conversation. The futility of his hope became clear before she reached the stove.

"Working with Suz has been an extraordinary experience, don't you think?" Miss Trudi asked.

Yeah, extraordinary. Though that wouldn't have been his first choice of words.

"She homes in on the heart," she continued, not waiting for an answer. "Perhaps Annette and I had a tendency to wander from the core subject."

She was talking about herself and Suz working together. He relaxed.

"I guess she's helped you," he said, "getting things pinned down so you'll like your new place."

"Yes, indeed. Her work has ensured that I will be very comfortable. Although I believe that in 'getting things pinned down,' it is your work she has made easier. You and she appear to work very well together. I thought so from the first."

"We've known each other a long time." In case he

wasn't clear enough, he added, "She's like another kid sister."

Miss Trudi laughed.

That wasn't the response he'd been going for.

An old-fashioned kettle whistled. A few more minutes, and he'd be done. If that happened before she resumed this conversation, he'd be a happy man.

Scuff, scuff, scuff, came the slippers. She pulled a chair over from the table and settled in.

"When I say you and Suz work well together, I meant that each of you brings specific strength to the union— business union. I have been talking with Miriam Jenkins— are you aware she is considering renovating her father's house into a bed-and-breakfast? With its location overlooking the lake and within walking distance of downtown Tobias, it could be ideal. Although she doesn't have the least idea how to go about it."

A thin edge of disdain in her voice made him wonder if there was history between Miriam and Miss Trudi. Suz would know.

Suz? No, Juney would be the one to know. If he wanted to ask, which he didn't. Suz's name must've come into his head because the idea might interest her. She was quite taken with Miss Trudi and the history of Tobias. She got that glint, between amusement and fascination in her eyes, and he—

"Max!"

"What?"

"Don't you agree?"

"Uh, it depends. On the circumstances." Like the circumstances described in whatever the hell she'd just asked him about.

The final screw came loose.

"Then you must agree. Because in these circumstances

it is entirely clear that it would be a marvelous partnership between you and Suz. A marriage of two strengths. It would allow Trevetti Building to provide services unlike those any other construction company could offer.''

In his brain, the words *you and Suz* and *marriage* were like water pouring into an electrical box, *pop-pop-popping* as it short-circuited the whole thing. He scrambled for something else to respond to.

''Partnership? Who said anything about a partnership?''

''You don't think Suz is worthy of being your partner?''

His head shot up. ''I never said that. If anything it's—'' He snapped his mouth closed and grimly returned to work. ''A partnership's not on the table.''

''It would be very good for her.''

He ordered himself not to look up at Miss Trudi again. Keeping the questions welling up in his head from spilling out his mouth was just as hard. *Help her? How? With what?*

''Do you remember Dora Aaronson? No, perhaps not, as she was quite a bit older than you. She was the most talented drawing student I ever taught.''

She lapsed into silence.

Max doggedly cleaned several decades' worth of grime out of the latch mechanism, then added a few drops of oil. What did Miss Trudi know? And what did she suspect? He wasn't going to ask.

She exhaled through her nose in what might have been exasperation.

''I had students before Dora who had exhibited aspects of the behavior, though not to so marked an extent. From them I gained experience in dealing with students who, to all outward appearances, perform beautifully, yet feel that they are inadequate, that their accomplishments are flukes.''

And sometimes they thought they were merely decorative. So Miss Trudi had spotted that in Suz, too.

"They fear they will fail at any moment and their house of cards will collapse, exposing them as the frauds they believe they are. Continuing to achieve and advance does not alleviate the concern. Indeed, it often makes it worse, for now they would have a greater distance to fall.

"Telling them they are accomplished is not sufficient," she continued. "They've learned to discount what they have been told. They experience it as a 'disconnect' between what people say about them and what they feel inside."

He paused in the act of resetting the mechanism. "Well, if they can't believe it when they're told they're good at what they do, how do they ever get over it?"

She nodded in apparent approval. "They have to be shown. By someone they have learned to trust and respect. That trust is built on the truth, especially hearing the truth when they have performed at a level below their best. The summer after her sophomore year in high school, Dora created a drawing that had won significant acclaim. With the best intentions, I am sure, her teachers, art-show judges, fellow students and certainly her family had passed over the mistakes she had made in composition, as well as execution."

"I knew by then that she did not believe in herself or her talent. She continued to draw because that was what people expected of her, yet she felt she was a fraud. I had tried so many things, but this drawing gave me the opportunity to practice honesty, a straightforward assessment. I told her that the work was not up to her standards.

"Years later she wrote to me after her first solo show in New York that my words had nearly stopped her from drawing." Miss Trudi looked directly into his eyes. "Except that she realized their truth. While others had lauded that work, she came to feel she had somehow fooled them all with the emperor's new clothes. Then I stood up and said what matched her experience—that the emperor was naked, her drawing was lackluster."

"When she executed a simple sketch of a wren lifting its head in song and I told her how moving it was, she believed me. And believing me, she allowed herself to believe a little in herself. That was the start."

Max broke the gaze. He placed the first new screw in the hole and applied the screwdriver. It went in like a dream and so did the next and the next, compared to taking the old ones out. The bright screw heads showed against the worn metal, but at least the lock wouldn't stick for these next few weeks.

"It was a valuable lesson to me in dealing with such students," Miss Trudi said. "To build their belief requires patience and skill, like the building of a brick wall, one firm layer at a time. You understand that, Max, I know."

He did. To take each step slowly in telling—no, showing—Suz her abilities. Lay one course of bricks securely before starting the next.

"All done." He wiped the door handle clean of any remnants of oil or dirt. "Should work fine now."

"Thank you. I am impressed once more at your skill in fixing things not functioning at full capacity, Max."

He shouldn't have been shocked, not after Juney's phone call.

But it had to be shock that rammed into his chest when Suz opened her room's exterior door—without needing to unlock the dead bolt because she hadn't had it on, dammit—and he saw her clothes in piles beside an open suitcase early Friday afternoon. Definitely shock. What else could it be?

He stepped inside without waiting for an invitation. It made sense to conserve the air-conditioning. Besides, he didn't want his crew distracted by the sight of her in a T-shirt long enough to almost hide the hem of her red shorts, yet short enough to start giving a man ideas—and fantasies.

"Juney said you dropped off paperwork on what you've done here."

"Hello to you, too." She closed the door, then picked up a blue skirt. "Yes, I gave Juney everything so she'd have the rest of today to go over it and call with questions. I also left Juney my cell-phone number to call me anytime to clear up problems left behind."

He grunted. He hadn't done much of a job of getting her to see her own value when she was expecting that there'd be problems with her work. "You're not waiting to see Annette and Steve when they get back Sunday?"

"I'll say hello, then head out. So I want things ready."

"Where are you going?"

"I thought I'd go back to Dayton. See my family."

Certainly her family had passed over the mistakes...

Miss Trudi had said that about Dora and her drawing. Could family have something to do with Suz's situation?

"Back to fix that emergency?" She gave a wan smile. He considered sitting on the bed. The upside would be he'd be in her way and slow her packing. The downside would be that he'd be sitting on her bed. He took the chair at the desk. "Are you ever going to tell me the whole story of that family emergency that almost kept you from the wedding?"

She cut him a look. "You want to hear the whole story?"

"Yup."

She drew in a sustaining breath. "They told me it was life or death. Something they couldn't talk about over the phone, but Mom and Dad's forty-five years of marriage would never get to fifty if I didn't come home right away. It turned out the huge emergency was that they were redecorating the house—they had a decorator, but they said they wanted to pay me to run the job like a general contractor, or it would fall apart."

She put the blue skirt on a growing pile to the right of the suitcase and picked up the sleeveless top she'd worn to bake banana bread in his kitchen.

"And when that was done, I must help my sister-in-law plan and run a birthday party for my nephew Brock, who happens to go to the best private preschool in Dayton, so the mothers of kids attending would be great contacts. Contacts for what? you might ask—I did. Oh, anything." She punctuated that with a one-handed airy wave. "And my cousin Amy, who's engaged to a Dayton boy whose father has a lot of friends in Ohio politics, can't possibly do the wedding arrangements herself. Why not? you might ask— I sure did. Why—because Amy is flighty. I pointed out that was fitting since she has an advanced degree in aeronautical engineering."

Another airy wave, this time with two hands because she had put the sleeveless top on the pile and hadn't picked up anything else, showed how her family had dismissed that point.

"Oh, she's fine with *technical* details, but for something like a wedding, she absolutely needed my help. For a fee. And think of all those lovely, lovely contacts among guests who would be so wowed by the wedding that they'd just have to know who'd planned it."

She spread her hands on her chest. "Little ol' me."

"Sounds like they were trying to help you start a new Every Detail."

"With important variations." She held up one finger. "Decorating, parties, weddings—those were all fine, but none of that grimy stuff we got into with Every Detail, where we helped people put on additions or muck out after a fire or flood. Oh, no, this would be much more genteel work. And it would be in Dayton." A second finger went up, followed quickly by a third. "Potential customers would come from among people my family knew or knew about, so they could make sure I was treated right."

"They wanted you home and they wanted to protect you—what's so awful about that?"

"Nothing—and everything."

That made no sense. He understood her family's reasoning—maybe too well. "Do you want to settle in Dayton?"

"I don't know." She sounded miserable. A surge of something eased the knot in his stomach. He wouldn't have tried to budge her from following any path that might make her happy. But misery? Yeah, he'd do his damnedest to budge her from that path. "It could be…comfortable. I love my family, I truly do, even when they're driving me nuts."

"You could start off like they said, then branch into work you and Annette did with Every Detail."

She gave him a look he'd gotten more than once from Annette, the look that mingled frustration and pity because he didn't get it. "You don't know my family. And maybe…" She bit her lip, then shrugged.

"Is there something else you want to do? Someplace you want to live?"

She sat on the bed, actually the pillows, with her back and head supported by the wall, one knee drawn up. She stared out the window, giving him her profile. "You mean, like have I dreamed since childhood of painting in Paris or studying music in Rome or writing in solitude on the moors of England? Can't say that I have.''

Words drummed in his head. His words to Miss Trudi and hers to him.

Suz started talking again, sounding almost as if she was thinking out loud. ''It would be so easy… If they'd waited until after Annette's wedding, I could have fallen in with their plans and stayed there.''

''How about staying here?''

She rolled her head against the wall to look at him, not seeming to take in his words. ''What?''

''Stay here.''

''And do what?''

''What you've been doing. You'd give Trevetti Building something to offer that no one else does—a complete package. One-stop shopping, but with lots of options. The business could expand.''

She sat up and her eyes went wide. He thought one emotion swirling in them was fear.

''Max, you know that working with Miss Trudi, I've simply been following Annette's plans.''

He'd thought she'd get around to that sooner rather than later. She put all she'd achieved with Every Detail at Annette's door.

And that made him more sure.

Whether it was Miss Trudi talking about building trust and truth or his thoughts about applying the Eric method, what they had in common was they needed time. The only way to get that was to keep her here. To tie her to him…so he could help her get over this.

''Besides,'' she went on, ''you're the one who gives me grief for flitting off. How long would it be before—''

''You're right, I couldn't let you flit off. Not once we'd

started offering the service to customers. You'd have to stick.''

''See? So—''

''You can't flit off, because I'm making you my partner.''

Chapter Eight

"Partner!"

"Partner."

"But...but if you want a partner, Annette would be so much better."

"You and I work better together." Suz could do no more than blink before he zipped right past that. "Besides, Annette will have her hands full with her new family."

He was right. Annette could give only a fraction of the time Suz could. Which meant that if she left, he'd carry the burdens alone again. Never getting time for himself.

But they'd work together day after day, possibly even more closely than they had so far. He would see through her like glass.

"Max, I don't think—"

"You're going to run out, Suz?" He didn't sound particularly surprised.

If he'd said "flit" again, she might have missed it. But

something about his tone made her recall his saying similar words: *she walked out—no, ran out.* His no-good deserting ex-fiancée. Was that how he saw *her?*

"No running," she heard coming out of her mouth. "I'll be your partner—but only if you let me buy into the business. Forty percent interest."

She would *not* run out on him the way that witch had. She could relieve him of some responsibilities—and cash-flow concerns—so he'd see he could pursue the dream he gave up years ago. And she'd do her darnedest to keep his illusions about her alive.

"No way. That's way too much for you to put on the line—"

As opposed to him, who put all his earnings, not to mention his heart and soul on the line for his business. "Take it or leave it."

The wild-horses-won't-budge-me look she knew so well slid to one side and something almost crafty edged in. Warnings pricked along the back of her neck. Facing anyone else in a negotiation she'd wonder how she was being snookered. But this was Max. How could she possibly be wary of him?

"I'm not jumping into this without something on paper," he said.

"Absolutely. A contract—"

"Not a contract. A written proposal of what you'd bring to the partnership beyond money."

"Sure, we can do that. As soon as we wrap up Bliss House." Which would give her plenty of time to talk Annette into doing the proposal.

He shook his head, not taking his eyes off her. "Now."

"Why? As long as we both know it's going to happen, we can formalize the partnership later on. We don't need—"

"Now. I can't tell people you'll be part of the team without knowing what you're going to do. With building you gotta always look beyond this job to the one after and the one after that. I need to line up clients, not wait until Bliss House is done. I need to know now."

Annette would be back the day after tomorrow. Figure a week for her to settle in and a week to pull together a proposal… "Two weeks."

"Tomorrow morning."

"What?" She sounded like a crow in a tizzy. "That's not enough time."

Even if she knew where Annette and Steve were, even if she would call them on their honeymoon…but she didn't know where they were, so she couldn't.

"Tomorrow morning."

"I can't do it." She was proud of those words. Not what they revealed, but that she didn't break down and cry. Because now that the corner of the curtain had been pulled back, he would see what stood behind it—not the Great Suz, but a fraud using flashing lights and special effects.

"You have to do it. On my desk tomorrow morning."

He hadn't even blinked. Did he not understand what she'd said? "Max, I told you, I can't do it. I can't—"

"You'll do it. Or no partnership."

Which meant he'd carry all the burden alone. "Max—"

"See you in the morning."

"But…dammit!"

She was swearing at a closed door.

A downpour gave way to mere rain sometime after she returned empty-handed from the library. What she needed was a how-to book on creating an overnight business plan, preferably with fill-in-the-blanks. No such luck.

After turning down Miss Trudi's offer of supper with a

brief explanation of what she had to do by morning, she holed up in her room.

She had sheets of paper strewn on the bed and nothing in the laptop when Miss Trudi arrived with soup, sandwich and chocolate-chip cookies.

The paper had spread to the floor and she was staring out the door—with blinds *and* curtains defiantly open—at mist turned to glitter by a security light when Miss Trudi came back with a thermos of tea and to say she was going to bed.

"Me, too," Suz said.

"You've finished your partnership plan, then. How lovely."

"I'm finished, all right, but it's not lovely."

"Come now, it can't be that bad."

Miss Trudi perched on the edge of the bed while Suz paced and ranted.

"…can't do proposals. I'll tell him what he wants is impossible. Sunday, I'll be on my way. It's better than if we'd gotten into a partnership and—"

Miss Trudi clapped her hands once, the sharp sound stopping Suz in midrant.

"Quit dramatizing, my dear. Simply tell Max what you would do for his business."

"That's what he wants, but—"

"This is one of those rare instances when what the man thinks he wants truly is what's best for him. So write on your little machine—" she fluttered a hand to the laptop "—what you have done in planning my new home. Write down the questions you have asked me and the answers you have elicited. That will show what you have done. Next, write what you could have asked and what answers you could anticipate if this had been a different project—

an office, perhaps, or a store. Finally, write the questions and answers if you had no restrictions of time or money.''

Miss Trudi pushed herself up from the bed. ''It's very simple, my dear.''

''Very simple,'' Suz muttered after she left. She opened the outside door and stepped into the mist, which dampened her face and settled into her hair and clothes. The outside air sashayed inside and swirled the papers off the bed, mixing with those on the floor, wiping out any order. It was a relief. Her work had been worthless, anyway.

She could give up now and go to bed. Start thinking in the morning about what to do with her life.

Write down the questions you have asked me and the answers you have elicited.

She could do that. Max would probably laugh, but at least she wouldn't arrive empty-handed.

Well after midnight, freshening gusts patted at the windows and door. She finished writing what she'd done with Miss Trudi, then changed into the boxer shorts and T-shirt she slept in. She was brushing her teeth when ideas about questions for an office popped up. She returned to the laptop.

The next thing she knew, she was holding the thermos upside down over her mug and realizing the tea was long gone, and she was so out of it that the laptop screen seemed to have faded.

She kneaded her neck as she turned to the window and realized the screen hadn't faded. The light around it had brightened. Now that she was aware of it, she heard birds raising a ruckus about the sun rising. She unfolded her legs from the bed with a groan and looked out. The scrubbed-clean sky looked as aqua as a tropical ocean.

A new day.

The day she had to show Max a partnership proposal. It

wouldn't matter so much if she hadn't envisioned giving him breathing room. Financially and with his time so he could take courses—if he chose to. She looked back at the laptop. Even with a lot of polishing and fixing, the proposal was bound to confirm for him that Annette had been the brains behind Every Detail.

Before she faced what level of drivel she'd left in that machine overnight, she needed caffeine. And baked goods. An almond croissant would be ideal, chocolate-chip cookies would do.

Head down, she poked her feet into worn slippers and shuffled down the dark hallway toward the kitchen. Old-house noises and the birds chirping outside swallowed her footsteps.

She'd stepped into the kitchen, dim here on the far side from the windows, and was halfway to the refrigerator when she became aware.

Not of anything in particular. Simply *aware*. Totally and elementally aware.

Her steps slowed, then slowed more. Finally came to a stop when the toes of a pair of well-worn work boots came within her head-down focus.

She closed her eyes. Squeezed them to try to shake the weariness and opened them again. Still there.

She ordered her muscles to execute the complex task of raising her head. And what was her reward? Max standing right in front of her.

He wore a University of Wisconsin sweatshirt that revealed the neck of a white T-shirt. If he followed his pattern, he would have the sweatshirt off in the first twenty minutes. The T-shirt would mold closer and closer to his torso as he worked, revealing each ridge and valley, every ripple of muscle.

Oh, God, if she didn't get those thoughts out of her head, he'd see it in her face. He'd know…

Desperation made her risk a look at his face to see if somehow he'd missed her cataloging his body.

He had.

Because he was staring at her body. Specifically, her breasts. Even more specifically, her nipples.

She looked down.

It was cold.

Well, chilly, anyway. That was why they jutted against her soft T-shirt.

A simple biological response to a meteorological fact.

Oh, Lord, then a heat wave moved in, making her breasts burn and tingle, and somehow they were swelling even more from the heat, pushing harder against the fabric as if they meant to break through it. Outbreaks of heat also burst to life in the pit of her stomach, up her throat, into her cheeks and, oddly, the palms of her hands.

"What are you doing…?" *What are you doing to me?* That was what she wanted to ask him. But her second-to-last unfogged brain cell waved its arms and screamed that that was *not* a good idea. "Here."

"Work." He didn't move. Didn't change the direction of his gaze.

"It's too early," she half wailed.

"Wanted to get ahead so later I could…we could… That's what you sleep in?"

The question seemed to come out of him against his will. It almost sounded as if he had his teeth clenched.

"Yeah."

"You never wore that when you and Annette visited."

"No." She'd worn sweats in the winter, pajamas otherwise.

She had to get him off the topic. She had to get his gaze

to stop throwing flames her body was only too happy to catch.

"You said you wanted to get ahead for later so we could—what? What could we do?"

Oh, that got his eyes to move, all right. His gaze snapped right up to meet hers and there it was between them, shimmering and crackling like a bolt of lightning, exactly what they could do.

He shifted his weight slightly. If his next move brought him toward her, would she be able to back away? Did she even want to try?

"Max."

She didn't know what she wanted to put into that speaking of his name—invitation, warning, pleading?

He released a breath through his teeth and took a step backward, then said, "Go over the proposal."

"What?"

"So we had time later to go over your partnership proposal. That's why I came early. Here." He yanked off his sweatshirt and held it out to her at arm's length. "Put this on. You're cold."

The last two words dared anybody to dispute that assessment.

She sure didn't have the energy to dispute it. She pushed her arms into the sleeves and let the oversize sweatshirt slide over her. The soft interior carried his warmth and scent. She wasn't cold anymore.

"What are you doing in the kitchen at this hour, anyway?" he grumbled.

"I'm hungry." Their eyes locked again. Desperately, she waved toward the refrigerator. "Cookies. I'm hungry for chocolate-chip cookies."

Breaking the look, she detoured around him and reached the freezer.

"You're having cookies for breakfast?" That sounded more like Big Brother Max, believer in breakfast as the most important meal. "You should have something better than that. You're going to…" As she turned from the freezer with three cookies, he looked at her again, eyes narrowed. "You've been up all night."

"Yeah."

"Doing the proposal?"

"Trying. I really don't think it's—"

"Show me what you have."

"Now?" Panic nearly swamped the word.

"An hour," he said.

"An hour? I have to take a shower and get dressed, uh, changed. An hour won't leave any time to look it over, much less revise it the way I know it needs. Maybe tomorrow—"

"An hour." He sounded oddly satisfied.

"But, Max—"

"Do a spell-check, but don't mess with anything else."

"Spelling's the least of my worries," she muttered.

"One hour."

"It's not a formal proposal. If you'd given me more time…"

Max didn't look at Suz seated on the swing on his front porch. She'd been interrupting his reading with related comments for twenty minutes.

"Suz, let me finish reading."

Okay, it hadn't been just her comments. It had been her distracting him. Sitting with her heels pressing against the edge of the swing, her arms wrapped around her bent legs and her chin resting on her knees, she looked about ten.

Except she also looked so much the way she had this morning when they'd stood close enough that he could smell the warmth of her tousled hair, that he could see the rounded form of her breasts through the clinging fabric, the points of them growing as they pushed out toward him…

A shudder went through him.

No wonder she was sitting that way. Her self-protective instincts probably told her there was a raving, drooling sex maniac in the neighborhood. God, what was the matter with him?

It wasn't as if he'd never before noticed that Suz had breasts.

He'd even seen her in outfits that, under certain circumstances, revealed the outline of her nipples. She never in any way flaunted her body, but some things a woman wore had fabric that tended to cling. And if the woman's body was responding to…something, changes happened.

He hadn't obsessed about them or anything. But he was male, after all. And she was female. Most definitely female.

And those changes sure as hell had happened this morning. The material of that T-shirt had cupped her breasts, softly outlining each curve, the one from her ribs up, the one from below her collarbone down, the one from each side and the dual curves leading away from the valley between her breasts. At the twin apexes of those curves, her nipples had pushed against T-shirt fabric that smoothed over her flesh the way he wished he could.

His gaze slid toward her. Could he see the nubs now, under the thicker material of this shirt?

What color were her nipples? As pale as the spent blooms of Miss Trudi's pink roses? Dusky? Or in between?

God, what was he doing, thinking about Suz that way?

This morning, when he'd walked into the kitchen and seen her, his guard was down because he hadn't expected to see her.

No, he hadn't expected to see her or to respond the way

he had. Not that he needed to be on his guard around Suz, for crying out loud.

A hell of a lot of good it had done to give her that sweatshirt. It had covered her clothes so it looked as if she was naked underneath, and that had his hands itching to slide under the hem and feel her soft skin, to pull her tight against him like—

A *thunk* practically jolted him out of his seat. It took several seconds to remember where he was, what he was supposed to be doing and to recognize the sound as Suz's feet hitting the floor.

That realization came just in time to prevent her from yanking the pages away from him.

"You don't have to finish it, Max."

"Why wouldn't I finish it?"

"You weren't reading. I don't blame you. I know it's not any good, so—"

"How do you know it's not any good?"

She looked confused. "How do I know? I wrote it. Of course I know."

He dropped his focus back to the printed pages. "Do you?"

"What's that supposed to mean?"

"Give me five more minutes, five *quiet* minutes, and I'll tell you."

"You shouldn't make such an important decision without giving me a chance to work on this and—"

He stood up with the papers in hand and started for the door.

"Max? Where are you going?"

"To the bathroom. I'm going to lock the door. If you stand outside the door and talk, I'm going to keep flushing the toilet to drown out your voice so I can finally get this read."

Maybe away from her his attention would stay on the pages.

He heard her huff of annoyance, but didn't slow his pace. She didn't follow him off the porch, so he satisfied himself with closing his bedroom door and sitting in the easy chair in the corner.

Doggedly pulling his thoughts away from other matters the two, maybe three times they wandered, he finished reading, then went back over the parts he'd read in snatches. Finally he made notes.

When he finished, he stared at the closed door for a full two minutes.

Max strode out onto the porch. Trying to twist around to see his face while she had her feet tucked up on the seat, Suz set the porch swing into such an erratic jig that she felt as if she was in a ship being tossed around by a hurricane.

She'd thought a gentle swinging motion would soothe her nerves. Now she needed Dramamine.

"It's good," Max said. "Very good."

She stuck her foot out to try to brake the rocking, catching only her toe on the floor, so the swing pivoted as far as the chains would let it.

He grabbed hold of one side and stilled the swing by putting his substantial thigh against one arm. He let go and put his hand out to shake.

Automatically she met his grip and even responded when he pumped her hand.

"Partner." He made it a statement of fact. A done deal. "I found cookies in the cabinet—I know how you like to mark important occasions. I'll give you a raincheck for something from the bakery."

"But—"

"We have a lot of work to do, so—"

"Hold on." Instead of taking a selection from the box of what looked to be pecan cookies, she put her hands to her forehead, trying to stop the whirling inside. "That's it? You're going to let me buy a piece of your business based on that? Don't you think it would be better to, uh, give me a trial period?"

"Are you trying to flit away already?"

"No! I just… Maybe a provisional partnership?"

"Okay." Then, when she'd relaxed enough to take a cookie, he added, "No buying into the business as a provisional partner, though."

"Max, there's no reason not to put my investment to good use."

"Yes, there is. I say so, and even with you as partner I still have the winning vote. I want you fully committed to this plan." He tapped the papers with three blunt-tipped fingers.

"Miss Trudi told me what to do in the proposal." There. It was out in the open. Now he'd see—

"Yeah? Did she write this? Are these her ideas?"

"Uh…"

"No. You did. So don't try to tell me Miss Trudi's responsible for what's here. Maybe she gave you a push, but it's your brain, your ideas that powered this engine. Take responsibility for once."

Where the heck had she put that one unfogged brain cell? He had her head spinning. "I take responsibility. I—"

"Good. I like what you put in about the package Trevetti Building can offer new customers, but first we have to bring off the Bliss House project. So, we'll start there. I want you to meet with the committee of craftspeople about designing display areas in Bliss House."

"I can't—"

He interrupted ruthlessly. "Suz, you can't do what you

can't do. So if you've done it, and you have—'' he tapped the pages ''—then you *can* do it. So no more excuses.''

''Excuses? That isn't—''

''Good, now let's get to work.''

Fran had recruited Suz and Max to help spiff up Steve's house before the newlyweds returned.

While Suz and Fran changed linens, dusted and vacuumed, Max and Rob mowed the lawn, edged and weeded, and Nell swept outside. Fran had stocked the refrigerator with milk and a few other perishables. Now she was arranging flowers from her garden into four vases. Suz waited to put them around the house, trying not to look out the window.

Not at Max. Besides, she couldn't see him from this window. She was watching for Steve's car. She heard a faint repetitive sound and looked down. Her foot was tapping against the floor.

Oh, God, she was nervous—nervous about what Annette would say about this partnership. Her own family hadn't been thrilled. What about Annette? Would her friend think it was a pathetic play for Max? Or that it was unfair to saddle Max with such an unequal partner?

Maybe she should tell Annette her hopes about getting Max to go back to school. But would Annette feel that reflected on *her* because taking care of her was the reason he'd quit? Or—

''Ready?''

Suz jumped. With a calm smile Fran held out two vases. ''These are for the bedroom and front hall, the others for the living room and kitchen. I'll clean the sink, and then we're ready to go.''

In ten minutes they were crossing the street to the back of the large house where Fran and Rob grew up, and where

Fran now lived. To the left, through thick foliage, she saw glimpses of the even more imposing house where Steve grew up. Max, Rob and Nell were on Fran's screened-in porch, drinking lemonade, with two more glasses on the small table waiting for them.

Nell was contemplating a future as a wedding planner or a circus owner when they spotted Steve's SUV turning into Kelly Street.

Nell dashed across the deep lawn and followed alongside the SUV as it pulled into her driveway. Steve and Annette got out with huge smiles. As if a magnet pulled them, they met at the rear of the SUV and stood side by side, their arms across one another's backs, while hugging Nell between them. The next few minutes were lost in greetings, half-heard questions and lost answers.

"Oh, Daddy, I'm so glad you're home!" Nell clasped her arms around his waist.

Steve looked misty-eyed as he gave his daughter another hug. "I missed you, too, sweetheart."

Tipping her head back to look at her father, Nell sighed in blissful satisfaction. "Now I can *finally* get a dog."

Through the adult laughter, Fran said, "We'll leave you three to settle in. Then come on over and have dinner. We're cooking out."

Rob prepared the grill, while Max, Fran and Suz returned to the porch.

"Everything's all set," Fran said in answer to Suz's offer to help.

"Good." Suz leaned forward, opening and closing her hands over the wicker arms. She flicked a look toward Max he couldn't interpret, then added, "Because I have something I'd like to talk to you about."

"Certainly." Fran looked curious but unruffled.

What the heck was Suz up to? She cut another look toward him. This one he thought he could pin down a little more. Was she afraid he might quash whatever it was she was doing? Or did she *hope* he might?

Either way, he was sitting tight and keeping his mouth shut.

"I heard—" she swallowed "—that you are the perfect person for a project at Bliss House, Fran."

"Me? I don't know anything about renovating—"

"After the renovations."

"—or selling crafts."

"Before the selling."

"You've got me intrigued," Fran said with a chuckle. "What?"

"You'd be perfect to rescue the gardens. Before you say anything," Suz added quickly, "think about it. Everyone in town tells me what a great gardener you are. You're familiar with the Bliss House gardens—you helped protect the prize specimens, right? You know how to research, so you could find information on the original gardens. But you're not so wedded to the past that you'll forget practicality. Also, I have it on good authority that you're always coming to the rescue, and heaven knows, those grounds need rescuing."

Fran's mouth drew up as if she wanted to grimace but didn't quite know how. "I've been thinking I need to get out of the rescue business."

"One more for old time's sake? And to benefit Tobias?"

Fran looked at Max. "She's dangerous."

Didn't he know it.

Before he could embarrass himself by saying that, Fran faced Suz.

"Do you have something in mind?"

"The design in front needs to draw people into the building. Pleasant, with a Victorian feel, but we don't want people touring the gardens when they should be inside buying. In back is where the gardens could be as accurate and intricate as you want. If you slow folks down as they come out, they might go back and pick up an item they'd debated about. During good weather there'll be tables outside the tearoom in the kitchen, so give folks there lots to look at. The sides need to be transitional, with vistas from those rooms—including the meeting room on the west side, with access through the French doors, so a sort of outside room would be ideal.''

Fran sat back. "You don't want much, do you?"

"Only what I know you can deliver."

Fran returned Suz's look for a time that to Max seemed to stretch into a week. If she said no, how would Suz take it?

"Okay," Fran said. "I'll work with you and Miss Trudi on the gardens."

Suz breathed out. "Great."

Max held back a grin as he ate and laughed and talked with his sister, his new brother-in-law and the others. Another bit of the unexpected from Suz. You'd think after knowing her for eight years...

Knowing her? Or trying his damnedest not to know her?

The image of Suz's arrival at the wedding took over his vision. It had felt like he was seeing her for the first time. Because he had been? Seeing her beyond the defenses he'd built up. Not another sister. Not a buddy.

God, had he felt this way about her all along?

Just then she looked over her shoulder, her face lit by candles on the porch railings, and their eyes met. A gut-deep certainty sent charges through his bloodstream. Suz didn't see him as a brother or a buddy. Those kisses had been as real for her as for him.

He forced himself to look away, pretending a great interest in Nell's plans for acquiring a puppy.

Because none of this changed anything. Eight years' habit of looking out for her still held—he would do what he had to for her good. And that didn't include him.

"Do you mind?"

Suz had asked to speak with Annette as the evening broke up. Attuned by years of friendship, they meandered to one side of Fran's lovely yard. In a rush, Suz spilled out the news about the partnership, including a glancing reference to Max's having more time to pursue any odd discarded dreams he might have lying around getting dusty.

Annette faced her, but all Suz could see was the outline of her face.

"Mind?" Annette repeated. "Let me see. You're taking work off my brother's broad but overburdened shoulders, giving his business a major selling point, investing money in it and relieving me of day-to-day responsibility at a time I'm trying to adjust to being a wife and stepmother, not to mention a soon-to-be dog owner. Oh, yes, and this also means my best friend is staying in town. Yeah, I really mind."

Annette hugged her, and Suz felt a tension flow out of her.

"I'll do my best. I promise."

"You always do, Suz." Annette sounded as if she believed it.

Suz was on a mission. Max wouldn't tell her what the deal was with his wrist, so she was going to find out.

She considered and dismissed Annette as a source. If there was something wrong and Annette knew, she would have told her. Suz scanned the landscape of Max's life, passed over Juney—if she knew, she would tell Suz in her own good time and not before—and zeroed in on Lenny.

It meant waiting until Max was not at the construction site while his workers were, which pretty much limited her opportunities to when he met with town and financial officials.

"Morning, miss."

"Lenny, don't you think you should call me Suz?"

"No, miss."

She gave him a conspiratorial glance. "Another Max edict?"

He chuckled, but gave her nothing more.

She put a hand on his arm and said, "I know you've been with Max for a long time and he not only relies on you, he respects your judgment. I wanted to be sure you didn't worry that I might interfere or affect your position."

"Oh, no, miss. I'm not worried. It'll be good to have you around." He shot a look at her. "Good for Max."

Heat crept up her neck. She ignored it and plunged ahead. "Oh, you mean because of his wrist."

Lenny immediately looked hunted. Definitely hunted. She hadn't grown up with four brothers without learning to recognize the signs of a man carrying a secret. She couldn't let him be burdened that way. To quote Maximilian Augusto Trevetti, it was for his own good.

"Yes, it's so sad when that happens."

"What happens, miss?"

"A man loses his touch. Some men sit behind a desk too much, get too accustomed to giving the orders. When they try to do something physical, they don't take into account how much ability they've lost." Lenny was a balloon about to pop. She added one more puff of air. "Probably showing off."

"Showing off! Max never showed off a day in his life!

If it hadna been for that fool kid Eric... Max was trying to stop him from—''

He clamped his mouth shut at the same time his eyes widened.

''Trying to stop him from doing what, Lenny?'' she encouraged softly.

''He made me promise. Not tellin' Annette, not tellin' Juney, not tellin' anyone.''

''He didn't say anything about me, though, did he. Besides, you've already started telling. If I ask him about it now, because I haven't heard the whole story...''

''Aw, miss...''

''He's hurting, Lenny. His wrist, maybe more. If I can help, I want to.''

He met her look for half a minute, then looked down.

''It was the Henderson job. The framing crew Eric was leading had finished some exposed interior rafters. Max was checking the work and caught sight of something shiny up on one of the crossties close to the ridge line. A screwdriver Eric had left the night before. He'd seen it, but the scaffolding was down by then and he was in too big a hurry, so he'd left it.

''Max, he couldn't do that. He worried something might jar it loose and somebody would get hurt. Besides, it wasn't the way to do a job.''

Lenny toed a pile of sawdust. ''I wasn't there, mind, or I woulda made sure they put up scaffolding. But what I was told was Max, he didn't want to make extra work for anybody other'n himself. So he used a ladder. Only, it meant standing on top of it like the warnings say not to. He got the screwdriver and was down one step when Muriel Henderson comes in, screeches how he'll fall to his death. That makes him jump, he loses his balance and down he goes. Tried to catch himself with his hand, like you do, natural, and *crrrk*. He told the guys it would mean their jobs if the story got to Annette any way at all. This town being what it is, that meant not tellin' anybody. 'Course they told me.''

And now he'd told her.

She felt the burden of Lenny's confidence. A little bubble of panic gurgled in her stomach at the thought of his relying on her. Lenny and the other men and Max. She'd think about that later. No time for panic now.

She understood how Max could dwell on what might have happened if the injury hadn't let him return to work as usual. And she saw how that fit with his regretting not having a degree to give him more options. Were those the crossroads Miss Trudi had talked about?

"Thank you, Lenny. I'll do my best to..." She swallowed. This wasn't the time for a halfhearted pledge. She'd delivered a promise to Annette already, and now a second one... Her heart slammed against her ribs, making her voice breathy, but she said, "I won't let you down."

Chapter Nine

"Hey, Suz. Wait up."

Max had spotted her as she walked from her parked car toward Bliss House's kitchen door at noon Wednesday. He skirted the covered stack of lumber and the flags marking the root cellar and met her at the steps.

He'd seen her only in passing since Monday evening, when there'd been an informal meeting to update Annette and Steve. Miss Trudi had insisted on holding it in the rose garden, even though the twilight brought out half the mosquitoes in the continental United States.

He'd sat apart. After spending the day putting in insulation in the attic of Miss Trudi's new home, he needed a shower, but he'd worked too late to get home and take one. Miss Trudi had said he could use her bathtub, but she had no shower, then had brightly suggested he use the shower in Suz's room. He mumbled something about not having fresh clothes and got out of that one.

"…we're incorporating plans for the grounds with the construction on Bliss House proper," Suz had told Annette and Steve. "Sparing special plants, selective earth-moving and directing machinery so it doesn't hurt the roots of any more plants than necessary."

"Great idea," Annette had said. Suz didn't even flinch— progress, he'd thought. "You know who would be great to design the grounds?"

"Yes. Fran Dalton. She's already at work on it."

That *yes,* assured and easy, was worth more to Max than any amount he would earn on Bliss House or beyond. She'd asked Fran on her own and she'd taken credit for it. Definitely progress.

"What sort of design are you and Fran considering?" Steve had asked.

Max had been vaguely aware of his sister's eyes on him. He didn't return her look. He'd heard all about the gardens already, so that didn't require his attention. But a lightning bug had been tracing loop-de-loops around Suz's head, lighting up her hair and eyes in a way that—

"Max?"

He blinked, taking a second to recognize it was the real Suz standing in front of him, not the memory, who had spoken.

Suz was half tempted to swat him. Maybe that would relieve some of her feelings. Why did the man have to stand there and look at her like he'd like to jump her bones when she knew darn right well he wouldn't do it?

"Uh, yeah," he said. "I got a call from Milt Portage about the flooring for the kitchen and bathroom. There's a problem."

That yanked her thoughts back on track.

"A problem?" If they couldn't get the washable wood flooring—her bright idea—as promised, that would delay

Miss Trudi's moving in and delay the Bliss House schedule. Sure, it would look great, but if it messed up the schedule…

"The figures are off."

She looked over his arm at the sheet on his clipboard. His T-shirt sleeve skimmed across her bare upper arm. The sun's heat seemed to distill Max's scent of hard work, clean sweat and sawdust. She backed away. She couldn't see the numbers, anyway, not with her eyes closed.

Max didn't seem to notice. "Looks like you added in the square footage for the pantry twice. I'll—"

"Oh, God." Gaining another step of safety, she pulled out her notebook and flipped to her copy. The error glared up at her. How could she have made such a mistake on such a simple thing? Addition, for heaven's sake. "I shouldn't have taken the easy route by trying to wrap it up while I was there. I should have told him to wait a day and have Juney do it right. It's all my fault. I screwed up."

Max slowly closed his mouth, his brows drawn down, though he seemed to be concentrating more than frowning.

"I'll pay for it, Max. It's my mistake and that's the least I can do. I wish I could do something so it wouldn't mess up the schedule." Oh, Lord, now he was looking at her as if he'd never seen her. "Max?"

"You're right, you screwed up."

Could words alone knock the breath out of you? He was going to tell her she didn't belong on the project. Send her away. End this strange collaboration. It was the only logical step after that comment. Except he hadn't sounded angry or upset.

"And you're going to make it right," he said.

"Of course. I'll pay—"

"Not money. You're going to Milt's shop right now and stay there until the two of you get this order fixed—with tomorrow the Fourth of July, it's got to get in fast. Unless he's given up smoking the world's cheapest cigars, you'll pay plenty. Then I want you to order the light fixtures. Get the specs from Juney. Do whatever magic you've been working to get Miss Trudi to make decisions and get the order in by the end of business Monday.''

"But I… The flooring…''

He crossed his arms over his chest, apparently thinking he looked ominous. In other circumstances she might have laughed.

"In Trevetti Building, the deal is, you make your mistakes right. Any problem with that?''

"No. But the money—''

"No money was lost. Milt caught it in time. He's waiting for you to get over there and fix the numbers.''

"Oh. Okay.'' It was definitely her responsibility to set things right, even if it hadn't cost the project money. "But the lights—''

"I'll call Juney so you can pick up the specs on your way back.''

"I don't know if I can—''

"You aren't thinking you get out of work because of this, are you? That's not the way it works. Nobody folded up their tent and quit when the figures were off on the cabinets and counter. They got busy making good on your idea to store trays and such.''

"But…''

Her protest faded because he had jogged down the steps.

Even as Suz drove away, she still looked like she'd been hit by a thunderbolt.

When he told her about the mixup in the numbers, she'd looked stricken, but not shell-shocked, an expression that made it damned hard not to pull her into his arms and tell her everything would be okay.

No, the thunderbolt hit when he didn't excuse her mistake but also didn't make a big deal of it.

He'd been about to pass it off entirely, say that he'd just tell Milt Portage to make the order right. But when she'd overreacted to the sort of human mistake anybody could make—it was the reason Milt rechecked orders—bells went off in his head. Bells that sounded a lot like Miss Trudi's voice.

...she felt she was a fraud.... Then I stood up and said what matched her experience—that the emperor was naked, her drawing was lackluster.

If he wanted Suz to believe him when he said she'd done good work, he couldn't let this slide. So he'd said, yes, she'd made a mistake and had to make it right.

That trust is built on the truth, especially hearing the truth when they have performed at a level below their best.

For a second there when Suz had closed her eyes and gone facing-a-firing-squad white, he had to grab his self-control with both hands to keep from undoing what he'd just done by telling her it was no big deal, by reminding her of all the good work she'd done, by dismissing her mistake.

Her confusion shifted toward anxiety when he'd given her responsibility for the lighting. Another chance to make a mistake. She'd hate that. She'd...

He pulled out his cell phone and hit redial.

"Juney? It's me. If Suz asks you to check behind her on the order for lighting, don't do it. Tell her you're too busy. In fact, you're too busy to check behind her on anything."

"I usually am, because you work me too hard. But that doesn't usually stop you from asking me to do more stuff."

"This time I'm telling you *not* to do more stuff, so you should be happy."

"I'd be happy if you made sense." Still grumbling, she hung up.

He shut off the phone, but didn't move.

If this worked…

Eric was doing better at recognizing his responsibilities, so why shouldn't Suz start recognizing her abilities? It was basically shedding old ways of thinking so they saw themselves realistically and adjusted their actions. Success would come when Eric left Trevetti Building for a better job or his own company, and for Suz…

Yeah, there it was, the thorn in the rose. Because success with Suz would come when she saw herself the way he saw her, including that she deserved far better than him.

That didn't matter. Couldn't matter. Because this was what he could give her. Chances to make mistakes, accountability for them and enough room to make them right.

God, if only he'd had the power to erase one mistake she'd taken on her shoulders, a mistake that had not been her fault at all.

He'd been watching some forgettable West Coast basketball game on TV that Saturday night in March. He could still hear the tremor in Annette's voice.

"Max, Suz's been in an accident."

He'd been off the couch by the end of that sentence.

"Is she—"

"She's not badly hurt. The guy who hit them was drunk, totally drunk—he's not hurt at all. But…oh, Max, Suz's date… He died."

His next memory was at the hospital, walking down a long hallway. Suz, pale and alone, sat in the middle of a bench where this hallway ended. She had a bandage on her temple with a wicked bruise blooming around it, a cut at the corner of her mouth and another bandage around her arm. She stared straight ahead. Unfocused, unblinking, every atom of misery showing in her eyes.

It wasn't until the third time he said her name that her head slowly came up.

"Max."

She sounded like a robot. In the next instant he was beside her and had her hand in both of his. She was icy cold, not just her hand but all of her. He could feel the chill through his clothes straight to his bones.

"Annette will be right back. She went…somewhere." Suz recited the words, like a child's lesson learned by rote, until she reached that last point, of where Annette had gone, and either Annette had not told her or the fact had been swamped by the horrors he could see replaying in her mind.

"She'll be right back. That's good."

He opened his jacket and wrapped it and himself around her, pulled her head in to rest the uninjured side of her face against his neck.

He learned later that if she hadn't been wearing her seat belt, it would have been much worse. As it was, the impact had thrown her against the passenger door with enough force to inflict the injuries. On the driver's side, where the drunk driver's car hit…

"Tad's dead, Max." It was that same reciting voice. "Another car hit his car and he died."

"I'm sorry, Suz. I'm so sorry."

"I should have done more. I should have known the right thing to do."

"The other driver was drunk, Suz. It was his fault. No one else's. Not Tad's, sure as hell not yours."

"I didn't do it right."

Suz forced herself to take care of the flooring order first. But with the figures checked and rechecked until Milt

Portage said his calculator was about to croak, she was back in her car heading toward the Tobias Library, where she'd promised to pick up Miss Trudi and Nell for a trip to an ice-cream shop—this one next to the wallpaper store.

It was bribery, pure and simple. The schedule was so tight to get Miss Trudi into her new place and out of Bliss House that Suz had worked up a day-by-day list of decisions Miss Trudi had to make. Today was wallpaper.

The more she knew about Max's operation, the larger the schedule loomed in her mind.

Trevetti Building had virtually no other income than the Bliss House project until well into the fall. The payments for Bliss House, which allowed only a thin profit margin in the first place, were tied to a strict schedule with harsh penalties for delays. So getting the work done was important both to get payments and to eventually free the crews for other jobs.

All that made mistakes like hers an unaffordable luxury.

What had she been thinking when she'd agreed to be his partner? Sure, her investment would help when the transfer was completed after the legalities Max insisted on. Maybe she did take a little work off Max's shoulders. And she was on hand to keep encouraging him to go back to college. But mistakes like this made her a dangerous liability.

But if Max agreed with that assessment, wouldn't he have been angry when he found out about her screwing up the order?

The voice in the back of her head asking those questions sounded unfamiliar, almost creaky. But maybe the voice had a point.

Yet Max hadn't patted her on the head and said it didn't matter. It did matter, and he didn't try to pretend it didn't. *You're right, you screwed up.*

She wasn't sure anyone had ever told her she'd screwed up.

If she'd bet on how Max would respond to one of her screwups, she would have said he'd be like her brothers—brush it under the rug and not let her get her hands on anything breakable again.

In an optimistic mood, she might have hoped he'd deal with it the way Annette did—homing in on making whatever was wrong right, working together.

He'd gone beyond that. He'd called her on the carpet for her error, then left her to clean up.

The deal is, you make your mistakes right.

Some mistakes were too big, too final to ever be made right.

But others, even potentially damaging ones, if you made them but corrected them, then what?

Max hadn't acted as if he thought she was an idiot or hopeless. He'd trusted her with the lighting. Trusted her? He'd pushed it on her. He wouldn't do that with someone who was an idiot.

Only as she spotted Miss Trudi and Nell waiting for her outside the library did another thought hit her. If Max was that forthright about a mistake, what about the times he'd said she'd done well?

"I don't understand why Juney won't take fifteen minutes to go over my figures," Suz said not for the first time.

"It's the Fourth of July—a holiday."

"Not today, but she's already said she can't next week."

"She's pretty busy," he muttered, also not for the first time.

"I know, but... Could you check my figures?"

"I'm even busier."

She stopped on the narrow walkway and looked over her shoulder at Max. They were on their third trip to his truck with the ''few little things'' Miss Trudi had insisted on bringing to the holiday celebration at Fran's house.

The rooftop deck on the Dalton house offered the third-best vantage point in Tobias to see the fireworks. The best was Corbett House next door, but with Lana Corbett still in Europe, no one had suggested using her house. Actually it was unlikely anybody would have suggested it even if she'd been in town. The second-best vantage point was from atop Bliss House—for someone with a death wish willing to negotiate those attic stairs.

Suz's expression shifted, and Max felt both wariness and anticipation slide into him.

''If you'll look at the course schedule for this fall, I'll do the lighting order without any more discussion.''

''You're doing the lighting whether we discuss it or not.''

''Max, there's no reason not to *look* at the schedule. One class, you could try that. You have to reapply and there could be a late fee, but as a reentry student you don't submit transcripts or test scores, and they have classes after four o'clock so people can work, then go to class and—''

''If you're thinking a degree would make some big difference in me or my life, it wouldn't. I'd still do what I'm doing, so what's the point?''

''Why are you so determined not to? It's like your wrist—acting as if you have something to hide.''

''I don't have anything to hide,'' he said too fast. ''That's—''

''Then what's the big mystery?''

''I did something I'd ream one of my employees for, okay? Any jackass should know better. Then I let a woman I've known all my life—''

"Who screeched."

"A woman whose screeches I've known all my life— You already knew."

She opened her eyes wide at the accusation. "How could I?" Her voice softened. "You were looking out for other people. Making sure Muriel Henderson didn't get conked someday by a falling screwdriver and avoiding making more work for your men. In other words, you were being Max."

A slashing motion of his hand dismissed that. "I could have left my business, my employees and myself in a hell of a fix if I'd been hurt worse."

"As I said, being Max, looking out for other people." Nothing soft about her words this time. "Is that what stops you from picking up the courses you need for your degree?"

"I have people who rely on me and I won't let them down."

"What about relying on yourself? What about letting yourself down? What about going after what you want?"

"Max! Max!" called Miss Trudi from the doorway. "Would you come carry this cooler?"

He held Suz's look, the one daring him to answer her questions, as he called back, "I'll be right there, Miss Trudi."

What had made her think she could sway Max?

Suz joined the chorus of oohs and ahhs on Fran's roof as a pinwheel of blue crackled and popped its way to yellow, then white.

Maybe she was wrong about the whole thing. As he said, it wasn't as if it would change his life—he was doing mostly what he wanted to do. So why should he bother?

Except she wasn't wrong. Not completing his degree ate at him.

Heck, he'd even told her about his wrist to sidetrack her. Far more than what he said it was the way his eyes became guarded. Even when he tried to joke about it, as he had the day he'd put the air conditioner in, there'd been that sense that he was protecting himself by not taking it seriously.

But he wouldn't admit it. Perhaps even to himself. *I don't have anything to hide.*

A trail of sparks whizzed skyward and Suz tipped her head back to track it. She pulled in a breath, waiting for the explosion of color and design. And waited. It didn't come.

A dud. She knew just how it felt.

"What the hell are you doing up there, Suz?"

"What does it look like I'm doing? I'm double-checking the measurements for the recessed lighting so I can order tomorrow."

He was already climbing the scaffolding erected for surfacing the vaulted portion of the ceiling. "It's Sunday, you're not wearing your hard hat, and you shouldn't be up here alone. In fact, you shouldn't be up here at all."

"You're not wearing a hard hat, either."

"I didn't plan to be up here." He stopped an arm's length from her. Writing something on the clipboard, she remained with her back to him. "As long as you don't screech…"

She chuckled. That was a relief. They'd hardly spoken two words to each other at Fran's on Friday. When he'd brought her and Miss Trudi back to Bliss House, she'd helped unload the paraphernalia and thanked him politely, all as if she were a thousand miles away.

Suz retracted the tape measure. Just before disappearing

into the case, the tab ticked the clipboard and tipped it out of her hand. It fell to the board beneath her feet and behind her, partway off the platform.

She turned and bent to retrieve it. The clipboard rocked and went over the edge.

"Suz…"

She straightened as the clipboard clattered on the subflooring below. She stood straight for an instant, then her toe caught against the uneven wood. Bent forward at the waist, she swung her arms to gain balance. In one stride he reached her. He grabbed her hips, pulling them back. He'd meant to stabilize her. Instead, he'd nearly knocked them both over when he overestimated the force necessary and brought her derriere flush against him.

Warm and solid and—heaven help him—moving, as her arm motions and other efforts to balance drove her up, then down, then up against him.

"I've got you, Suz."

If she would relax and let him handle the situation, everything would be fine. But she kept flailing, and his hold on her right hip was going to go.

He gave her another yank back and adjusted his right hand before her momentum carried her forward against his hold. Now his hand was up under her shirt, spread against her ribs and absorbing the hot smoothness of her skin.

"Hold still, dammit."

He spread his legs as wide as he could on the narrow platform, Both arms were around her. His right thumb and index finger brushed the lower curve of her breast through her bra. She jolted back against him.

"Don't move." Maybe it had been instinct at her abrupt move, but his hand had advanced, cupping that curve of her breast, his thumb brushing its point.

"I've got to move. This isn't… I'll…"

He felt her flesh swelling beneath his hand, the nipple hardening, and answered with his own swelling and hardening.

What was he doing? They were eight feet in the air on a narrow platform, yet laying her down on rough boards and plunging inside her was all he could think about. It was a conspiracy. A conspiracy of his body and hers.

He pulled in air and forced his hold to the relative safety of her waist.

"Max. I—"

"Give me…a minute."

"Oh." She shifted her weight, just the faintest adjustment. It was enough, because she gave another "Oh." This one laced with comprehension and surprise.

"I'll go down first," he said. "If you feel like you're falling—"

"I'm not going to fall."

A level of physical discomfort accompanied him down. It was a pleasure compared to his thoughts.

Falling…

God, he was falling for her. The generator on his willpower had about run dry. He had to do something. And fast.

Suz deserved…

His thoughts snagged on that thought. *Deserved.* If she was with someone who could give her everything she deserved… He'd have to back away if she belonged to someone else. The right kind of man.

He knew what he had to do.

"Don't you lecture me, Max. I was fine until you came up there and… Well, I was fine."

He looked at her, then away. Propped his hands on his hips, then dropped them. He shifted his weight to the balls of his feet. His jaw flexed. Finally he spoke.

''You want to go to the country-club dance Saturday night?''

Her mouth opened. Nothing came out except a rasping cough. He started to move behind her, but she gestured for him to stay put.

She closed her mouth, swallowed and finally croaked out, ''Yes.''

Chapter Ten

Good Lord, a date with Max? What was she thinking? She knew all about dates. You went out once or twice, then the guy either saw too much of what you really were or resented your holding him at a distance. And poof! He disappeared—unless he kept calling and you had to tell him no thanks as sternly but politely as you could.

Considering those scenarios with Max made her feel as if the knot in her stomach were being pulled tight by opposing teams of Romanian weightlifters.

But when he'd asked the question, she'd been at a distinct disadvantage.

Her nerve endings had still been doing a celebratory samba. Okay, her nerve endings and her lungs, which had pulled in a couple gallons of air.

It had seemed unreal standing on that narrow walkway above the ground, with Max holding her tight back against him. So tight that she felt his heart beating, his erection pressing against her and his breath stirring her hair.

Unreal, yet so very real.

And when he'd asked her his question, the truth had come out—yes, she wanted to go to the dance with him. Which had surprised the heck out of her. Before she could think of a good excuse to take it back and substitute a more reasonable response, he'd said, "Good," and turned on his heel. Stopping at the doorway and he'd ordered, "Stay on the ground from now on."

Keep her feet on the ground. Good advice.

She hadn't been able to test the success of her efforts, since he'd avoided her since Sunday. Which also meant she hadn't been able to call off going to the dance with him. Oh, she supposed she could have called his cell phone. But that would have been so cold. Besides, she needed to see his face to know how he was truly responding to whatever excuse she'd come up with—if she had come up with a good excuse, which she hadn't.

So here she stood in Bliss House's kitchen, hand on the doorknob, pulling in a breath before opening the door he'd knocked on a moment ago.

"If you would prefer that I open the door," Miss Trudi said, advancing from the counter, "I would be happy to—"

"That's okay, I've got it. Thanks."

She opened the door and walked out, making Max back up quickly to keep from being run over—or having her plastered to his front—then closed the door behind her.

"Uh, hi, Suz. You look beautiful."

A ball of heat burned in her chest, sending one column up her neck and into her face, while the other slid down to curl at the base of her stomach. Other men had called her beautiful. But Max…she believed it when Max said it.

"I hope it's okay. It's the only dressy dress I have with

me.'' She smoothed down the red silk. "It's the dress I wore to the wedding.''

"I know.'' She looked toward him for the first time, but he'd stepped into shadow as he gestured for her to precede him. "Shall we go?''

The drive was silent and awkward. She dared several glances his way—he wore the same suit he'd worn to the wedding—but couldn't for the life of her think of a topic of conversation.

After he parked and came around to open her door, the contrast to the truck's efficient air conditioner finally gave her a topic—the weather.

"God, when is this heat going to break?''

"Pretty soon you'll be complaining about the opposite— a cold front's supposed to move in late next week. And you know what they say about opposites.''

She swallowed, then ventured, "They attract?''

"They cause storms.''

So much for that topic.

"I didn't think you came to social events at the country club,'' she tried again as they went through the flower-covered archway into the grounds where the wedding reception had been held. This gathering was smaller and much less varied than Steve and Annette's friends.

"Jason Remtree from the bank and others have started inviting me.''

"That's nice.''

"They do it so they can grill me extra beyond the limited meeting schedule Steve set up. Even tried it at the wedding.''

"So why do you come?''

He stopped and turned to her as if to respond, but Rob Dalton greeted them. His warm smile didn't quite erase the wariness in his eyes. "Good evening, Suz. Max.''

"Hi, Rob." She felt a sudden pleasure at seeing her friend, not worrying about what to say to him. "I didn't know you were going to be here."

"You didn't?" He sounded confused beneath his usual politeness and looked from her to Max, then back to her. "I've been looking forward to dancing with you again."

"A dance would be great. But...should I have known you'd be here?"

Looking at Max now, Rob said, "I don't know. Should she have?"

Shifting to see more of Max's face than his profile, she caught the tail end of a look he sent Rob. Amusement appeared to be mixing in with Rob's puzzlement. Max had his I'll-take-care-of-it expression in place.

"Suz, let's take a walk. We'll be right back, Rob."

Puzzlement was contagious. She sure had a case of it now. Taking a walk—a lovely idea—implied the two of them would be away from the general flow of the party. So why tell Rob they'd be right back?

But as Max led her down steps that zigzagged the hillside to the lakefront, she couldn't rouse much enthusiasm to solve that particular puzzle.

A persistent breeze furrowed the lake and tossed the scent of roses high and wide. Clouds quick-stepped across the sky, making the stars blink bright when they escaped cover. Music and human voices came in soft snatches.

And Max's warm, capable, strong and gentle hand cupped her elbow as they reached the bottom step and started out onto the pier.

At the end, they stopped, and he dropped his hand, still not talking. The wind was stronger here, the sounds from the country club fainter.

"Tobias must special-order nights like these."

He turned his head toward her without meeting her eyes.

"This is as gorgeous as the night of Annette and Steve's reception," she said in explanation.

As gorgeous as the night they'd stood on his porch and he had kissed her for the first time. But not the last time.

"I shouldn't have…that night, after the reception…it was a mistake, my mistake to let things…" *Mistake?* But he didn't give her a chance to ask for a clarification. He kept talking. "Rob's a good guy. The divorce—that can happen to anybody. You know that, don't you?"

"I know Rob's a good guy." She pushed her wind-whipped hair behind her ear. "What I don't know is what he's got to do with this."

With us, she thought.

Staring out over the lake, he went on as if he hadn't heard her. "He comes from a good family. Educated, has had a lot of success in business. Steady, dependable. He can give a woman a good life." He glanced at her, then away, so the moonlight glimmer of his eyes was like a flash of lightning that disappeared before she recognized what it illuminated. "Rob's the sort of guy you belong with. The sort of guy you deserve. He'd treat you right."

The lightning struck her.

Rooted her right to the spot. Stopped her breathing. Fried the synapses of her brain.

The stars blinked out, the music turned discordant, and the scent of roses was long gone. He'd brought her here, not to spend the evening with him, not for a date with him, but to spend it with Rob Dalton.

You want to go to the country-club dance Saturday night?

Max Trevetti had fixed her up. The idiot intended to send her off on a date with another man.

No, she was the idiot. She'd let herself get dreamy about a night under the stars with Max. Wondering if—hoping!—

the sizzle of the kisses and touches they'd shared would blend with the soft magic of starlight and music to break through the resistance Max kept himself cloaked in and, to be honest, through her fears.

That was why she'd told him the truth. Yes, she wanted to come to this dance—*with him.* She'd have gone bowling or to the movies or to the Toby to play darts just as happily.

She'd hoped for a breakthrough. Instead, she'd gotten a six-foot-plus, broad-shouldered moron of a matchmaker.

"...my mistake," he was saying again.

"Mistake? Your mistake?"

He might have heard something in her voice, because he turned his back to the lake and really looked at her then. "Suz, you have every right to blame me for letting that happen—"

"Blame? Oh, I blame you, all right. I blame you for *this.* I blame you big-time for this."

"This? But—"

"There was a mistake, all right. I made the first one thinking... Ha!" The sound she made took imagination to recognize as a laugh. "But now I know better. Mistakes? You want to talk mistakes? You take the prize for this one, Trevetti."

"I just wanted—"

"What's best for me. Don't say it. I know. That's all you've ever wanted for me or from me. Well, I'll tell you what's best for me now. This!"

If she'd thought about it, she never would have done it. If he'd thought she might do it, she never would have succeeded in doing it. But she caught both of them by surprise.

She placed her palms on his broad chest and pushed.

Max Trevetti stumbled back a step and fell off the end of the pier into the lake, his grunt of surprise drowned out by the slapping splash.

She spun around and headed for the shore. She was on the first step up the hillside when Rob appeared above her, coming down the steps in a hurry.

"Is everything okay?"

"Just fine."

"What happened? I thought I heard—"

"Max and I had a difference of opinion, that's all. I'm ready for that dance now."

They'd reached the same level, and Rob looked over her shoulder toward the pier and back to her face. Sounds behind her indicated Max was climbing out of the lake, while bringing a satisfying quantity of water with him.

"Listen, I don't know what's going on, but I have to say I was surprised when Max said you wanted to come to this dance with me." He paused—maybe because he knew she wouldn't have heard him over her gnashing teeth. "Fran said you and Max... Well, if I'm in the middle of something and you'd rather I disappeared—"

"Are you backing out on our dance?"

Perhaps she sounded a little fierce, because he backed up a step and raised his hands in surrender. But he also grinned.

"Absolutely not."

He looked over her shoulder again—she suspected to make sure Max was all right. Of course he was. Max was always all right. So all right that he had time to screw up everyone else.

Apparently satisfied, Rob tucked her hand in the crook of his arm.

"I'd be delighted to have that dance now. As long is it's a safe distance from the lakeshore."

Suz would leave if she could. Not only this dance, but the town, the county, the state.

But they were partners. Max wouldn't keep the money if she walked away. Besides, she couldn't walk away. He needed help so he didn't work himself into the ground. So he maybe, eventually, just might give himself a chance to fill a gap in his gut he wouldn't even acknowledge.

She wouldn't leave him the way his father had. She wouldn't die on him the way his mother had. And she sure as hell wouldn't run off on him the way his fiancée had.

They were partners.

"Is it bad?"

She blinked, taking a second to recognize that the speaker was Rob, the man she was dancing with.

After their first dance, he'd procured glasses of wine, steered her past clusters of fellow guests with passing pleasantries and found a quiet place to sit. After a short time he excused himself. He returned quickly and said, "Max's truck is gone from the parking lot. There appears to be a wet trail leading up to where it was parked."

If Max had had to march, dripping wet, through the middle of the dancers, it would have served him right. Still, it was nice of Rob to have checked, and she said so. He responded by asking her to dance again. She said yes because...what difference did it make?

"Is what bad?"

"The headache that's making you frown so fiercely." His tone combined amusement and sympathy.

"It's fine."

"Oh-kay." Skepticism divided the word in two. "Tell you what, why don't I take you home? I'm danced out."

"Two dances danced you out?"

"Yup."

She didn't have the energy to protest, to tell him she would find her own way home. Weakly, she let him lead her to his car and drive her to Bliss House. Weakly, she sat and waited for him to come around the car to open her door, then escort her past the construction area with its safety lights and to the door with the Max-installed dead bolts.

"Let's have dinner," Rob said. "How about tomorrow night?"

"Rob, I'm…" What could she say? *I'm stupid?* Too stupid to grab on to a great guy because, well, just because. "I'm not comfortable dating—" at the last second she gestured fleetingly at the wedding ring he wore "—newly separated men."

He looked at his hand as if surprised to find the ring there. "I suppose I should take it off." After a pause he looked up again. "I'm not newly separated. The divorce is final."

"Oh." She'd thought when he'd said his marriage was over that night she and Max had seen him and Fran at the Toby, he'd meant emotionally.

"Not many people in Tobias know. A client—a friend— went through a divorce a year ago that wiped him out financially and emotionally. One thing he told me was that when you're separated and want to spill your guts, your friends know better than to start the flood by asking questions. After the divorce, when you're trying to look ahead, not back, that's when they ask all the questions. I'm not in the mood for questions, so I've let folks think the divorce process wasn't as far along as it was. But I thought Max would have told you. He asked me straight out earlier this week."

Naturally. Would Matchmaker Max fix her up with a guy not yet divorced? He'd be stripped of his Big Brother wings.

"Max Trevetti." Her voice wobbled on the name—with anger. Definitely anger. "Max is…"

She shook her head, frustrated with her inability to adequately express her frustration with the most frustrating male on the planet.

Rob grinned, taking her elbow and leading her to the door of her room.

"Max Trevetti," Rob said, "is the reason that when we go out for dinner tomorrow night, it won't be a date, but a meal between friends."

One second Max was doing fine.

He came out of the Toby after Sunday supper. Maybe he hadn't taken advantage of the congenial company by sitting alone in a corner and turning down all offers for conversation or darts. But at least he hadn't sat at home in front of the tube and eaten cereal, which was all he had in the house—not even the makings for an omelet like the one Suz had made him.

He hadn't wanted conversation, so what? He'd done what was right for Suz. He'd known it wouldn't be fun. His having fun wasn't the issue.

The next second the headlights of a car turning into the Toby parking lot had sliced across the passenger compartment of a car going in the opposite direction. This car had thoughtfully stopped to let the turning car go ahead.

In that second he saw a tableau he couldn't get out of his head.

Rob and Suz, turned toward each other in the front seat of Rob's expensive, elegant car, looking into each other's eyes. Smiling.

Something rose in him. Primitive and raw. A kind of rage he'd never known.

It was over in a snap of the fingers. The first car finished its turn. Rob's car headed on down the highway, probably taking Suz back to Bliss House after some gracious dinner. The kind she deserved.

While Max stood in the dark parking lot alone and wondered how he could live in Tobias if Suz was added to its population as Mrs. Rob Dalton.

"Max, this has got to stop."

He looked up at his sister. It was Friday night—no, Saturday morning, because it was after midnight—and she stood between him and the TV, hands on hips, glaring. He wondered why she was here at this hour, but not enough to ask. It had been a hell of a week. Working all out, they'd made real progress. Sure, some of the men had grumbled. Too bad.

"Stop? The game's only in the third inning."

"You think I'm talking about a baseball game?" She looked at the screen behind her. "These aren't even the Brewers. Since when do you follow... Is this Japanese baseball?"

"Yeah. The Yakult Swallows and Chunichi Dragons. Game of the week."

"I don't care if it's the game of the year." She clicked off the TV. "I can't believe you would sit here watching teams from the other side of the world play baseball in the middle of the night when you should either be sleeping or talking this out with Suz so you don't drive all your employees away."

"There's nothing to talk out." He realized his error in addressing the Suz part of that diatribe first when Annette's eyes lit up with a that-was-significant light. "Our employees are fine."

"Wrong. I've had phone calls from five of them. The ones who—"

"They shouldn't call you. Give Juney the names and I'll set them straight."

Annette's "Ha!" stopped him. "Juney called twice herself," she said with ill-disguised triumph. "As I was saying, the ones who didn't beg me to give you a rabies shot asked why you're making Suz so miserable."

"I'm not doing a thing to Suz."

"Not doing a thing? Try fixing her up with Rob for the country-club dance and not bothering to tell her. No, she hasn't said a word and neither has Rob. You know this town—someone overheard and blabbed."

"I told her eventually." He glanced away under the pressure of her glare, then back. "Besides, all I've ever tried to do was for her own good."

Annette stared at him. Abruptly, her shoulders slumped and the tension went out of her. "Oh, Max." She sat beside him, patted his knee and said again, "Oh, Max."

"Cut that out. First you come in here acting like I've done something terrible to Suz, and now you sound like I'm some feeble-minded idiot who deserves pity. The way I treat her is no different from how I treat you."

Pushing aside her purse, Annette shifted to sit on the coffee table to face him. "No different?"

"No different. When I saw you with a guy I didn't approve of, I steered you toward somebody else."

A spasm gripped his gut. He'd steered Suz away from someone he didn't approve of for her—himself—and toward Rob. So why had he felt that way seeing them together Sunday night?

Okay, and Saturday night. Both when she'd walked up the steps with her hand tucked in Rob's arm and when he'd spotted them dancing on his way to his truck.

"Yeah, you did," his sister agreed. "Back when I was sixteen. When I started seeing Steve in college, you warned me about the Corbetts, but you didn't meddle. This spring when I saw Steve again, you didn't interfere.''

"You knew what you were getting into. It's different.''

"Oh, Max, yes, it's different. Absolutely different. And if you want proof, I have some.'' She dug into her purse, pulling out a photo folder like those Juney had left lying around.

"Look, if you're going to pull out pictures of me,'' he said, "I wasn't expecting her, that's all. Everybody's reading a lot into a picture—a couple of pictures—and they don't mean a thing.''

"Really?'' She dropped a photo in front of him.

He had one hand at the small of Suz's back. His other hand clasped one of hers to his chest. Contradicting what that hold on her communicated, he was looking away. She'd lifted her head and pulled back slightly, still within his hold. She was looking at him.

My God, how could he get hard at a photograph of Suz looking at him?

How could he not?

"Doesn't mean a thing, huh?'' Annette stood. "Did you know Rob's left town?''

Left? He'd left Suz? He'd kill the guy…except part of him wanted to clap him on the back and buy him a round at the Toby.

"I'll leave you with that bit of information and with that picture.''

He wasn't even sure when the door closed behind Annette. His thoughts were too loud and insistent to leave room for much else.

What they boiled down to was, he didn't give a rat's ass what Rob Dalton did. All he cared about was how Suz felt about what Rob did.

* * *

Suz had just completed the most miserable week of her life and here at her door at Bliss House stood the cause—Max Trevetti. Not only for what he'd done, but for what he'd made her confront about herself.

There'd been good in that, she supposed. She'd recognized that for all her self-doubts, she *had* left home for college and had created a new business with Annette. She and Annette had a long talk about their past partnership. She couldn't doubt Annette's sincerity in her respect for what Suz had contributed to Every Detail.

If self-confrontation ended there, it might not have been so bad. Annette had made one allusion to Max, which Suz had sidestepped. But she'd also looked at herself in an emotional mirror and there stood a woman who was nuts about a man who'd thrown her a surprise blind date.

She wasn't feeling charitable.

"What are you doing here?"

"According to the Suz Grant theory that baked goods cure all pains, these might help." He extended his arm to present a white bakery bag.

She didn't take it from him. "Help what?"

"I know Rob's left town."

"Yes, he has."

He waited, clearly expecting her to say more. She didn't. She wasn't going to help him one bit.

He pulled the bag back, opened the top, then extended it again. "I thought… There's nothing anybody can really do except listen. I can listen."

"Can you?" She selected a French doughnut and bit into it. Not helping him didn't require turning down pastry. She turned her back, leaving him to follow if he wanted. "You haven't done such a hot job so far."

He came in, closing the door. After leaning around her

to put the bag on the night table, he went to the far side of the room, testing the air conditioner's force with his hand, fiddling with the plug.

"I listened. If Rob had said he was going to cut his leave of absence short, I wouldn't have—"

"Thrown me at him?"

He faced her, the air conditioner forgotten. "That was—"

"For my own good?" Her words sounded brittle when she'd been aiming for carefree. "Actually, Rob hasn't cut his leave short. He's in Chicago temporarily to check out something about a company buying property here."

She took the last bite of doughnut, fished a napkin from the bag and wiped her hands.

"Good. Glad things are going well for you two. Rob can give you a good life. He's educated. He's from the right kind of family. He's—"

"Oh, for heaven's sake! If you start talking about the kind of man I deserve or someone being good enough for me, I'll…" She'd spun around from the night table and taken an involuntary step toward Max. Now she crossed her arms at her waist and stilled. "It's what we feel about each other that isn't good enough. We both know there's no chemistry. No—" a stronger woman wouldn't have looked at him; she couldn't take her eyes off him "—heat."

She felt the heat. Pouring off him and reaching out to her, burrowing deep, deep inside her.

"Suz…" He took a step toward her, then stopped. "If I touch you now…"

One lousy, treacherous tear slid from the corner of her left eye and skidded down beside her nose.

"Suz." He reached for her, had her shoulders in his hands.

She batted them away. "No. I won't have your sympathy."

"Sympathy? That's not what…" His hands cupped her face. Large, solid, slightly scratchy Max hands holding her so that they looked into each other's eyes. "Sympathy is not what has me shaking and sweating in my dreams at the thought of having you in my bed. Sympathy is not what has me hard and hot. Sympathy is not what has me wanting to be deep inside you. Now, Suzanna."

He could push the moment. One kiss and the heat would carry them. He released her face, brushed the back of his fingers across her cheek, then dropped his hands to his side. But he didn't back away.

The brown of his eyes burned dark and intense, and she felt the heat from him and for him meet and merge, to ignite a place inside her she knew would never be extinguished.

Their other touches had been impulses, almost accidents, as if they had to be caught off guard before they could let themselves touch each other. This would be deliberate. Each movement a question, an answer. Each a choice.

Their mouths touched, only their mouths. As soft as a first kiss. Their heads tilted, finding the right angle. As sure as a lifetime of kisses.

His hand at her waist, hers to the back of his neck. Her parting her lips, his tongue's entrance. His hand sliding between them to cup her breast through her shirt, her lean to open the way. Her shift of her hips, his press to hold her tighter against him.

They sat together on the side of the bed. He drew her shirt over her head, combing her hair with his fingers. She pulled white cotton from his jeans, pleated the fabric up over the hard, flat surface of his abdomen, then tugged slowly upward to watch the shifting ripples as he freed himself.

Her hands' success with the snap of his jeans sucked breath from them both. The slide of a zipper became an accelerant.

At his hands, disposal of her shorts was a simple lift of her hips. In a progression of touches and slides, they worked back to the head of the bed. He dragged down the spread until their feet could push at it.

She touched his face and he kissed her. Heated intent seared into her with each stroke of his tongue.

Breathing hard, he pulled back enough to gaze down at her. He made a sound, then rolled to reach over the side of the bed. He pulled two foil packets from his jeans pocket and put them on the night table, then rolled back to look down at her.

"If you want me to stop, just tell me."

Another choice.

"What if I don't want you to stop?"

"Then show me."

She skimmed her knuckles from the depression at the base of his throat, down the muscled center of his chest, lower, over his abdomen, pausing to burrow under elastic, then lower. To find him hard and smooth and hot.

He made a sound that rumbled from his chest through his throat. Yet she understood when his hand covered hers and drew it away. It would be so easy to take the choice away on a tide of fire. But that wasn't the right way, not for them, not for now, not for what would follow.

He hooked the straps of her bra and lowered the lace-trimmed fabric. He touched her then. Roughened fingertips, callused thumbs, hardened palms against the tender flesh spilling over the top of the fabric and, through the fabric, the equally tender flesh swelling at his attention.

She breathed to the ragged clock of his touch, her hips pitching toward him for more contact. His arms went around her, his hands working the hooks to free her, dropping her bra beyond the bed.

He murmured, ''Rosy,'' then covered one nipple with his mouth, sucking and licking until she arched with the tormenting pleasure of it.

Choice long made, her need raged.

''Max…please.''

If only she'd known those two words were all she'd needed. His briefs, her panties gone in a heartbeat. The condom required multiple heartbeats, yet the impatience he showed brought another kind of satisfaction.

Impatience released in a low groan as he eased between her legs. Arms locked, he looked down at her. A flash of heat so intense she gasped with it covered her. Slowly his gaze traveled up her body. She saw him look at her breasts, the swollen, pointed results of his attention drawing a pulsing reaction felt where he was poised to enter her. A rolling tremor in response lifted her hips, and the tip of him found entrance.

His gaze touched her mouth, then met her eyes. She gasped. The air half drawn in, he stroked into her, and a second gasp built on the first.

''Suzanna.''

Her gasps fueled the heat. Faster and deeper. Tears slid from her eyes, but she never closed them. Never stopped looking at the man watching her, the connection of their eyes as powerful as where he entered her body.

So when the heat exploded into a fire that roared through her body, consuming her and creating her, she saw it reflected and amplified in those dark eyes.

''Max!''

Chapter Eleven

Suz dug into the bag again. She didn't encounter any doughnuts, but something was in there because the bag still had weight.

Max leaned against the pillows, watching her with that left side of his mouth—her side—lifted in a grin. Even more satisfying was the gleam of heat glinting between those thick, dark eyelashes

He'd eaten his share of doughnuts, plus licked the sweetness methodically from her fingers and palms and wrists. She'd objected when he advanced to the inside of her elbows, proclaiming she wasn't that messy an eater, but she hadn't objected long.

Which was when the second condom was used, after extended unhurried exploration, and the reason she needed sustenance.

"Aha!" It wasn't a doughnut, but her fingers grasped something.

A banana. The peel still yellow, but well past the crisp stage Max preferred. "What's this?"

"A banana."

"Thank you, Mr. Produce. Why did you bring a banana?"

"My version of humble pie."

"Max Trevetti eating humble pie. Now this is something I'll enjoy."

"I'll do it. I'll tell you I'm sorry about that thing with Rob, but—"

"And tell him."

"—I'd much rather see you eating that banana."

His tone put an entirely different light on his watching her eat a green banana weeks ago in his kitchen. She felt a flush of heat and desire surging, along with a strange sort of shyness, considering the past couple of hours.

"Right now I need something more substantial than watching you eat humble pie. Let's raid the kitchen."

"Miss Trudi…"

"She's spending the day on a cruise of retired teachers on Lake Geneva. She won't be back until after dinner."

She pulled on his T-shirt and boxers. He wore only his jeans, unsnapped.

Like kids afraid they might get caught—or adults eager to get back to what they'd been doing—they zipped around the old-fashioned kitchen, surprising Miss Trudi's hermit-like cat, Squid, who stalked off.

In no time they were in the hallway's dim twists and turns. They turned the last bend, the open door in sight. Max leaned across their loaded hands and kissed her, the sliding of his tongue immediately setting her ticking to his rhythm. She drew away.

"We have to…get to the room…." She moved sideways, toward the door. "Put this down and—"

Max stopped her with his mouth and body, pressing both to her. Their full hands held to the sides while the friction of his hips against hers, his bare chest against the cotton-covered tips of her breasts wound her tighter and tighter.

Milk sloshed out of a glass he held and spilled down the front of the T-shirt she wore. She giggled at the jolt of cool liquid, then stopped abruptly as his hot mouth fastened over her nipple, drawing on her through the damp fabric.

"Max…Max…" She was panting. Trying to find words. "Have to…put this down…"

He jerked around, took the last step into the room and half threw the two dishes and the glass he'd carried onto the dresser. He snatched the plates and bottle of water from her and added them to the jumble. One hand on her wrist, he drew her into the room, slammed the door and immediately pressed her back against it with the hard weight of his body.

He wrapped his fingers around the T-shirt neck, so that his knuckles grazed her collarbone. Caught in that sensation, the crisp *rrrrrip* jolted her.

"Max!"

He had torn the shirt from neck to hem in one motion.

"I'll get another," he rumbled, pushing the fabric off her shoulders so it fell to the floor.

It wasn't the T-shirt, it was the passion it represented. *Max felt this way about her.*

That revelation brought a thousand questions on its tail. Her mind refused to contemplate them. Not now, not yet.

Max pushed at the boxers, which were so loose on her that one touch dropped them to the floor. She stepped out of them. Denim rubbed tender skin as he pressed against her at the same time he dug in his pocket, pulling out another condom packet, opened his jeans and drew it on.

He lifted her up, her back against the door.

His hands under her bottom, he licked and kissed her breasts. Her legs wrapped around his waist, her heels and calves pushing his jeans lower. He held her above him until she made a sound of impatient demand. With a guttural growl, he let her slide down onto him.

"Suz, wake up. I'm taking you to my house."

She muttered into the pillow ending with "...stay here?"

"Because Miss Trudi will be home, because we'll starve and because I'm out of condoms."

That got her moving. They showered together. She put on loose shorts and the blouse that tied at her waist while he called in a pizza order.

The pizza delivery turned into his drive just behind them. They sat on the porch swing to eat it. He kissed sauce from the corner of her mouth. She nipped cheese from the tip of his finger.

As moonlight painted the lake, he drew her into his lap, giving one hand the luxury of stroking her long, smooth leg from her bare toes to her hip under the hem of her shorts.

She fell asleep first. When he awoke, the lights across the lake in Tobias were down to a vigilant few. He carried her into his bed, slid off her shorts, unbuttoned her out of the blouse and crawled in beside her. A man his age had to be happy that desire alone hadn't killed him today.

Then she stirred against him, her long-fingered hand trailing down his side before slipping forward and curling lightly around him.

Oh, hell, he'd die happy.

Islands of memory floated amid murky impressions. The memories were stark moments caught on a tape in her mind, ever ready to rewind and play back in full detail.

The moment she should have seen coming.

"I love you, Suz." Tad looking across the red tablecloth, grasping her hand, his face hopeful, determined, yet resigned.

"I'm so sorry, Tad. I don't feel that way about you."

She'd said a great many other things before and after that—about enjoying his company, about his strengths, about the fault being hers not his—but that was the one statement that came out of her memory stark and clear. Because that was the statement that had turned off the hope and the determination in his face.

The moment before the accident.

Looking at Tad's profile as he accelerated smoothly when the light changed from red to green. Hoping to see there something other than disappointment and hurt. Recognizing that the white car hurtling toward the intersection from their left was not going to stop for the red light it faced, was going to broadside Tad's blue compact.

"Tad!"

The jerk of impact, the floating sensation of being driven sideways. Sounds coming sharp, then muffled, like someone playing with the tape's volume control.

Then blank. Not a long one, though, because the sounds were still echoing when the next moment came.

Tad looking as if he had draped himself over the steering wheel to rest. But with the steering wheel now nearly on the passenger-side floor. The partially collapsed roof and the driver's door compressing his lower body into an impossibly small space. His face turned toward her, as if at the last moment he'd looked away from what was coming.

She pushed back the ceiling fabric and brushed his hair from his forehead, then saw blood. She took her glove off and pressed it against where she thought the blood came from, trying to stop its flow.

He murmured. She took his hand and felt a surge of hope when his fingers tightened. She told him help was coming. She heard voices of people who surely would help them.

"Hang on, Tad."

She hadn't known what else to do for him. Where else was he hurt? He didn't answer.

Someone yanked her door open, rattled off questions she didn't bother to answer, then said the one important thing— an ambulance was coming.

"The ambulance is on its way, Tad. You hear that? You hang on. We'll get you to a hospital and everything will be okay."

There was enough light now that she saw his eyes.

"Tell my family…"

"You'll tell them, Tad. You will. Just hang on. Don't think about anything else. The ambulance is almost here. I can hear it."

"Tell them…and you…love."

The moment Tad died.

She slipped into a blur of firemen and EMTs. They transported Tad to the hospital. Time of death was declared an hour later. But she knew he'd died there in the car, with the light gone from his eyes and his final words spoken.

The murky sea of impressions washed over the tape then, leaving few moments.

A small one came of sitting somewhere with Max's arms wrapped around her, hearing the beat of his heart, strong, steady, never giving up.

Max's presence became a buffer between her and the worst of it. Max notifying the school. Max with her while she gave her statement to the police. Max calling her family. Max meeting Tad's parents at the airport. Max holding her arm during the campus memorial service and again at that first court hearing for the drunk driver.

Max wiping her face when she threw up before meeting Tad's parents to tell them about his last moments.

That was one duty Max had not been able to shelter her from. And he couldn't shelter her from what went on in her head and her heart.

Suz saw the midafternoon sunlight, felt the beginnings of hunger after the cold pizza and cereal they'd eaten hours ago, heard Max's breathing beside her. So she knew she was not dreaming, but thinking and remembering.

She knew he was awake, too.

With her back against the headboard, her knees drawn up and her chin resting on a pillow atop them, she started talking.

"When I was a little girl, not even in school yet, I decided to make a cake. I guess a lot of kids do that, mixing flour and sugar and making a mess. Except my family took that mess and baked it and ate it. I remember their faces as they chewed and chewed and smiled and said what a genius I was. And I agreed. Then I took a bite. It was awful." She gave a weak chuckle. "It's a miracle I ever tried to bake anything else."

He rolled to his side, propping his head on one hand, but said nothing.

"I suppose that's when it started. I didn't set them straight. I thought somehow I'd fooled them. Of course it didn't end there. 'Oh, look at the incredible thing Suz has done—she's the next I.M. Pei or better than Monet or destined to be an astronaut.' And I *knew* the sand castle was a lump, the fingerpainting was a mess and my paper airplane took a nosedive.

"Don't say it, Max. I can hear you thinking it already—so she got crazy in *preschool?* But it went on happening.

I kept thinking the grades would stop coming, because they'd figure out how little I really understood—or remembered, God! I couldn't remember half the facts a week after a test. But it never happened. Then I was out of college, and Annette and I were starting the business. She was so unhappy about Steve, and I was her friend, so she felt loyal to me. She has such a generous heart.''

''And a hard head. She wouldn't have had you around as a friend much less as a partner if she didn't know how good you were.''

''I think…I think I know that now—thanks to you.'' She looked at him, over the edge of the pillow. ''You're not subtle, but you are effective, Trevetti. It isn't like I think—thought—I'm a total idiot. I knew I could do some stuff. But people would say I was this marvel, and all the while it felt like my best skill was faking it.''

''Most people feel like they're faking it most of the time.''

''Maybe. But—'' this is where it got hard, really hard, but she had to say it and he had to hear it ''—most people don't kill someone as a result of it.''

''What kind of bull—''

''Just listen, Max. You said you were good at it. Now you have to prove it.''

He'd bolted upright. She hadn't moved. Tension stretched with the seconds before he slid back to rest his shoulder against the wall. ''Okay, I'm listening.''

''I used to think that if I'd been as smart and cool under pressure as everyone said I was, I could have saved Tad. If I'd known first aid or CPR or something. But that wasn't how I failed him. I failed him because I couldn't let people close for fear they would see I wasn't the Marvelous Suz.'' She tried a grin, not sure it worked. ''I thought of myself as being like the wizard in *The Wizard of Oz,* hiding behind a curtain, fooling everyone but liable to exposure at any second.

"Anyone who threatened to get too close, I pushed away. That's what I did to Tad. He told me that night that he loved me. I told him I didn't love him—how could I risk letting anyone inside that curtain? And when the accident happened, I told him the ambulance was coming. I begged him to hold on, to fight." Tears slid down her face, linking under her chin. "He gave up hope. I'd killed his hope."

Max had her shoulders in his hands, holding her, trying to get her to look at him.

"He had massive injuries. No amount of hope could have saved him. You couldn't have done anything. Not if you'd known first aid, not if you'd been the top trauma surgeon in the country. Not if you had loved him. He didn't die because of you."

"You don't understand."

"Listen to me, Suzanna Grant, I do understand. God knows I understand letting down someone who's died and what it's like to live with that. I promised my mother—swore to her—that I wouldn't drop out, that I would get my degree. Knowing I was lying through my teeth even as I said the words. I knew I had to quit to fulfill the bigger promise—that I'd look out for Annette. But she wanted both promises. So I lied so she could die in peace. And I've lived with that.

"I lied. You told the truth. If we'd done the opposite, it still wouldn't have changed that someone died before they should have. We did what was there to do at that moment."

She sucked in a breath that came out a sob for Max.

He wouldn't go after his degree because he felt he'd forfeited that right when he'd made his choice, and sealed it with a lie to his dying mother.

''She wouldn't want you to punish yourself, Max. You couldn't keep both promises at once, but you could do it now. You... Even if you had to let go before, you can't be afraid to grab hold of a dream again. Oh, Max...''

Tears took over the words. For him, for his mother, for her, for Tad. For the past.

Max wrapped her in his arms, her head against his chest, letting her hear the beat of his heart, strong, steady, never giving up.

Promise me, Maximilian. Promise you stay at university. You finish. For me.

I promise, Ma. I promise. For you.

He hadn't thought of that lie to his mother for a long, long time.

He'd made his choice even before she'd asked him to make two pledges that couldn't exist side by side. Made his choice, put his head down and bulled ahead. No looking back.

Not until he broke his wrist.

And then the might-have-beens and what-ifs had rolled over him like a wave that had been building for fifteen years.

The things he'd told Suz about how a degree wouldn't change his life, they were all true. He couldn't go back to that twenty-year-old with all the possibilities in the world. Maybe he didn't even want to.

So why had throwing out those course schedules she'd been peppering his house with been so damned hard?

You couldn't keep both promises at once, but you could do it now.

Suz was wrong. He couldn't keep his promise to his

mother even if he went back to college now. Because he wouldn't be doing it for her anymore. He'd be doing it for himself.

Suz would have said the emptiness beside her woke her, if that was possible. Max, already wearing a fresh T-shirt, was zipping a clean pair of jeans.

She blinked the clock into focus. Six. Sunday evening.

"Where are you going?"

"It's looking like a bad storm's coming. I'm going to check on the site."

As if he hadn't done that thoroughly before leaving. "I'll go with you."

She felt leaden, sunk in an emotional hangover. She didn't know how to address what they'd said, how to interpret his silence. She didn't want to leave. But even more, she didn't want to be here if he was wishing she'd leave. Once at Bliss House, she'd have a choice—stay there or return with him. More important, he'd have a choice—ask her to come back with him or say nothing.

He shot her one quick look, but there was nothing to read in it. All he said was, "Sure. If you want."

Neither of them said more as she quickly dressed and they headed out.

In the few minutes between leaving the house and the truck's AC kicked in, air stuck to her skin like a swimsuit soaked in hot water. But as they followed the road around the lake's eastern curve, then north through Tobias toward Bliss House's hilltop, she saw only a moderately cloudy sky out the passenger window. Thunder was a distant, muted rumble.

Max turned left onto the street behind Bliss House, one of the highest vantage points in Tobias. He muttered something, more of a sound than a word, but his tone had her turning to look west.

From the western horizon a pool of murky gray-green swirled with black spread like a dark blanket being drawn up over the sky.

"My God."

Before she could say more, her cell phone rang. It was Miss Trudi.

"Oh, my dear, I'm glad I found you. Are you somewhere safe?"

"Just pulled in behind Bliss House. I'll come inside in a minute."

"I'm not at Bliss House, Suz. I'm with Fran and Nell at Fran's house. I'm not at all sure Bliss House is the safest place. And for you to be there alone!"

"Max is here."

Beside her, Max had turned off the ignition, and said quietly, "I'm going to check things."

He was out of the truck before she did more than nod. She opened her door, intending to follow him, but the wind made her miss something Miss Trudi said, so she pulled the door closed and asked her to repeat it.

"I said that as long as you are with Max, everything should be okay. The weather forecaster has said we could have strong thunderstorms and there is a tornado warning for the area."

"But the sky's not that yellowish green it gets with a tornado. Besides, I thought Tobias never got tornadoes— all the trees and the lake. Isn't that what you said?"

She crossed her legs, then uncrossed them immediately. Her skin felt so sticky she was afraid her legs might stick together permanently.

"That color is characteristic, but not essential for the formation of a tornado. No tornado ever has struck Tobias, and they are certainly not as common in Wisconsin as they are in Oklahoma or Kansas. Some hypothesize it is because of Lake Michigan to our east and Lake Superior to our north, which prevent the air from superheating. Tornadoes prefer a clash of cold and hot air, with a low pressure system—''

''Miss Trudi? Miss Trudi? You're breaking up. Must be the cell phone. Gotta go. I'll call you at Fran's later.'' As much as she enjoyed Miss Trudi's wide range of knowledge, she wasn't in the mood for a meteorological lecture. She turned off the cell phone and dropped it into her purse, which she left on the truck floor. She would need both hands to help Max.

She found him checking the plastic covering over the large stack of lumber.

''Miss Trudi says there's a tornado warning.'' His grunt said he wasn't surprised. ''What can I do?''

''Pick up anything small and loose that could get ruined by rain or thrown around by the wind.''

She used an empty mortar bucket to gather an errant screwdriver, two blocks of wood and a brick, and was reaching for a broom when a piercing wail seemed to crawl right under her skin. It paused, then started again.

Max came around the corner at a run. ''Tornado siren. We gotta get in the main house. Leave this stuff.''

''But…'' She looked at the things in her hands, looked at the sky, now swirling almost over her head, and dropped the half-filled bucket. If there was a tornado, a lot more than these little things would be tossed around.

Max took her hand and sprinted toward Bliss House's back porch, tugging her through the barrier of wind. She kept up, but gulped in air that was more humidity than oxygen.

Rain started coming down—no, not down, sideways—as they reached the porch overhang. They stood there, hands still clasped, gasping for breath.

The wind through the trees sounded like an angry ocean, the sound pounding at them in waves, as if they were a beach. The sound deepened until it rumbled. But it kept going, never stopping the way thunder did. Then it seemed to condense into one deep-throated roar. A roar that was way, way too heavy on the bass, so the rumble went beyond a sound to become a physical sensation. Reverberating in her bones, through the porch floor and into the earth, where it seemed to shake the ground.

And now the wind sucked at them the way waves did at sand, trying to drag them to its will.

Max pointed to the west and she saw one of the swirling masses of black clouds slowly stretch down, thinning into a point where it seemed to reach to the ground, like a narrow ice-cream cone. A second dropped down, this one wider. And nearer.

The pressure pushed at the outside of her ribs while her heart pounded them from the inside and her lungs strained to pull in air. Yet she stared at the fattening cone advancing on them. Growing bigger and darker—yet not entirely dark.

"Look, Max. It's beautiful."

He stared at it, too. He must have seen the silvery glitter sparkling out of the darkness. Whirling and whirling, constantly changing the colors and light, like a sequined dancer twirling against a black backdrop.

Max swore, wrapped his hand around her arm and yanked her toward the house. "It's glass. Glass and metal and a hell of a lot of other things that could cut us to—"

His last word was swallowed by the growling roar. He shoved her inside and slammed the door behind them. "Basement!"

Released from the storm's fascination, she caught his urgency, remembering the way from her tours with Miss Trudi.

"This way!"

She reached the door first, switched on the lights, and nothing happened. She spun around and ran right into Max's chest.

"No lights. We need candles."

His curse wished electricity and absent flashlights to blazes. "No time."

He pushed past her, starting down the steep steps using one hand to feel along the wall, while holding the other out to her. She clasped it and used her free hand the same way.

"There's a broken step," she warned. "Third from the bottom."

He grunted. He had no way of knowing when they reached the third from the bottom, but at least it was a warning.

"Here. Go close to the wall."

She felt with her foot, found the break-away slant and edged around it. Another second and they were at the bottom, hands clasped, their breathing audible in the relative stillness of the basement.

"We have to go to the southwest corner." He started to pull her toward the right.

"No! That's a myth." She didn't remember how she'd learned that, but she was certain of it. "We want to get as far away from the tornado as we can."

She pulled back, tugging him to the left, toward the southeast corner, and at the same time she desperately tried to visualize the configuration of boxes, trunks and old furniture. Max followed her into the rough aisle that slithered through the accumulations of more than a century. He released her hand, and for a second she felt adrift and alone.

"Both hands in front of you," he said, while he grabbed the fabric of her blouse at the small of her back in his fist.

Then she understood. He was leaving her hands free to

search the space ahead to avoid being hurt without releasing the connection between them.

They seemed to inch across the space, though the journey couldn't have taken even a full minute. When her hands touched the ornately carved oval of a picture frame, she knew where they were. Bending, she stretched her hands out and found the cloth-covered, horsehair love seat that she'd considered the most hideous piece of furniture she'd ever seen.

"This is it. As far as we can get. There's a love seat here we can sit on."

"No." He moved ahead of her, and with her eyes adjusting to the wispy light, she made out that he was tipping the love seat upside down to balance on its arms and the top edge of its back. "Under it."

She was already moving when his hand found her leg and tugged. In seconds they were both on the floor. He maneuvered her into the angle of space under the love seat, then closed off the triangular cave with his body, his arms wrapping around her.

She hooked her legs over his, drawing him in closer.

The love seat's musty smell was almost overwhelming. She pressed her head against the juncture of his neck and shoulder and took in his scent. She felt his chin against her temple, then a softer touch against the top of her head, as if he'd rested his cheek there.

Far overhead thunderous *thunks* echoed as the house sustained blows from wind-driven projectiles. A horrible cracking and ripping sound seemed to carry through the old walls and into the stone foundation.

"You'll be okay." He made it a vow, a pledge of protection.

"*We'll* be okay."

She thought he kissed the top of her head. "Yes. We'll be okay."

She tipped her head back, trying to see his face. She didn't know if it was sight or memory that let her make out the strong line of his brow, the sharp slant of his cheekbones, the decisive ridge of his jaw. Sight or memory, it was the bedrock strength and honor of the man that she saw.

"Max—"

"Don't say it. Not yet."

If he hadn't been stretched out along her body, she would have curled up with the pain that drove into her gut with as much force as the tornado displayed above them. There might not be any more time, but he didn't want to hear that she loved him.

He must have heard the sound that escaped her. His arms tightened around her.

"No, Suz. You don't underst—"

"I'm going to say it, anyway. Even if you don't want it. I—"

"I love you, Suz. That's why—I wanted to say it first. I want you to know, to always know I said it to you. Not an answer, not a *me, too*. Whatever else happens, know this— I love you. I will always love you."

"Oh, Max." As tears welled and slid free, she reached to touch his face. Her fingertips found his ear first, then his cheek, his lips. She held her touch there, using it to guide her mouth as she raised her head. "I love you, too."

She replaced her fingers with her lips, felt his lips part to hers and kissed him so deeply and so long that the sensation of love almost seemed to become visible behind her closed eyelids.

Max shifted, turning her to her back, so he was over and around her, protecting and possessing.

She held him off for one second. "Whatever else happens, I have always loved you. I will always love you."

A series of crashes and what sounded like an explosion came from above them. They held on to each other more tighter, kissed deeper.

Chapter Twelve

Max might never have let her go if Suz hadn't started coughing. Somehow it made him aware that the larger noises around them had stopped. The tornado was gone.

He backed out from under the love seat, drawing Suz with him to ease her coughing. As he straightened he felt a brush against his neck, and realized what had caused Suz's coughing. Blows against the old house had dislodged decades of fine dust, which had floated down onto his back—and into Suz's face.

He pulled up the hem of his T-shirt to wipe her face. Through a coughing paroxysm, she ran her fingers along his arm until they touched the back of his hand.

It was a good thing she was coughing, or that touch would have been enough to overcome the common sense drumming at his head that he needed to get her out of this dust bowl, not make love to her on a basement floor in the dark and dirt.

They felt their way up the stairs and into the kitchen, where nothing appeared disturbed. She lifted the receiver from the wall telephone, listened, then shook her head. He tried the light switch. Nothing.

Then they opened the back door.

It looked as if the world had been put in a blender, then the contents dumped. A stop sign and its pole were wrapped around a high limb of a nearly denuded oak. A garbage can sat on the roof. Shreds of clothing clung to buildings and plants. One bush had not only lost its protective wrap, but looked like that old sight gag where someone's hair stood straight on end. All the windows in the new construction were gone. What appeared to be a pair of overalls was plastered over one gaping hole. Paper fluttered everywhere.

The shed they'd used for storage was gone. Simply...gone. A hard hat and random chunks of wood were all that indicated where it had been.

Suz's hand tightened on his as together they stepped outside. Their shoes crunched through a rubble of crushed glass, plastic, vinyl siding and items torn to such fine pieces there was no telling what they'd been.

The tornado had taken out a third of the stacked lumber, littering a few remnants along the path of destruction heading east and ramming one shard into the trunk of the old maple tree. The rest was nowhere to be seen. The remaining two-thirds of the stack, the cover long gone, had been skewed around, leaving some lengths barely balanced, but seemingly undamaged.

"Look." Without releasing his hand, Suz retrieved something from under a sodden sheet from last week's *Milwaukee Journal-Sentinel*. It was a small amber-colored glass.

Intact. Eerily unscratched.

He made a sound of disbelief, but kept moving.

Beyond a corner of the building, he saw that the cement wall had become the final resting place of a two-by-four—driven into it like a nail into a board.

"Oh, my God."

At Suz's hoarse words, he looked to the west and saw Kelly Street, now a jumble of cars on their sides or roofs, at least two crushed under the fallen mass of old oaks and maples. The houses on either side of the street appeared intact, as if the storm had used the street's center yellow line as a guide wire.

Mentally following the storm's track, he whipped his head around to the east, but no clear path showed in that direction.

"It must have lifted," he muttered.

"Thank God." She'd clearly had the same fears he had—that the path had been headed for the residential heart of town, including Steve and Annette's house, as well as Fran's.

Tobias had come through relatively unscathed, as long as the tornado hadn't skipped back down and…

Almost to the street, they'd turned the corner to see the fourth side of Miss Trudi's new home. Twin blows stopped him.

Most of the back wall was gone. It looked like a giant mouth had bit it off and swallowed. There wasn't even rubble to show for it. Beyond that, the main house came into focus—with two-thirds of its roof gone.

The damage horrified Suz, but what chilled her was the way Max's face went still.

"We can fix it, Max." She hoped he didn't hear that edge of desperation in her voice. All his work, all his sacrifices. *Don't let this dream go, Max.*

He shook his head. Worse, he released her hand as he moved ahead, doggedly continuing his circuit of the construction site. She hurried to catch up with him.

"Max, we'll rebuild. It'll take longer, but I'll invest more—"

"No, you won't." Three words formed a solid wall she didn't think any tornado could break through, and that left her on the other side. "You're not going to throw away your money, too. But don't worry, it'll get completed. Maybe not for this Christmas, but it'll be finished."

"But your business—"

"It doesn't matter. As long as everyone's okay. That's what counts." He turned then, enfolding her in his arms. "I'm thankful beyond words that you're safe."

She hugged him back, her mind racing. The tornado still threatened Max, yanking another dream from his grasp. How did you get someone to hold on with all his might?

Releasing her, he moved away, inspecting the ragged edge of a wall the storm had torn away.

"Yeah." She pushed a grin into her voice, trying to get him to respond. "Saved by lust. I bet we're the only people who rode out a tornado by making out."

He remained solemn. "It's probably a pretty natural reaction. Life in the face of danger."

Great. He was already dismissing what had happened in the basement as a natural response to the possibility of being blown to smithereens.

She continued on ahead of him.

Was his lack of expression to avoid showing her what he felt about this horrible damage or showing her what he didn't feel about her?

Must be the shortest duration for a declaration of love on record.

Irony got in a few jabs, too. Here she'd learned that she really did have some of the abilities people had been giving her credit for all these years, except where it really counted—in helping Max. She'd tried so hard to help Max see that he had a right to follow the path that would make him happy, and she'd failed.

If she couldn't do that for him, what good was loving him?

"Suz! Don't move!"

She obeyed the concern in his voice rather than the command. "Why?"

Eyes on the ground, she'd been picking her way through debris. Now she spotted a small orange flag two feet to her right. But it was the only one left of the several that had marked the rectangular area of the root cellar, making it impossible to tell exactly where the cellar was.

"The ground could be weakened. Stay there." Max edged closer to the lopsided lumber stack "I can't be sure which point of the cellar that flag marks—it could be under you or on this side of the flag."

"You mean where you're standing?" Her voice climbed.

"It's okay. We had the lumber restacked to be clear of the root cellar. As long as I stay here, I'll be fine. Now, reach out and grab my hand."

He planted a foot close to the base of the stacked lumber, then the other a stride closer to her. Bracing over that forward leg, he reached toward her.

She took one step toward his hand and gained confidence when nothing happened. She drew in a breath in preparation for the next step.

A rumble sounded, fainter than the raucous tornado yet ominous, and with a muffled curse Max and his outstretched hand disappeared.

The breath she'd sucked in came out as a scream. He was gone. Swallowed by the ground. She barely took that in when a different sound, staccato and higher-pitched, started.

She couldn't even scream.

The earth beneath the lumber was also giving way, the lengths clattering down, down into the dark emptiness that had swallowed Max. Pieces snapped off as they crashed against each other, those falling from the top of the pile broke those below, and still others drove down into the opening like spikes. All on top of where Max was. The cascading horror seemed to go on forever.

"Max! Max!"

She pulled loose boards off, tossing them to the side. She didn't realize she'd been calling his name until the crash of falling boards tailed off enough that she could hear her own voice.

"I'm here," she heard Max say.

She stilled, wanting to gabble out prayers of thanksgiving, pleas that he get out, incantations for his safety. She forced herself to speak calmly. "Are you hurt? Can you move?"

"I'm not hurt. Not badly." His voice sounded strained. "But I'm pinned. Board across my chest and others on top of it."

Pressing down on him. He couldn't breathe. That was why he sounded strained.

"I'll get help. I'll call…"

But the telephone didn't work. Her cell phone… She'd dropped it in her purse and left it in the truck. She looked around. The truck was gone. Gouges in the mud showed it must have been dragged sideways. She followed the path with her eyes and saw the truck half a block down on its crumpled top in the middle of the street, the doors flung open. Even if her purse had stayed inside, could the cell phone have survived?

Max's voice came. "Might take...too long. You do this."

She covered her mouth with her hands to keep from protesting, but he must have heard it in her silence.

"You can do it, Suz."

"My God, if I pick the wrong one..." They could all drop down on him, increasing the weight, crushing him. Or stabbing—

"You won't. Counting on you."

Don't! Don't count on me, Max! I'm not the person you think I am, capable of coming through for you. If I fail you like I failed...

Through the damp, earthy smell of the storm, she thought she caught the sharp scent of friction-burned metal. Tad's face became the only thing she could see, the light fading from his eyes...

No amount of hope could have saved him. You couldn't have done anything. Not if you'd known first aid, not if you'd been the top trauma surgeon in the country. Not if you had loved him.

But this was different. It had to be. Max said he wasn't badly hurt. If she could get him free...

"Believe...in you...Suz. You...believe."

Oh, God, she had to believe. Because she couldn't fail.

She cleared the loose, easy boards first. Now she slid one board free from the tangle. Then a second. A third. That allowed her to lift off a fourth.

Slow. She was too slow!

She studied the pile of wood in front of her. She pulled

out a broken-off piece and used that as a lever to pry off three at once. That was better, and— "No!"

She reached toward the boards as if that could stop them from shifting and settling with a creaking groan. Then came a crack of a board below giving way.

"Max!"

"Okay. I'm okay." Then there was another movement, this time from the bottom of the pile. It seemed to heave and move slightly to the left. She heard his breaths as deep gasps.

"Oh, Max, what have I done?"

"You made it better." He sucked in another breath. "I've got more room."

"Thank God. Then we can wait, then, until I get help."

There was a pause. It allowed her to hear the faint creaking she hadn't heard before. The creaking of a board under extreme stress.

"Better not."

In that laconic reply she heard how dangerous this truly was.

"Listen, Suz. There is no one in this world I would rather have up there than you. There's a board that should be coming out up there at about a forty-five-degree angle, pointing toward the main house. That's the *last* one I want you to move. Understand?"

She eyed the board streaked by water. "Yes."

She set to work then, pulling boards, sliding them, prying them when she could. Rain made the wood slick. She kept working. Splinters drove into her skin. She kept working. Her hands bled on the wood. She kept working.

She saw small patches of his jeans, one of his T-shirts. Max spoke to her. She wasn't even sure what he said; she concentrated on the sound of her voice, drawing it in to fire muscles that screamed for her to stop.

And then the scream was outside her body. Different, yet familiar.

She straightened with a jerk. The tornado siren. Oh, God. Not another tornado! She looked west, and another boiling mass of dark clouds was rolling toward them.

"Go inside, Suz. In the basement, under the love seat. Use blankets—"

"I am not leaving you." She knew she sounded more indignant than heroic.

"I'll be okay. Root cellar—that's where people used to go."

Her gaze went to that angled board again. The one holding so many other boards off his body.

"Those root cellars had roofs and they didn't have piles of boards all over them that a tornado could turn into missiles."

"Suz—"

"I'm not going. Now are we going to do this, or am I going to stand out here doing nothing until the tornado scoops me up like Dorothy?" Without waiting for an answer, she wiped her hands on her shorts and took hold of another board. "Here we go."

But it would take too long at this rate.

There had to be something... *She* had to do something.

Her gaze went back to that angled board. She stared at it. Taking apart the angles, gauging where Max was, judging the consequences.

She looked back over her shoulder at the clouds rumbling closer, lightning slashing down.

"Max. If I can clear a small space for you, can you pull yourself out of the hole without help?"

He hesitated. From doubt about her or about his own physical ability? "I can do it. But what—"

She gulped in air. "You have to trust me. Can you trust me?"

"Yes." No hesitation. Her eyes stung. She blinked hard—no time for that. "Tell me when."

She found a rope, looped it around the angled board, wiggling the loop down as far as she could. She forced herself to draw on it slowly and steadily, pausing to wiggle it lower to improve the angle. The boards that rested atop it shifted, yanking at her arms.

"It's okay!" Max called out. "Keep going."

Her arms trembled with the ache as the angled board took on the weight of more and more shifting boards, until it seemed like a single, narrow dam holding back a flood.

"A little more."

She tightened her grip on the rope, getting a better purchase where rain and blood hadn't made the surface slick, and pulled more.

"That's it! Hold it there."

She heard the rip of fabric, then saw movement on the far side of the hole. Joy at a glimpse of dark hair shot through her and her hold slipped, giving back a few precious inches to the lumber.

She gasped, grabbing more tightly, digging her heels in, straining her thighs and back and shoulders to hold on. Just hold on. Just hold on…

"Let go, Suz. You can let go."

And Max was there, his arms around her, opening her cramping fingers from around the rope, letting the dam burst with a clatter of boards, turning her into him.

Max. Real. Alive. She buried her face against the swath of his chest left bare by the torn T-shirt and didn't mind the taste of dirt against her lips. She could feel and smell him. That was what mattered.

He was saying things to her, she didn't know what. It didn't matter. He was talking. Max.

"Look."

The order of that one word did get her to lift her face. His face and hair were streaked with dirt and he had a scratch over one eyebrow. But he was grinning. Wrapping her in his arms, he turned ninety degrees so she could look that direction without moving her head from his chest. Now that was service, she thought groggily.

And then she saw…the huge dark cloud breaking into isolated patches of meteorological sullenness, the last rays of the blood-orange sun streaming through at the western horizon.

And then a familiar SUV pulling up with a screech of brakes and doors flying open, as Annette, Miss Trudi and the others who had become her friends poured out. Behind them, Lenny arrived in his truck.

Suz let her face drop back to Max's chest, absorbing that comfort.

She was aware of worried voices and tender hands, but mostly she was aware of Max's arms around her, his heart beating solid and strong beneath the skin under her cheek.

"Oh, Max," she heard Annette say at one point. "What are you going to do? There's so much damage."

"Suz says we're going to fix it. So we better get started."

Suz smiled as a velvety dark cloud from inside her head swept over her, and she passed out.

Eight days later Suz parked her car in front of Bliss House and walked around back, carrying a box with four gallons of stain-killing primer she'd been sent for. It was heavy, but this was easier than trying to find a spot to park in back, which was crowded with more pickups and SUVs and vans than the block had ever seen before.

Besides, she'd grown muscles in the past week and a day—physical and emotional muscles.

That first night, she'd come around almost immediately. Someone had called an ambulance and the EMTs had treated her hands and checked Max over. They'd wanted both of them to go to the hospital, but they'd refused. By then, other people were arriving. Eric and others from the construction crew, subcontractors, friends and former students of Miss Trudi, former clients of Max's.

Before full dark, they had tarps over the gaping hole in the back of Miss Trudi's new home and the roof of her old one. Annette had organized the unskilled volunteers into cleanup crews. The whine of chainsaws sounded as workmen disposed of uprooted trees. And casseroles had blanketed Bliss House's large kitchen table. When it was too dark to do any more, the group used battery-powered lanterns and flashlights to gather around the back steps.

Steve had just arrived and reported there were injuries and damage, but no fatalities. The tornado had skipped across the county, touching and lifting, touching and lifting. Apparently it had stayed on the ground longest as it tore through a dairy farm on the western edge of the county— and around Bliss House.

A voice from the back—she thought it was Fran—asked how far behind schedule this would put them on Bliss House and how much it would cost.

When Max hesitated, Suz stepped out of the protective circle of his arm almost for the first time since he'd come out of that hole and told them about the steep scheduling penalties the bank had insisted on, and how Max had put up his own money to get started.

A murmur shimmied across the group, then Milt Portage called out, "You need any flooring, I'll cover it—and install it."

An electrician matched that offer. Eric and Lenny said they'd work without looking for overtime. Annette, Fran and several other women said they would do whatever they could to help. Sitting on the steps, she and Max took the names of volunteers on legal pads Miss Trudi provided and assigned tasks for first light.

It was after midnight when Suz stood up, then nearly toppled over from leg cramps. Max's arm was back around her before she could even blink.

"You're coming home with me," he'd said, handed his pad and hers to Annette, then led her to a truck. She didn't find out until the next day that he had commandeered Lenny's truck.

He'd practically carried her into his house, where the only damage was trees littering the yard. They showered together, holding each other up, rinsing the worst of the dirt, dust, mud and blood from their bodies and hair. They fell into bed, spooned closely. Sometime during the night she awoke and turned to him. He kissed her gently, almost sweetly. Then they made love with a desperation she'd never known before.

He woke her near dawn with slow, tender touches that gave way to the same kind of joining.

It set the pattern for the days that followed.

They wrung every minute of work possible out of the daylight hours, and beyond daylight starting the second night, when Max called in a favor to acquire a generator.

When Suz couldn't think straight anymore, Max would

scoop her up, take her to his home and his bed, and make love to her until thinking straight was no longer even a goal.

The one thing they didn't do was talk.

Oh, they talked about the work, sure. That second day Max called her over to the back steps where he and Lenny were running figures.

"As my partner, you better hear this," he said, then explained the difficulties of tying in what they had to replace on that back wall with what had survived the storm. Things like replacing the twelve inches of the flooring joists bitten off by the storm while keeping the structure sturdy. The costs and the man-hours weren't pretty.

"But if we take shortcuts, it won't last, so—"

"What if you make those rooms a foot shorter?"

The two men stared at her.

"It's the narrow end of the living room and the guest room above—I don't think Miss Trudi will object to loosing a foot. We could use a bay window downstairs to make it look longer, and she'd get a better view of the gardens."

The two men still stared at her.

"I just thought…I mean, we don't have to do it exactly the way it was, do we?"

"It might work," Lenny said at last.

Max glanced at his foreman. "Damn right it might." He kissed her then, a short but thorough kiss that had Lenny chuckling and her feeling weak-kneed. "I'll call the architect and engineer."

It wasn't quite as simple as she'd thought, but working with what the storm had left, instead of trying to restore it to the original dimensions, saved a lot of time and money.

She put the box down with a groan, then looked around. Missing trees, vanished foliage and an unusual number of new vehicles demonstrated the tornado's damage. They had remedied most of what the storm had undone, but had to catch up on the time they'd lost.

She scanned the regular crew and volunteers, but didn't spot the particular white T-shirt she was seeking.

A sensation on the back of her neck like the stroke of a gentle finger made her turn and look up. There he was, on the roof of Bliss House, checking the plywood deck put on in preparation for the shingling. Except at the moment, he wasn't doing that. He was looking down at her. He waved.

How fitting. The two of them close enough to see each other, but too far apart for communication other than gestures. Not that it would matter if they'd been standing side by side—or lying side by side.

They didn't talk.

They didn't talk about what they'd said to each other in the basement during the tornado. They didn't talk about what they hadn't said to each other for the thirty-six hours before that.

She smiled, knowing that from this distance he would see the smile, and not the tears in her eyes.

"You shouldn't be carrying that," Max said.

Suz put down an overfilled box of old photographs with a grunt, straightening slowly as she pushed damp hair that had escaped her ponytail off her forehead. She produced a tired smile.

They were moving Miss Trudi's furniture and paraphernalia into rooms that were painted. A couple of more days and Miss Trudi's new home would be habitable. Work on it would continue, but next week they could start on the main house. Suz had suggested a party at the Toby this Saturday night to celebrate. Max would have doggedly kept working, but she'd seen the need to mark milestones, and from everyone's reaction, she was right.

Max itched to grab her wrist—her hands still bore signs of how she had abused them to free him—and drag her away from the heat and mess and muscle-aching work. Trouble was, he might not come back himself.

"Suz, why don't you take a rest?"

"Why don't you?"

"That's what I'm doing. Just standing here holding this wardrobe."

"Which must weigh a ton, even tipped on its edge like that. And you've obviously been doing something even more strenuous, because you've torn your T-shirt."

Careful not to upset the balance of the heavy mahogany piece, he looked down at his shoulder where a nail had caught the fabric. He grinned and narrowed his eyes at her intently. "We're hell on T-shirts, aren't we?"

She didn't grin back, but he saw the response in her eyes. Oh, yeah, he could definitely take her home right now and not return.

"Speak for yourself. You're the destructive one. By the way, why *are* you holding the wardrobe like that?"

"Annette went to get pads to keep the feet from damaging the floor."

"Max." The strain in her voice came from something beyond physical exertion. "I want to talk to you—about taking classes. The late-fee deadline is—"

"There's no way, with everything going on."

"We'll be on schedule by the time classes start. Okay—" She held up hands of surrender as he opened his mouth.

Shifting her hands to her hips, she walked to the living room's newly added bay window. How many hours before his hands could cup those hips, hold her tight to him? How long before he sank into her, drove them both—

"Interesting."

He blinked away from thoughts a damned sight more than *interesting*. "What?"

"I was just thinking of something Miss Trudi said when you showed us the construction. I was preoccupied then with—" she flipped one hand as if to divert a mosquito "—fears about that idea for the floor plan, but now… And it all fits."

"What fits?"

"What she said. She said that once you make up your mind, there's no changing it without a whole lot of evidence to the contrary. That's why, when you've had to let go of a dream, you think you can't grab hold of it again. But you *can* change your mind—your heart—Max, so you won't be afraid to grab hold of a dream again. Wanting me was the evidence to the contrary that made you stop seeing me as a kid sister. And now the tornado's the evidence to the contrary."

He couldn't dispute that wanting her had wiped out any delusions about his feelings toward her being brotherly, but… "The tornado? How do you get that?"

"Because this—" she gestured at the room "—is the evidence that the tornado was the evidence to the contrary. You had a dream of building this. It got knocked down. And look what you're doing—rebuilding! And not just stoically, thinking it's going to be the end of your business. No. Because the tornado—what happened after the tornado—with you and me and all the people who've rallied around you is the evidence to the contrary that's changed your mind. So you're rebuilding and you're believing Trevetti Building will go on building for years and years, and I'm so proud of you."

It had never occurred to him not to rebuild. All these people were relying on him. As for the future, *his* future…

What about relying on yourself? What about letting yourself down? What about not going for what you want?

Her eyelashes sparkled with tears as she smiled. Then she nodded, and he had the oddest feeling she knew what had just gone through his mind.

"Wait a minute, Suz. Where are you going?"

At the doorway she stopped and looked back at him. "I'm going to find you the evidence to the contrary so you can grab hold of a dream again."

"Max, it's my fault."

Eric planted himself in front of Max as if dynamite wouldn't blast him out. But Max felt mellow. The gathering at the Toby was winding down, which meant he could take Suz home and to bed. He'd told everybody there'd be no work tomorrow, the first day off since the tornado. Oh, he'd stop by to check on things, but otherwise, he intended to spend an entire lazy day with Suz.

"What is?"

"The root-cellar roof collapsing. That lumber falling on you that you almost… It's my fault. That day you called me onto the carpet for not seeing to my responsibilities, I checked and the new guys had stacked it too close to the root-cellar flags. I shoulda made them take it down and redo it. But I thought it was good enough. I thought you were too much of a stickler. I moved the flags marking where the pit ended by a foot."

Max looked at the young man's set face, saw the expectation that he would be fired. And the relief that he'd said his piece, anyway.

"You were wrong, Eric."

"God, I know and—"

"Why tell me now?" The truth flickered across Eric's eyes: expecting to get fired, he'd waited until his departure wouldn't hurt the project so much.

"I want you to know I'll never cut a corner on safety again."

"Good. But what I meant was that you were wrong to think it was all your fault. It was partly mine for not paying closer attention to what you did and then to where I was going that day. Mostly it was the tornado's fault."

"You shouldn't need to check on me," Eric said grimly.

"No, I shouldn't. But I knew that I *did* need to check on you. If I ever again feel that way, you're gone. Got it?"

Eric stared a moment before realization that he wasn't being fired spread across his face. "Got it. Yes, sir. I definitely got it."

"Good. Then get back to the party. And come Monday, get to work." Before the younger man had taken more than a step, Max called him back. "One more thing. I wouldn't mention this to anyone if I were you. If it got to Suz…well, let's say I wouldn't want to be you."

"No, sir," Eric agreed emphatically. "I just… You're a hell of a lucky guy, Max—I mean you and Suz. You deserve it, but still, you're a hell of a lucky guy. Hold on to her."

…so you can grab hold of a dream again.

Max Trevetti rocked back on his heels. The kid was right.

He was a hell of a lucky guy. And he did deserve it. Suz had told him so.

Suz tugged against Max's grip on her hand, redirecting him toward the front door. "Max, let's sit on the porch for a while. It's a nice night."

If he said no, if he touched her, would she go with him inside to his bed, because that was what she wanted more than anything else?

No, *almost* more than anything else.

Sometimes a man can't know what he can do unless he's shown—most times by a woman.

She wanted more than anything else to do that for Max. To help him see all the things he could do—anything he put his mind to. Starting with going back to college. To prove to himself that he could.

As he'd helped her prove to herself that she could.

Could make mistakes.

Could survive them.

Could face a crisis.

Could handle it.

Could accept that not everything that went wrong was her responsibility, and some things that went right *were* her responsibility.

Above all, that she could believe that she *could.*

"Okay. I want to talk to you about something, anyway."

Without releasing her hand, he sat on the swing, drawing her with him. She reached out and snagged the package from behind the planter.

"Me first," she said. "This is for you."

By the porch lights' mellow glow, she saw him looking at the tissue-paper-wrapped rectangle as if he didn't know what to do with it.

"What is it?"

"That's the idea behind unwrapping—finding out what's inside. Go ahead, rip it open. That's the best kind of paper to rip, that's why I used it.'' He pulled at the ribbon with his free hand. She released his other one. ''You need two hands to do it right.''

It would take a lot more presents to get Max into unwrapping with abandon, but he did get the ribbon off and peeled back the paper.

His mouth quirked. ''Underwear? You're giving me underwear? Least you could've done was make it sexy underwear.''

It *was* sexy underwear now that it belonged to him.

But if she said that, they might not continue this conversation. ''Your supply of T-shirts is falling dangerously low.''

He leaned toward her. ''I don't mind sacrificing more for a good cause.''

''There's more,'' she said hurriedly, leaning back. If his lips connected with her neck… ''Look between the shirts.''

He flipped up the first one and found the newspaper clippings. ''Those are stories about people who've gone back to college after twenty, thirty, even fifty years. One woman decided at eighty to get a degree—and she had to finish high school first.'' She nudged the next shirt and he raised it to reveal a printout. ''These are statistics on reentry students at the University of Wisconsin, how old they are, how long it takes them to finish. You'll have lots of company, Max.''

He couldn't possibly see the print in this light, yet he seemed riveted. Or maybe he sensed what waited between the last two T-shirts.

Without prompting, he pulled up the next package and revealed a solitary snapshot, square and fading. A dark-haired boy stood behind a log, looking out across Lake Tobias. On the log sat a thin, dark-haired woman, looking up at him, her face so full of love and hope for the boy that it could break any heart, especially the heart of the woman who loved him now.

"She would be so proud of the man you are." Suz's voice came out barely a whisper. "She would be so proud of all you've done—including the lie you told to spare her. She would want for you what you want for yourself."

"I have something to show you, too." He sounded odd. He stood, his motions jerky. "Wait a minute."

He took out his keys, unlocked the front door and disappeared.

She tried to breathe. When she'd talked with Annette, spilling out all her hopes, fears and theories, Annette had been so sure this photograph, from among the few they had of their mother, would open Max's mind and heart to reclaiming an old dream. Maybe she should have said something different. Maybe she should have—

He was back.

He faced her, feet slightly spread, hands at his side, jaw tense. "I've decided to make some changes in Trevetti Building."

She wrapped her hands around the swing's front edge on either side of her legs, squeezing hard, hoping physical pain would offset the other kind.

"I understand. It's your company. You want things back the way they were, so I'll—"

"No, I don't want things back the way they were. I want things better. Starting with you moving your things in here for good."

Tears sprang to her eyes. "Oh, Max."

"I'm not done." His tone stilled her heart. "The changes are that you're going to take on more responsibility—you and Lenny and Juney. Maybe even Eric. After I'm done dividing my time between the company and classes, maybe we can think about expanding—"

"Classes?"

He held out a sheet of paper to her. "It's amazing what you can do by the Internet these days. You might not be able to see it in this light, but it says my application as a reentry student to the University of Wisconsin has been accepted. I thought I'd wait until next semester when—"

"Oh, Max!" She launched herself out of the swing and into his arms, knocking him back a step. "I'm so glad, so glad."

Laughing, he gathered her in, took two more steps back and sat in the chair, shifting her across his lap. "Don't you want to know why?"

"Because you realized that you can do anything you set your mind to. And that you deserve everything you've ever wanted."

He chuckled. "Not exactly. It's because of you. No, don't get that expression." His kissed the spot between her eyebrows. "I'm not talking about trying to remake myself into some fancy, white-collar kind of guy. Although you do des—"

"Max."

"Okay, okay." His chest rose and fell with a deep breath. "You know, you were right, Suz. About me. Making up my mind about what's possible and what's not. It hurt to quit school. It hurt a lot. I guess I didn't want to risk that hurt again. But how could I not risk it after what you've confronted?" His hold on her tightened. "You think I didn't know you were fighting demons when you got me out of the root cellar? You think I didn't know that you were fearing you'd failed Tad, that you might fail me?"

He wiped the tears sliding down her cheeks with his thumb.

"But it wasn't only then. It was every day working with you. How you were afraid you might fail and you tried, anyway. With you in front of me, how can I possibly be afraid to reach for what I want? I won't let you down—or myself. I'm going after what I want. A degree. And you.

"I love you, Suz. I want us to be married. But this will be a long haul. There's no guarantee on college—I wasn't a hotshot before and now the question is if I can think halfway coherently. Plus, Trevetti Building's no sure deal. If I get hurt or the economy goes bad or about a hundred other things. I'm not the best bargain around. I don't expect you to wait until we know if—"

She sat up, thumping her hand against his chest for emphasis. "I don't expect to wait for anything, Max Trevetti. You're marrying me now."

He kissed her again, settling back in the chair, settling in.

"Suzanna Grant, your loving me is the most unexpected miracle in my life. You're more than I will ever deserve."

She snuggled against him. "I know. But it's for your own good."

* * * * *

SPECIAL EDITION™

A twist of fate forces a blushing bride
to leave her groom at the altar. Years later,
new circumstances bring them back together.
Now the entire town of Tobias is whispering
about the inevitable happy event in...

Wedding of
the Century
by
PATRICIA McLINN
(SE #1523)

**Available February 2003
at your favorite
retail outlet.**

**And you won't
want to miss
her stunning spin-off:**

The Unexpected
Wedding Guest
(SE #1541)

Available May 2003

Where love comes alive™

Visit Silhouette at www.eHarlequin.com   SSEWOTC

Silhouette

SPECIAL EDITION™

and

bestselling author
LAURIE PAIGE

introduce a new series about seven cousins—
bound by blood, honor and tradition—who bring
a whole new meaning to "family reunion"!

SEVEN DEVILS

This time, the Daltons are the good guys....

"Laurie Paige doesn't miss..."
—*New York Times* bestselling author
Catherine Coulter

"It is always a joy to savor the consistent
excellence of this outstanding author."
—*Romantic Times*

Available at your favorite retail outlet.

Silhouette®

Where love comes alive™

Visit Silhouette at www.eHarlequin.com   SSESD

Silhouette Desire
presents the continuation of

LONE STAR
LSCC
COUNTRY CLUB
EST. 1923

Where Texas society reigns supreme—
and appearances are *everything!*

Shameless

(SD #1513)
by

ANN MAJOR

On sale June 2003

A lonely ex-marine
must decide:
Can he snub the
heartbreaking siren
he's sworn to
forget...or
will he give
in to her mind-
blowing seduction...
and a last chance
at love?

*Available at your
favorite retail outlet.*

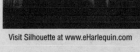

Silhouette®
Where love comes alive™

Visit Silhouette at www.eHarlequin.com

SDLSCCS

We're proud to present two emotional novels of strong Western passions, intense, irresistible heroes and the women who are about to tear down their walls of protection!

Don't miss

SUMMER
Gold

containing

Sweet Wind, Wild Wind
by *New York Times* bestselling author
Elizabeth Lowell

&

A Wolf River Summer
an original novel by
Barbara McCauley

Available this June wherever Silhouette books are sold.

Silhouette®
Where love comes alive™

Visit Silhouette at www.eHarlequin.com   PSSG

eHARLEQUIN.com

Sit back, relax and enhance your romance
with our great magazine reading!

- **Sex and Romance!** Like your romance
  hot? Then you'll *love* the sensual reading
  in this area.

- **Quizzes!** Curious about your lovestyle?
  His commitment to you? Get the
  answers here!

- **Romantic Guides and Features!**
  Unravel the mysteries of love with
  informative articles and advice!

- **Fun Games!** Play to your heart's content....

**Plus...romantic recipes,
top ten lists,
Lovescopes...and more!**

**Enjoy our online magazine today—
visit www.eHarlequin.com!**

INTMAG